SUCH A FANTASTIC GIRL

E. D. RICH

E. D. RICH

Carmel, IN

LCCN: 2025915342

Ebook ISBN: 979-8-9995816-1-7

Paperback ISBN: 979-8-9995816-0-0

eli.duncan.rich@gmail.com

Cover design by Alex Dickson

First edition 2025

Acknowledgements

In the process of getting my first novel (*It Could Have Been Murder*) finished, I failed to acknowledge the individuals who were instrumental in bringing my book to life. I would like to take this opportunity to give a shout out to Kara MacGregor and Mary Ray—two ladies who are fantastic beta readers. My son, Alex, would be a brilliant book editor and very candidly told me when things weren't working in the story. My husband, Kyle, also took a turn in reading my book as it went along, and, God love him, he knew when he should smile and nod. My good friend, Lauren Cardinale, was an invaluable hypnotherapy resource, and she was vital in making the Berlin chapter ring true. And Guy Brown wouldn't have been Guy Brown had I not borrowed a last name and ear injury from my cousin, Doug Brown, who is a really great guy, nothing like Guy Brown. I'd also like to thank Pam June and Chris Fontanez—whether either of you knew it or not, you were instrumental.

Such a Fantastic Girl was inspired, at least initially, by my niece Ellen Gardner. Thank you for going out for drinks in the summer of 2024! There were a few more beta readers this time around: Mary Ray, Jennifer Sturges, my husband (and he didn't hold back on the constructive criticism with this book), Lauren Cardinale, and Jan Carnaghi, a long-time friend who is also a psychiatric mental health nurse practitioner. I would also like to thank my friend from college, Kyle Steele, who connected me with other authors and people in the book world, and provided incredible advice at exactly the right time. Karin Gillespie also provided tremendous insight that I keep going over time and again, and her counsel keeps me just a little bit more sane. My developmental editor, Sara Oestreich was a godsend, and she didn't hold back when it came to getting the manuscript in shape.

Of course, neither book could have happened without the support of my husband and son, sisters, parents, in-laws and extended family, and wonderful friends both near and far.

PART ONE

THE SESSION
SARA - AGE 42

It was hot outside and humid. My hair was plastered to the back of my neck, and even having it pulled into a ponytail didn't lessen the stickiness, and certainly did nothing to mitigate the near-constant low buzz of mosquitoes. I double-tapped the track pad on my laptop to launch the video therapy session. It was long overdue. In the deepest recesses of my belly, I felt a weird churning sensation I knew to be trepidation and nerves and my own awareness that I had done harm to people I loved. I should never have done harm. I took an oath, but I put myself first. I watched the computer screen, and a small woman appeared.

"Sara, hi. Mary Burgess," she said introducing herself. "How are you today?" she asked.

"I'm okay, I guess. Nervous, I think. Definitely ashamed." The words were inadequate for how I felt. I felt ashamed for not caring more, for not feeling terrible about not putting my children first. I should feel like a Grade A asshole, but mostly I felt bad for not feeling like a Grade A asshole.

"We are going to unpack everything. There's no need for you to get so mired in overwhelming feelings that you can't see your way out of the situation you see yourself in. We're going to get to a point where you can feel comfortable with the decisions you make for yourself." The therapist's head seemed to expand onscreen, but that's when I realized she was moving closer to her screen to see me better. "It's going to be a lot of work. What I need from you is commitment. I need to know why you want to go through therapy now, and I need to know your whole story. Do you think you can give me the whole story?"

I nodded, not trusting myself to speak, the knot in my throat portending tears, and I felt like I had cried every tear I had over the past few years. The well should have been dry, and yet ugly tears hid in the wings. This feeling. What I felt right now. This was why I didn't want to go through therapy. But I also knew that I didn't feel human, and facing things head-on was the only way I could become a functioning human being again. All I could do was keep nodding, and Mary smiled, acknowledging my agreement.

"Great. Then, let's start with something easy. Tell me about you when you were growing up. What were you like?" I watched a little light on the side of the screen turn green. "Oh, that's the session timer," the therapist said. "We also record all the sessions and load them into your electronic medical record. The little light freaks people out sometimes."

"I totally get it," I said. "Sometimes, I think when I see a patient, it's going to be a quick in and out, and then as I'm leaving the room, there's the 'Hey, doc...by the way...' and it's always something complicated. Do what you need to do. You won't get any complaints from me."

She peered back at me. I peered back at her.

"All righty," I said, and I cracked my knuckles. "Me. Growing up. I was a good kid. Didn't cause trouble. My mom always said I was fantastic—a fantastic student, athlete, daughter, friend...a fantastic girl. I was such a fantastic girl for a long, long time, becoming a fantastic woman, doctor, co-worker, wife, and mother. Then this thing happened, punching me right out of being fantastic and into something else. For what seemed like a long time, I crawled around in the dark, scrounging for my fantastic self, and I never found her again. I had to be something else."

"Stop," Mary said, holding up a hand like she might be directing traffic. I wasn't prepared for hand signals, but even over the distance between our computers and cameras, I shut my mouth. "Why were you fantastic? Why weren't you just good or amazing or sometimes human? That's a lot to put on a kid. The word fantastic and fantasy aren't just randomly connected. Were you a fantasy?" Mary looked concerned and confused, like what I had told her was something akin to growing up and practicing blood sacrifice.

"My parents had trouble conceiving. They went through a lot to get pregnant and stay pregnant, and I think by the time I was born, I was the concrete result of a shared fantasy." Mary's face took on a look of concern and caring, which vanished almost as quickly as it had appeared. I thought it wasn't that unlike the mask I wore for my patients; but was it a mask? I really did care for my patients, and it was easy to care for them because at the end of the day, they were things I could put away and not worry about until next time.

I continued, "Yeah. Sounds strange, but they had a shared dream, and they dreamed it every night for five years before I was born. They weren't shy about telling me I was a miracle, and I think I must have gotten used to thinking that everything I did was special, magical, beyond my own limited perception," I said. I let my answer percolate a little bit. What would I have told a patient who answered me like this? Mary smiled, but it wasn't a happy smile. It was the smile of commiseration and understanding that best intentions don't always yield the best results. I could see her sitting back in her chair, her hands clasped on her desk. I wondered if she had children, if she'd had trouble conceiving, if she had suffered a loss. I watched her pupils zipping back and forth while she processed my response. She was thinking ahead several steps, shaping the session in her mind.

"Not to be a broken record, but that's a lot to put on a kid. You were an only child?"

"Yes. My mother's uterus ruptured after I was born. God shut down the factory, permanently," I whispered. "I don't think anyone should feel sorry for me or my parents, though. I had a fantastic childhood. We traveled, volunteered, went and did things, and my parents allowed me to grow into a woman who wanted to help people, who wanted to pursue medicine. I think if I didn't have my profession throughout all of what's happened over the past years, I don't think I could have gone on some days."

Mary said, "Then I'm glad your work has been able to sustain you in some way. Do you think your work also allowed you to hide from facing your problems, really addressing them? Allowed you to go on without making some critical decisions?"

"I mean, probably. Not making a choice is still a choice, and I failed to make some vital choices. I ignored my daughter who was wasting away in front of me, and I left just days before my ex-husband took her for a psychiatric evaluation and therapy for her eating disorder. I did harm. I was a terrible mother. I was so caught up in my own stuff that I quit being a parent, quit taking care of this vulnerable person, and I almost killed her."

Was I a monster? I thought about one of those Godzilla movies where the monster is stomping on buildings, cars, people, without any regard for the destruction. I thought about King Kong. He destroyed everything just to have the one thing he wanted more than anything, and in the end, he didn't get it. In the end, well, it didn't end well for him. I thought I was Godzilla and King Kong all wrapped into a fantastically dysfunctional package.

"Stop," Mary said, again raising her hand in the 'halt' gesture. "You aren't the only character in your story. Got that? We are going to pick this thing apart, though, and we are going to work through accepting responsibility, and we are also going to develop coping skills, and only you will know what your limits are, but we will work toward it together." She paused. "You do need to know, though, and I've seen this with many patients, you were never alone. Never. Everyone—your parents, friends, husband, children—wanted to help you, but they didn't know the secret handshake to get access to your feelings, emotions, and psyche. You didn't know either. So. I want to begin by focusing on the good stuff. I want to know Sara James during her best, happiest, most fantastic days. How does that sound?"

"It sounds all right, I guess. Do you think they will ever be able to forgive me?" I was pretty sure the people of Godzilla's fictional Tokyo didn't forgive him. People were unpredictable, though. Being welcomed back with open arms was probably a pipedream. Every time I thought about reaching out to Jen and Bryan, I chickened out. I wrote to them plenty, but I never mailed anything, never emailed. My ego and cowardice were my Achilles' heel.

"Maybe yes, maybe no. Humans are funny creatures, and you are going to have to accept what your family is willing to give you. It may only be an olive branch, or it could be the keys to the castle. It could be a lump of coal. Whatever it is, when you've done the work, it's going to have to be sufficient. The timing of everything was at a pretty critical developmental time in your kids' lives. They aren't going to forgive you and celebrate you because you finally dealt with your grief. It doesn't work that way."

I nodded. Of course it wouldn't work that way. Wishful thinking. Cleaning up my mess wasn't going to be like emptying a dustpan and looking around and having a completely clean floor.

"Tell you what," Mary said. "You have a chance to feel like a human again, reset the mechanism inside yourself. You will have to have the courage to accept whatever the consequences may be. Things happen in life, and we are on a need-to-know basis, and, still, we hunt for meaning. Why did this or that happen? It doesn't make sense even though I lived a good life, and I did everything I was supposed to do. But here's the thing: Life doesn't always make sense."

"Do you have homework for me? Should I be journaling, cutting things out of magazines and making a collage or a vision board or something? I feel like I should be doing more than just talking. It's funny, though. Talking is the one thing I didn't do with my family when I had the chance."

THE HAPPY FAMILY: A REFLECTION

JEN

Once upon a time, there was Mom, Dad, and me. Then they decided, "Jen should not be alone. Let's give her a sibling." Along came Bryan. And things were good for a few years, and Mom and Dad decided, "Jen and Bryan need pets. Let's get some animals." But then Mom and Dad looked around our small suburban yard and decided, "Yeesh. This is inadequate for Jen and Bryan's animals. Let's get some land." And Mom and Dad moved us to a house with several acres of land, and our nearest neighbors were still right next door, but the door was a half mile away.

Mom and Dad decided, "These animals need their own homes." And Mom and Dad first built a chicken coop and filled it with little hens, but Mom was adamant no hen should be red. "There will be no little, red hen. Do you hear me, Rob?"

We knew a few stories about chickens: Chicken Little, and The Little Red Hen. I liked Chicken Little better because we all knew the sky wasn't going to fall. The Little Red Hen was kind of sad because the little hen had to do everything herself, even after asking for help. In the end, she wound up sharing, but I didn't think she really needed to do anything for the other animals because they had their chance to help. I think Mom wanted all of us to know these chickens were a family project and everyone was going to participate, which was fine with me. The chickens were cute.

Mom and Dad were nearly ready to call things good when they realized Bryan and I couldn't really play with the hens. When we got near them, they pecked us. Dad said, "Let's see if the kids are allergic to dogs and cats." We visited friends with dogs and cats. We were allergic to cats. Mom and Dad decided against adding a cat to the family. We did all right with dogs, though, and our family grew by two, Sage, a beagle, and Rosemary, a standard poodle. Rosemary turned out to be the alpha, and Sage was perfectly fine to follow her lead. For a while, though, the chickens thought they were the alpha, all of the chickens, and then Rosemary grew much larger than the chickens, and she became their protector, and all the avian and canine beings quickly got with the program. Sage was happy to be included and was the junior protector of the chickens.

What I thought was just a larger yard was actually a small-ish farm. Mom worked as a doctor. She drove to work every day, and when we started school, she walked with us each morning from her office to our elementary. Dad worked from home as some kind of computer science guy, and in the summertime when he took breaks in his day, he would urgently request us to help him in the vegetable patch. When we went to the grocery for our weekly provisions, the only produce we ever bought would be something we weren't growing. Mom and Dad decided if we liked something well enough, we would figure out how to grow it. Mom and Dad cooked together. In the kitchen, Mom was the alpha, and Dad was happy to take direction because all the work eventually made itself into his stomach and ours.

Our first experience with death occurred when one of the hens died. None of the other chickens wanted to be near her, and there was a flurry of activity in the coop the morning we found the dead hen. Mom said, "I don't want to hear any jokes about the little, dead hen." Dad pinched his fingers together and ran them across his lips to indicate he was closing the imaginary zipper. We held a funeral for the little, dead hen, burying her near the woods behind our vegetable patch. Bryan and I were sad, because there would be fewer eggs to collect, but we didn't cry. We weren't friends with the chicken, and we weren't going to cook her and eat her, either.

Dad said, with all of us gathered around the small hole we had dug, "She was a good chicken. She provided a service to this family for several years, or would have if she hadn't succumbed, and now she's running free in the farmyard in the sky."

Mom tried to give Dad a stern look, but she was also trying to hold back laughter. Bryan finally did cry for the chicken, thinking it was his fault the chicken had died.

Mom pulled him to her and squatted to eye level with Bryan. "Honey, eventually everyone dies. It's a fact. What any of us can hope for is for the life we live and lead to mean something and add to the collective good."

"What Mom is saying, kids, is to live good lives. Think about your actions and your choices and how they impact the people in your lives and the lives of people you don't even know yet. Think about how you affect the world you live in." Dad spread his arms wide, seeming to invite the entire world in for a hug.

"Is this why you guys get mad when we use paper towels?" Bryan asked, rubbing away the tears from his cheeks.

"Kinda. Yeah," Mom said.

"Our garden footprint?" Bryan asked.

"Carbon footprint, but, yeah," Mom said. "I like garden footprint better, though."

We planted a few sunflower seeds around the chicken's grave. We replaced the hen with a pretty blue and brown one, and then a red because it was the only color the store had that particular day, and then a few more white ones because, eventually, the all the hens reached their expiration dates. The expired hens joined their friend back by the woods, and over the course of the summer, we had several sunflowers, which turned the loss into something bright and lovely.

One day, Mom and I were sitting on the porch swing, and I asked, "Mama, why don't we eat the chickens when they die? Are they different than the chicken from the store?"

She said simply, "We don't eat pets."

I didn't think of them as pets. I thought of them as egg machines, but Mom thought differently, and I didn't question her. For all I knew, she came outside to play with them after we went to bed. But I decided to accept her explanation. "I would never want to eat Rosemary or Sage," I told her. "I promise."

She smiled.

Eventually we had a pair of sheep and a goat. The sheep were nice. They were soft. The goat was his own man. We called him Jiminy because, according to Dad, "He looks like he's always judging me." Bryan and I each named one of the sheep. Bryan named the female, and I named the male: Jolene and Axl. Our family liked music, and our parents wanted us to know the songs marking different parts of their own lives.

Our mom said, "The first time I ever heard 'Sweet Child o' Mine,' I was lying in a tanning bed."

Our dad liked The Doors. "They were way before my time, but I met this woman when I was first out of college, and she did dry cleaning delivery. She had been a hippie and had actually seen The Doors live. She said to me, 'You know you're a good dancer if you can dance to the song The End.'" Dad played "The End," and none of us could do much more than sway.

One day, Mom called Dad from work. She was a little frantic, and as the call progressed, she was coming close to a full-on panic attack. She had a patient who couldn't pay a bill, and Mom was fine with it, but the patient wanted to pay her something and brought her a miniature horse. "We know nothing about horses," she said. "What are we going to do with a miniature horse? I think this thing is worth way more than what these people owe on their bill. Do you think they just don't want their little horse anymore? Oh, my god. What are we going to do with a miniature horse? We know NOTHING about horses, regular or miniature. Can you come pick it up? It's in my parking lot. What are we going to do? Oh, my god. What are we going to do. With. A. Horse?!"

"Kids," Dad said. "Your mom is in a panic. We're going to need to go help her. Get in the truck and put on your seatbelts." He scrubbed a hand up and down the side of his face, looked at us in the rearview mirror, taking a beat to run both hands through the mop of his hair. I swore I heard him whisper, "And the hits keep coming," but I'll never know for sure. I never asked.

Dad made a couple quick calls to friends to see if anyone had any kind of trailer we could borrow for a couple hours. Our dad was in the truck within 30 seconds of completing his second phone call, drove around ten minutes to the home of one of his buddies, picked up a trailer, attached it to the back of the truck, and ten minutes later, we were in the parking lot of Mom's office. And there he was. A miniature horse the color of butterscotch, his mane a beautiful blond. Bryan and I were immediately in love with the horse.

We sprang from our seats in the truck, racing to where the tiny horse was holding court. He was surrounded by adoring fans made up of passers-by and Mom's patients. And there was Mom. She was wearing her lab coat and holding the end of a rope or leash or lead or rein, and then I knew in my bones, and it was soul-crushing for a moment, but only a moment: We knew nothing about horses. We didn't even know the terminology. With the chickens, sheep, and goat, we'd had plenty of time to do research and learn about them before they became permanent fixtures. But this exquisite little horse? We were ill-equipped, to say the least, but we had one thing, and maybe this one thing would make everything ok. We had a barn.

Mom handed the horse off to one of her office staff and walked very quickly to where we were standing. She probably would have run, but I think she was trying to play it cool and preserve a smidgen of her dignity. "Jesus, Joseph, Mary, and all the saints," she said in a single breath. "You're here! Finally! I've been standing out here with a growing crowd for almost a half hour. Oh, my god. I don't know what we're going to do with this thing. He has a name. It's Henry, but I think I want to call him Jesus, Joseph, and Mary and all the saints." She took Bryan and me by the hand, walking back to where Henry stood.

Dad hadn't said a word, but he wore a smirk. He ambled along behind us, and upon reaching where Henry stood, Dad took command of things. He patted Henry, smoothed his hand down his mane, and dug a carrot out of his back pocket. Dad kissed Mom, telling her, "Don't worry about a thing. We have Henry well in hand, and we'll see you after you get home tonight. Everything is going to be just fine. Jolene, Axl, and Jiminy are going to enjoy Henry, and I think Rosemary, Sage, Jen, and Bryan will, too."

Dad expertly led Henry to the trailer, tied him up, and called to us, "Jen, Bryan. Let's head home and get Henry squared away." We ran back to the truck, strapping ourselves in. This afternoon would be epic, or so we thought.

When we got back to our house, I took the crappy old laptop out to the front porch and began searching for information about miniature horses. This horse was going to be a lot more work than we thought. Whoever thought they were paying a bill by giving Mom this horse gave her and our family a financial obligation that probably cost more than the bill they were trying to pay.

"Dad, we need to go to Tractor Supply. We need to buy a bunch of stuff for the horse," I called into the house.

"Can it wait?" he asked, joining me on the front porch.

"Probably not until tomorrow. We need to go today. I think the horse is going to be a lot of work."

"Kiddo, I like how you think. You are a problem solver, and this world needs more problem solvers who are willing to do some research, just like you're doing right now. Make a list, and we can go to the store in about an hour. Sound good?"

"Great," I said.

THE GHOST: A REFLECTION

BRYAN

Our mom, what can I say? Maybe she was Teflon; maybe she was just plain squirrelly. Having a regular job as a physician in a suburb, two children, a husband, a home, some land, and a few animals—it may have been too ordinary a life for her. She shut down on doing mom-type things and even being a loving person. She had been fun and cool, and then she became someone we didn't know.

She began to check out when I was 12 and Jen was 13. Heck, it may have been even before, but it definitely became apparent around junior high. Mom began taking shifts in the emergency room at the hospital. She would work in her office until around 6 pm, Monday through Friday, and then she would work nights on Fridays, Saturdays, and Sundays. On the nights she was home, she sat alone in her office reading medical journals on her laptop. Around 9:30 or 10 pm, Jen and I would get ready for bed, and Mom would absently say, "Goodnight, you two. Love you." Sometimes she would make eye contact, but more often than not, the routine was rote. And it sucked. She sucked.

One night, after Mom said her half-hearted 'love you,' Jen said, "I just want to ask her: Do you really?"

"Does she really what?" I asked.

"Does she really love us? Jen said, giving me that look that older kids give younger kids for asking stupid questions.

"You don't think she loves us?" I asked.

"Well, when was the last time you got a hug or kiss or, like, anything nice from her?" Jen said. "I'll tell you, Bry, I can't remember."

An then I thought about it, and I couldn't remember either.

***

Dad cooked, and we helped. Mom had given up doing anything in the kitchen, and she wasn't ever home to sit down to dinner with the rest of us, usually arriving from work after we had already eaten, then going straight to the treadmill for a half hour run. By the time she finished, our homework was done and we were getting ready for bed. After doing her thing, she would disappear. Sometimes I thought her journals were sucking her inside, and one day we'd find an open magazine on the floor with her beating her fists on the page to try to escape. If she had been sucked into a magazine, at least there would be an excuse for her not tucking us into bed anymore or taking part in the life of our family or acting like she gave a crap about any of us. If we didn't take it upon ourselves to pop our heads into the office, I think she'd suffice going days without seeing us. Not going to lie: It was weird.

Weirder still was our own behavior the nights she was home at a time where we could interact like a family. She seemed like a dinner guest, and we treated her like one. Jen and I were like Stepford children, trotting out our A+ work from school, using our manners, trying and failing to generate interesting conversation—anything to impress her enough to want to go back to the mom we used to know. Jen and I racked our brains, trying to figure out what we did wrong to make her into this stranger in our home, in our family.

My sister and I were at a loss, completely. Mom had simply left the building, and the person playing Mom was doing the worst job ever.

One Saturday morning, I overheard Jen talking to Mom.

"Mom," Jen said. "I need to talk to you about something."

"OK. Shoot. I don't know if I can help, but I'll try," Mom responded.

"I think I need to get a bra. Like an actual bra, not a sports bra, and I don't know where to go, what to look for. I think I need you to take me somewhere for a fitting. I talked to my friend Kim, and she said her mom took her to this place where they would do all the measurements and make sure you had the exact right bra for your size, shape…everything. I know your work keeps you from being able to take me on a weeknight, but I was hoping we could go on a Saturday. Maybe even today?" I could hear the hope in Jen's voice, and the desperation.

"I see," said Mom. "Well, today, I was planning to get a nap in before I go to the ER, and you're right about not being able to go on a weeknight. I'll have to look at the ER schedule to see when my first Saturday off might be. If I'm doctor-of-the-day, I can't really ask off." She paused a moment. "Um. Yeah. Let me check tonight."

Mom seemed to think a moment then asked Jen, "Do you think Kim's mom would be willing to go to this bra place with you?" I was stunned and had to stifle the gasp of shock that wanted to make its way out of my mouth.

I wanted to stick my head into the room and yell, "Be a freaking mom! Your daughter is asking you to be a mom." Jay-sus. I mean, how out of touch was this person who worked as a doctor every day?

"Uh, I don't know," Jen said. I know she was trying to put on a brave face, and I could tell she didn't expect the question from our mom.

When I told Dad what I had overheard, his face grew red. There was a mix of emotions playing across his face. There was anger, sure, but there was heartbreak, too, in the glassiness in his eyes. "Leave this with me," he said in a very serious tone. "Thank you for talking to me about this. I can only imagine how Jen is feeling."

The following weekend, our mom did take Jen to the bra place. Jen's whole affect brightened. Our mom had decided to participate in Jen's life by taking her to get a fucking bra.

They didn't make a day of it by getting mani-pedis, which I knew Jen was hoping to do, and they didn't have lunch somewhere fancy. Also something I knew Jen wanted to do. No. They went to the bra place, then they came home. It depressed me to see how elated Jen was to have this scrap of time with Mom, who went to her bedroom, closing the door behind her, and sleeping the rest of the day. I saw the light in Jen's eyes dim a little. Jen began to be small. She was quieter when Mom was around. She shrank, I guess. I noticed. Dad noticed.

Jen stopped eating. She would run all the time. It wouldn't be unusual for Jen to eat lettuce and cucumbers—plain. It was disgusting. I walked by her bedroom one morning while we were getting ready for school. Jen was just pulling her shirt down and was facing away from her door. I saw all the ribs, all the vertebrae. There was still meat on her bones, but Jesus, Joseph, and Mary, the flesh on my sister was disappearing, and so was she. I didn't know what to do. My mom was useless. I went to my dad. He was the only other person who had even the tiniest clue what was going on in this house. But things weren't right and hadn't been right for a while. And I think I had begun to hate my mother, which made me feel terrible. Who hates their mother?

One Saturday afternoon, Mom was gathering her stuff to go her ER job. She had forgotten her laptop. I was busy trying to ignore her and the flurry of activity she had kicked up trying to escape her home and family. She looked right at me and asked, "Bryan can you do me a favor?"

"Depends. What do you need?" I responded in a flat tone.

She looked at me quizzically. "Can you get my laptop from the office?"

"No," I answered. "I am very busy. I cannot help you." I made certain to have eye contact with her as I got my phone out of my pocket and began playing a stupid game on my phone. I moved to one of the wing chairs, lazily settling myself in it, slouching into a corner, and slinging my legs over one of the chair's arms. It was the first time I had ever been openly defiant to an adult, and it scared and thrilled me at the same time.

"Excuse me," she said. "I'm your mother."

And I looked up from my phone, pointedly looked her in the eye and said, "Oh. Are you? I had forgotten. Thought you had, too." Then I removed myself from the chair and the room and walked out of the house. I had no idea how all that was going to go down, but I didn't want to stay there and find out. A few moments later, Mom's car disappeared down the drive.

I had no idea if Mom would involve Dad by telling him about my behavior, and I felt that I should tell him what I had done and said, but more importantly why I had done what I'd done. Dad was in the garden, pulling weeds. I told him everything. "Did I do the wrong thing?" I asked.

"No, Bryan, I don't think you did. You did and said the right things. She doesn't think you guys notice. Now she knows. We all know something's broken," Dad's tone was resigned. He looked up at the sky, squinting into the sun, then looked at me, surveying the scenery. "Where is your sister? Has she eaten anything?"

"I think she had egg whites for breakfast. Just egg whites. Then she immediately left to go for a run." I looked at my watch. "She's been gone," I looked at the clock on my phone, "Dad, she's been gone for...100-ish minutes."

"Let's go for a ride," Dad said. "Go get in the car. I've got to grab some car keys. We're going to find your sister."

When We Were Young: A reflection

Sara

How did I get here? I know I sound like a Talking Heads song, and there are times I think the song was written about me, about the older 30- or 40-something version of me.

Rob and I met when I was 22, in my first year of medical school. My friends were hosting a party following a big biochem exam. I was in the kitchen, rooting around in the fridge for one of the sours I had brought to the party, and when I turned around, there was this guy. "Are you getting stuff out to make nacho cheese? This party needs nacho cheese. So many chips, and no dip."

I held up the can in my hand and popped the top. "What do you need to make nacho cheese or any kind of dip?" I asked.

"Mind if I take a look in there to see what I'd be working with?" Rob asked.

"Please. Have at it," I said. "I'm Sara, by the way." I gave an awkward wave, and did this weird head bob thing that I swear I had never done before.

"Hi, Sara. I'm Rob. I'm going to be very up front with you and tell you I drank one of your sours. It was delicious."

There was an awkward pause. I didn't expect his openness and confession. "No worries," I said. "Do we have the makings for a dip?"

"Indeed," Rob said.

"Not that I'm checking you out, but I am checking you out. You look like a swimmer. Are you?" I am not usually brazen or forward, but on this particular night, I was pulling out all the stops.

"If I had a dollar for every time someone asked me that question, I'd have one dollar," he laughed, and it was a full-bellied laugh that after a few seconds degenerated into the fringes of hysteria. "But now, the dip." He proceeded to pull out the necessary ingredients and then worked expertly in the cabinets to get bowls and some serveware for the dips he quickly fixed.

I commented, "You certainly know your way around this kitchen."

"I was Devin's roommate last year. When he and Terri got engaged, I figured I needed to find my own place. I still know where everything is, and I'm here about once a week for dinner—which I usually cook. Devin and Terri are terrible cooks. They always have ingredients on hand, and I love to cook."

"What's your signature dish?" I asked, leaning against the counter, watching him put the dips into various bowls to go next to the chips and crackers which seemed to be multiplying like rabbits.

"I hate to limit myself to one dish, but I would say my cooking tends to lean Italian and Greek."

I exclaimed, "You know what? My favorite foods are Italian and Greek! You, my friend, may have earned the privilege of feeding me."

Rob looked at me in speculation, like I would look at a piece of tissue under a microscope. "Have I?" He raised a brow. "Am I feeding just you, or is there a boyfriend in the picture? See, I need to know how impressive my cooking would need to be. If there's a boyfriend, then I'm not wasting time with fresh spinach in the spanakopita. If there's no boyfriend, then you get all the fresh ingredients."

"Nope. Just me. No boyfriend," I answered, and I swear, if I could smile coquettishly, I would have.

"Ah," Rob said. "Would it be presumptuous of me to ask you to a dinner I'm not cooking? A restaurant? I could even follow up the meal with a movie or something—in an actual theater."

"I would be delighted to dine with you, Rob, and, you're not being presumptuous. I am single, enjoy having a meal, and a movie would be the cherry on top." We sounded like idiots. Flirty and formal-sounding, especially because we were anything but.

We made plans and swapped phone numbers. I liked his confidence, how upfront he was, and I really liked the swagger he brought to his approach. And the man could cook. I wondered how many dates before he would make dinner for me.

He took a peek in the freezer and brought out a bag of pizza rolls. "What do you think—does this party need some hot food, too? I guarantee these will disappear within five minutes of my putting them on the table."

"Right? They are unhealthy, made with questionable ingredients, and completely loaded with sodium, but I love them so much. I could probably demolish a whole bag of those things in a sitting," I gushed.

"Same," he said.

I followed him around the rest of the night, and, maybe, he followed me around, too. There was something about him. It could have been the lack of pretense, maybe his comfort in his own skin, but I liked him as a person right away, and I knew deep down he was someone I could love. And the thing about love is when you aren't looking for it and it's standing in front of you, it's a scary thing. It's Michael Myers jacking up your prom kind of scary.

We were replenishing food--chips or dip or veggies or something. I wasn't paying a whole lot of attention to what we were doing. I just had this giddy feeling inside me, like a bunch of little birds twittering around an earthworm. It was something special, and there was the lingering wonder of which one of them was going to get the worm. "Huh," I said. Rob looked at me, waiting for the rest of the thought. "I was just looking at you, and I could've sworn earlier that you had brown eyes, but now on closer inspection they're kind of hazel or something. I don't know. Maybe a little bottle glass green?"

"Yeah," he answered. "I like to think of them like a mood ring. Depending on my mood, sometimes they're cloudier or clearer. I can't tell you which moods do what because I'm obviously not able to see my eyes, unless I'm standing in front of a mirror." He stopped talking, rearranged some of the vegetables on the plates and said, "I think I must think you're too cool for me because I just sounded like a moron."

"You didn't answer my question earlier," I said.

Rob looked at me curiously, "And what question was that?"

"You're built like a swimmer. Were you a high school or college swimmer?" I picked up the last pizza roll on the table and popped it into my mouth.

"Ah. I could have $2 now. I swam in high school, played water polo in college—but just intramurals. It was fun, but I don't think I've ever had a harder workout," he answered.

"What about you? You're built like a runner. Did you run cross country in high school or college?"

"Both," I said. "I was a really good high school runner, but an average collegiate runner. Now, I just run for fitness."

"So...we were both right. Very good observational skills," he said, following the comment with some brow waggling.

Two days later, we went on our first date. Dinner and a movie. There are two foods I never ate when I went on a date: Salad and spaghetti. I was terrible at getting a bite-sized piece of lettuce on the fork, and I was always nervous there'd be part of the lettuce sticking out of my mouth because I couldn't fit it all the way past my lips. I had the same fear with spaghetti, but there was the added fear of making a mess with red sauce. For our first date, we went to a diner, and I had a patty melt, and I did not ask the server to hold the onions.

Rob said, "I am impressed. No weird salad order with this and that on the side, and no croutons, and blah, blah, blah. Thank you for eating like a normal person."

I laughed so hard, it turned into cackling. Then he was cackling, too. The movie theater showed old movies and featured "Cool Hand Luke." We did not laugh or cackle during the movie, and after, walking back to the car, Rob held my hand. It was magic. I wanted to hold his hand forever, to feel the warmth and strong security of his palm against mine.

The first date was followed by a second, then a third, and a fourth. We talked on the phone every day, and we texted. We saw each other when we could, but med school was demanding, and I was not the best at biochemistry and needed to get some tutoring, which cut into my free time. I was counting down the days until the end of the semester when biochem would be behind me, and I could come up for air for a bit. Every time Rob and I were together, though, there was this feeling that would give me a rush, like together we could make some kind of magic, like anything could happen as long as we had each other.

I fell hopelessly in love with Rob, and I didn't want to keep quiet about it. I wanted him to know, but deep down I hoped he would say it first. Someone had to say it first, and I decided I'd just take the plunge, pull off the Band-aid, let the cat out of the bag, all the cliches.

We were driving down the highway, sunroof open, windows rolled down. Rob was driving, and the music blasting from the stereo competed with the noise from the road. My hair was going wild with the air blowing in through the windows, and we were singing along at the tops of our lungs with Motley Crue, and I couldn't hold back. I leaned forward and turned the music down. He took his eyes off the road and looked at me. "Sara. Is everything ok?"

"I just wanted to tell you I love you," I said.

"Well, I love you, too," he responded matter-of-factly, like it was the most normal thing in the world, like we said it to each other every day. I think I expected more of a heartfelt reaction, and the wind was blown out of my sails; but he did say he loved me, too. Should it have felt more momentous? Maybe, but the guy was driving, and we could talk about our mutual love later, and maybe he or I would feel differently then.

"Oh. Okay. I really wanted you to know how I felt," I said, a little sheepishly.

He smiled at me, and I could see all the emotion in his expression. "I'm going to kiss you and other stuff as soon as we get off the road. Okay? You're going to feel to your very core how deeply I care for and love you." Suddenly, I got it. Timing. It was everything.

We had already slept together, but it was different after the love discussion. We had a connection, and even now, I know we still share it. At the time, I felt sure Rob was probably my one great and true love.

And Here's When Things Go South

Rob - age 39

I can pinpoint when Sara's life went off the rails. After Bryan was born, we felt our family was complete. We weren't trying for more children, but we weren't preventing it either. And, we were pretty good at missing Sara's fertile window. When Jen and Bryan were in junior high, though, we were a little sloppy after a friend's wedding.

We fell into the hotel bed, and the last thing on our minds was the viscosity of Sara's cervical mucus or when her last period had been. We mauled each other. It was an exceptional wedding reception.

We'd had a few cocktails too many and couldn't keep our hands off each other. We left the reception, packing ourselves like sardines into an elevator with a bunch of college kids who were in the same hotel for a fraternity or sorority dance. As soon as the elevator stopped on our floor, we pushed our way out of the car and ran down the hall toward our room. I had the room key card in hand, and we spilled through the door, pulling off our shoes and clothes, dropping them wherever.

The sex was explosive, and then we passed out. When we woke the next morning, Sara pulled out her phone while I was brushing my teeth and said, "Uh-oh."

"What?"

"We might have made a baby last night. How do you feel about a baby?" she asked.

"I feel a baby would be a surprise, but I support whatever you want. If you want a baby, then I want a baby. We'd all want a baby. But if you don't want a baby, then I'm on board with you—no matter what." I walked over to the edge of the bed where Sara was looking at the calendar on her phone. Sitting next to her, I pulled her onto my lap and held her. "Whatever you want."

We sat still a moment, and Sara put her arms around my neck, nuzzled me, and said, "You are a unicorn, my unicorn, and I love you. I guess we'll wait and see over the next few weeks what happens."

At the time, we were both 39, and Sara stayed active. She ran every day, maintained good nutrition, and lived a healthy lifestyle. About four weeks after the wedding reception, she realized she had missed her period. She took a pregnancy test, and, it was positive.

We decided not to tell Jen and Bryan until after the first trimester. Every night, though, Sara and I talked to the baby, telling it about its sister and brother and about our animals. We read to it, played our favorite songs. We were nearly out of the first trimester when Sara miscarried.

It was around 10 pm on a Wednesday night. I remember it was a Wednesday because we had just been joking about it being Hump Day and doing the Humpty Hump. But it's weird, this odd stuff we tend to remember. Sara had gone into the bathroom to brush her teeth before bed, and she called to me with distress in her voice, "Rob. I need you. Can you please..." Her voice dropped off, and I heard a thud.

I ran into the bathroom, and Sara was lying on the floor. Her toothbrush lay on the floor next to her, and I saw the blood. It was blossoming out from under Sara's nightgown like a sick rose. I didn't know what to do, but on some level, I knew Sara was miscarrying. I called 9-1-1, and the ambulance came. I called my mom to come watch the kids while I followed the ambulance to the hospital.

Sara roused in the ambulance with a little bit of smelling salts, and she asked what was going on. The paramedics had put a monitor on her to see if they could pick up the baby's heartbeat. Sara asked about the heartbeat, and the paramedics didn't make eye contact with her. They were trying in vain to see if they were missing something. But they weren't. There was no heartbeat. She would have to wait until she had an ultrasound at the hospital to see what was going on in her uterus.

The ultrasound revealed that Sara was no longer pregnant. We were no longer expecting a baby.

I cried. Sara cried. We cried together. We didn't even know the baby's gender, but we loved our baby and felt the loss deeply. They sent us home the same night and advised Sara to follow up with her gynecologist. We arrived back at our house bone weary with red, swollen eyes. Sara couldn't stop the tears from rolling down her face. She buried her face in my mom's hair and whispered to her, "We lost the baby."

My mom cried, too, and the two of them held each other, shaken by their tears. I had called Sara's mom before we left the hospital, and I knew she was on her way to our house. When her mother arrived, the two moms divided and conquered. Sara's mom led her to our bedroom, urging Sara to lie down and get some rest. My mom held me, and I cried some more. Until we found out we were expecting, we didn't know just how much we wanted this third child, and the loss felt primal.

Eventually, my mom went home, and I went to bed, holding Sara close. Sara's mom stayed the night in our guest room. In the morning, her mom got the kids ready for school. Sara called her office and asked to have her patients rescheduled. She called her OB/GYN, and their office already had her hospital records. They wanted her to come in for a D&C later in the day and were working her in as a favor. Sara hung up the phone and collapsed onto me in despair, her body heaving with sobs. I stroked her hair and held her close. We would weather this together. We would go through grief counseling. We would do whatever it took for as long as needed to get our lives straightened out. We could never forget this loss, but we could learn how to cope with it.

The following day, both sets of grandparents took Jen and Bryan out of school, and they all left town for a long weekend. I said, "I think we need to see someone about grief counseling. I think I need some direction, and I need to be able to cope with the loss. We could go together, or we could each go by ourselves. What do you think?"

Sara stared at me like I had three heads. "Are you crazy? I am a doctor in this town. People will recognize me and think I'm unstable. I can't afford to run into a patient or someone I know."

"No one is going to think you're unstable. People seek therapy for a lot of different reasons. If you're so worried about being seen by someone you know, we don't have to see someone here in town," I countered.

"You can do what you want, but it's a firm 'no' for me. If I think I'm depressed, I'll write myself a prescription for an anti-depressant."

I didn't bring it up again until after a few months of my starting grief counseling. "Sara, I think you should consider going in for grief counseling with me. It has helped. What happened...it was horrific. I found you lying on the floor in a pool of blood. My first thought was that I had lost you." I had to stop talking. I was getting choked up remembering that night and recalling all the weird little details that were so unimportant but stood out in my memory. The tiny things that now seemed to layer on top of the seriousness of the scene that had played out. I wiped away a few tears with the back of my hand. "Any way you look at that night, it was traumatic, and there's no shame in needing support.".

She reeled on me. "Do you know how idiotic you sound when you talk about processing your feelings and emotions? You weren't the one who had a life drained out of you, spread all over our bathroom floor. Your body wasn't the one to fail our baby. You didn't have a constant barrage of hormones flooding your body for almost three months, and you're never going to be able to feel this loss like I'm feeling it. Go to your counseling. Enjoy it. Get on with your life, but I can't stop feeling like I've lost something and I'm never going to get it back." She turned her back on me and went into our home office and shut the door. She had been doing this every night since shortly after the miscarriage. Some nights, I could hear her crying behind the closed door, and other nights it was silent.

Many nights she slept on the couch in the office, and on the nights I felt her climbing into bed with me, she never reached out for me. Never sought any human connection. I would roll over, stretching my arms to wrap her inside an embrace, and she would push my hands away. In the mornings, she would be gone from the bed, almost like she was a momentary fragment of a dream, dissolving with the sunrise. She hurt, and she carried the burden of the hurt, shutting everyone out of her life.

Extreme Life Makeover

Sara - Age 41

Every day seemed like the same day. I saw the same patients with the same problems and gave them the same prescriptions and instructions, had the same conversations. As mundane as my work seemed, work was my coping mechanism. It was the one part of my life I could compartmentalize, and I think I did it well.

One night, while reading (in an attempt to escape my husband and children), I came across an ad for Doctors Without Borders. Initially I wasn't very serious about it, but then I started thinking maybe a change of scenery would be a great move. Different patients, customs, worldview, problems—it might wake me up. Being somewhere else in the world might help me gain insight into my own situation, and if not, then I was no longer geographically located where I had experienced this hugest of personal losses and come apart at the seams.

I interviewed, and I didn't think about anyone but my own interests and well-being. I would be needed in a way I wasn't currently needed in my job. The people who would be my patients were traveling from hours away, in some cases. If I couldn't make my own corner of the world make sense, I could do something to make this other spot on the planet better.

The offer came. I was overjoyed and paralyzed. I had to put in my notice at work. Letters had to be sent to all my patients. I had to tell my parents, Rob, and my kids about the new job, and, more importantly, I had to tell them I was going alone. I chickened out of telling my family right away. I did a shitty job handling my husband, and in the process alienated him even more than I had already. Oh, and I left it to Rob to tell the kids. I couldn't face them, and I was ill-equipped to answer any of their questions. The kids had already started to view me with disdain, and I couldn't blame them because I was little more than a morose housemate to them. I had been watching their faces grow more and more sullen with each passing day, and even though I knew I had the power to change things for them, I did nothing.

It was when I had to explain to Rob what I was doing that I realized I'd already been running away for two years but hadn't left home.

Sara's Plans

Rob - age 41

"Rob," Sara said one night after she had eaten dinner—by herself, in our home office. She hadn't even seen the kids. She came home, hit the treadmill, and disappeared into the office, only coming out after she heard me turning out lights and going through the ritual of goodnights and sweet dreams with Jen and Bryan. There was something in her tone that gave me pause. I looked at her, and she was biting one of her nails. She was nervous about something. She would not make eye contact with me. "I've been looking for a change. I'm going to take a post in Africa with Doctors Without Borders."

"Oh, yeah?" I said. "You don't want to deal with the borderless situation right here at home?"

"Don't be like that," she said, giving me a look like I was being childish. Was she chiding me? And my ire began to climb the upward slope of a rollercoaster, knowing full well how angry I would be when I reached the top of the hill.

"Be like what—a concerned parent and spouse? I mean, do I, do the kids even figure into your decision? It seems like a very big decision to make unilaterally and drop on your husband." Sara wrapped her arms around her middle and began pacing back and forth across the room. She wouldn't make eye contact with me. "When would you be leaving? When would the rest of us be leaving? Are we leaving? See. Part of marriage is communicating. I think maybe you've forgotten about that. I haven't." I felt my face heating, and my voice was breaking throughout what I thought could be a productive dialogue with my wife. Her face reddened, partly in anger and partly in embarrassment. She still wasn't making eye contact with me, but she was getting riled up—which was a big change from how she'd been for the past two years.

"God, Rob. I knew you were going to be like this," she said. She sighed, shrugged her shoulders, and started to turn away.

"Nuh-uh. We're talking about this. When is this supposed to be happening?" I pushed.

"Three weeks," she said softly. "I would leave in two weeks for orientation." I stared at her.

This was some big news and, frankly, no lead time. It was a recipe for disaster. I could work anywhere if there were electricity, wi-fi, or a cell signal. I knew people in some locations where there was no running water, no carpet or flooring. Africa could go either way with access to phone and internet

"Three weeks," I sighed, then blew out a big breath. "We can't make plans that fast," I said.

"You guys wouldn't be coming with me. It's just me. By myself." She looked down and pulled the cuffs of her sweatshirt over her hands. She did not have the guts to look me in the eye to say she was running away.

I took turns standing and sitting to focus on something other than anger and lashing out. She was leaving her job, partnership, and her family—in three weeks. Wow. There were a lot of words bubbling up, and all the censoring I had been doing for the past two years hadn't amounted to anything; Sara was still unhappy, and as it turned out, she was so unhappy she felt she had to escape.. Nothing had gotten better, but, in fact, had gotten worse. I had kept a tight lid on everything for two years. Two years. We had all been walking on eggshells with Sara. She didn't get a free pass to be horrible. Sara's face wasn't difficult to read. Even though she wasn't looking at me, I saw contrition, and it gave me hope—false hope in our case—that things weren't as bad as I thought.

"How many people are you going to destroy and let down and make feel as miserable as you do? Is that what's going to make you happy—watching the rest of us crumble in misery? Are you paying any attention to the two children you already have? The two pregnancies that didn't end in miscarriage? Do you notice how thin my daughter is? Do you notice she eats hardly anything and goes on runs that sometimes last up to two hours? Do you want us all to become a tragic landscape for you to perch your life on...and for what? So we can feel like you feel? Is that what you're doing here? You can't or won't be happy until we've all been baptized in your pit of despair?" Sara was crying, tears and grief marking her face, and she was so very silent. I had kept quiet about everything since the day she said I sounded like an idiot for pursuing therapy.

"You don't know, Rob. You don't live in my head. You just don't know," Sara whispered through her tears. She was shaking her head and drawing in on herself, and all I could do was continue twisting the knife

"I keep thinking I miss you, the 'you' from before the miscarriage—that you'll come back to us and everything will be better. But it won't. Come. Go. Stay. Get the fuck out. I don't care. I've been watching you harm the two people I love most for two years. I want to love you. I remember the fantastic woman I fell in love with, but she already made her decision and left two years ago. She just didn't have the common courtesy to tell us. And you know what, Sara? You need help. I have made excuses for you, bent over backwards for you with our kids. I didn't want to tarnish the image of the mother of my children, but Jen and Bryan aren't dumb. They don't know why you're a terrible mother because—news flash—you are a terrible mother, and everyone in this house knows it. Didn't used to be, but you have won ALL the prizes over the last two years." I took a breath, and now Sara was looking me in the eye, and I saw indignation there. I wanted her to be angry. I wanted to see something that showed me she cared about something besides her inability to deal with her own misery.

"Fuck you, Rob. I expected more understanding from you," Sara said, and it sounded eerie because she didn't raise her voice.

"Believe me. You had plenty of my understanding throughout the past two years," I answered, my voice the polar opposite to hers. I was loud and wasn't going to worry about volume unless one of the neighbors called the cops.

"You know who the biggest casualties are in all this? Our kids, and they don't even know the whole story. You ignore them, look at them with pure indifference and a dash of disdain, disgust, disregard...I don't know...but it's something other than pride or love." I walked out to the porch, sat on the top step, and I cried.

Ripping off the Band-Aid

Sara - age 41

I couldn't put it off any longer. Rob, the kids, work. They all had to be notified I was leaving. Rob laid the guilt trip on thick, and he managed to have a Part 1 and Part 2 to his guilt trip. He concluded Part One by storming out of the house. If he wanted me to feel bad, I felt bad. But I had felt bad for two years already. Now, though, the bad feeling was guilt. I looked out the window and saw Rob sitting on the porch steps. He held his head in his hands, and his large body was shaking.

I went outside and joined him on the steps and didn't say anything. Rob broke the silence, speaking quietly into the night, "Bryan is an empath. He sees and feels everything, and he's holding on to the barest shred of regard for you. He's holding out hope. I guarantee, though, he will give up on you as soon as you leave your going away party—because we will do a sendoff because, I guess, maybe it's the right thing to do. But his focus is on his sister—losing both of the two most important women in his life will crush him, and she is the most important female in his life because she is present."

This was something that I used to know. I had known my kids like I knew my own name, and hearing Rob describe them to me like strangers...had they become people I used to know? I listened to the crickets chirping in the night. There were fireflies lighting up tiny pockets of darkness, and they seemed to be choreographed in concert with the cricket song. It was a beautiful night for early summer, still mild but warm enough not to make me want to throw on a jacket.

"You have to stay somewhere else until you leave for Doctors Without Borders. You are a doctor, and you're harming people in your own home. I'm taking Jen to her pediatrician appointment tomorrow. Let me ask you something. Are you so caught up in your own trauma that you can't see the flesh disappearing from our daughter on a daily basis? Do you know what she ate yesterday? Celery and ice cubes. You aren't a safe space for her anymore because you've repeatedly rejected her."

I wasn't a safe space for anyone, not even for myself. Doctors Without Borders. It was extreme. It was overkill for avoiding my problems. But it could provide some redemption, maybe reverse my karma. I felt something light tickle my arm, and looking down, I saw it was a mosquito. Nature's vampires. I watched the insect take a good hit of blood from my arm. Eventually, the site would itch, and it would niggle at me, and I would scratch it and scratch it for relief, and it would deaden some of the numbness that was part of my every day existence.

"I'm not a place of comfort or support for anyone, Rob. My parents always told me how fantastic, amazing, and magical I've always been, but you know better than anyone. I completely checked out of being a wife and mother and have been none of those things."

"I haven't told your mom. She would be so disappointed in you and then feel like she and your dad did something wrong raising you. But she has noticed something is wrong with **my** little girl. Has she mentioned it to you? I'm assuming you talk to your mother...but maybe not." I felt myself getting hot and imagined my face getting red.. I couldn't tell if it was anger or embarrassment, but I just kept looking at Rob, and knowing I had let him down caused some of the righteous indignation to ebb from me.

"After you're gone, it's going to be all hands on deck to save my daughter. Thanks so much for your partnership. My daughter is going to see a fucking eating disorder psychiatrist to deal with her eating disorder. *My* daughter has been performing, trying to divine why she can't make the most important woman in her life love and accept her. God! Why am I still talking to you? Nothing gets through. Pack a bag and go to your parents' house." I stayed put, remaining silent. My tears had dried, and I looked at his dear, dear face with anger and fatigue. I think this was the first time I had ever seen Rob this angry.

Rob paced back and forth across the porch. He had been seized by nervous energy because he was finally uncorking everything that had been collecting in his head. He had been patient for two years, but I had finally reached the end of his patience, and I couldn't blame him. "And, yeah, we are done. There's nothing left between us. I don't even know if I can be your friend, because who you are right now is someone I would never consider a friend. Come back for your party, but don't expect a ticker tape parade or red carpet. I just didn't foresee any of this when we exchanged marriage vows. I never thought I could ever grow to despise you and, lo and behold, I do despise you."

Rob's pacing stopped, and I looked up at him. Words as weapons. Silence as a weapon. We both hit grand slams, but knowing he despised me felt like a gut punch. His voice sounded like it was cracking, like he could barely contain his anger and sadness, and he wasn't a guy who cried. The degree of frustration and the flood of emotions were a lot. For both of us.

"I am sorry you despise me, and I'm sorry to be dumping everything on you right now, in the eleventh hour," I whispered. I thought I was telling the truth, but I knew in my heart of hearts, I had been holding back until the very last minute.

"You know what's funny? Your patients are relative strangers compared to your goddamned family, and they get better treatment and attention than the people you once loved. I'm assuming there was a time you loved us. Maybe not. Maybe we all just fit into some fucked up narrative in your head, and you didn't like the story's direction and chucked us like leftovers in the fridge. I'll make up an excuse or something for the kids. Hell, that's what I've been doing for the last two years anyway." He gave a low laugh, probably part of it nerves, and part of it the relief for saying what needed to be said.

I did not know what to say. I couldn't respond. Any words I could possibly say were going to be salt in a very deep wound. All I could do was stare at Rob, stunned because he had been the peacekeeper in this house for two years while I hid, and everyone has their limits. I guess he had finally hit his. My announcement was the nail in the coffin. I went back into the house, into our bedroom. Rob didn't follow me, and he was still rooted to the spot where I'd left him when I returned with a duffle bag and suitcase. I removed my wedding and engagement rings. We were done. We had both known it for quite some time during the prior two years. We weren't partners. I wasn't fit to be anyone's partner right now.

The Send Off

Jen - age 15

There was a loud boom that went off in my head when Dad told us Mom was going to Africa to work for Doctors Without Borders. I was surprised our house didn't collapse. I was even more surprised when Dad said Mom was leaving in two or three weeks or whatever. It didn't matter. She was leaving. Dad was disgusted, though. She left the house maybe two weeks before her going-away party. I heard Dad speaking very loudly. Bryan and I heard bits and pieces (the louder bits and pieces), but we opted to stay upstairs and out of the fray.

Was it a surprise? Not really. She had been running away from us for two years, but the physical abandonment was something new and different. I wondered how many months ago she had begun pursuing something with Doctors Without Borders, and she didn't have the common courtesy to say anything until three weeks before she was scheduled to leave. God! She was the worst.

She had a problem and didn't trust any of us to help her, and I had a problem, and I didn't trust her either. In fact, my indifference and increasing dislike and disregard for her fueled my running. I ran harder, faster, and longer. I wanted to challenge her to a road race or a long distance run and show her she wasn't as fantastic as she thought she was.

Dad was the one who told us Mom was leaving. She was such a chicken shit. She didn't even have the decency to have a heart to heart with us or anything. It ratcheted up my dislike.

Bryan kept his cool. I didn't think of myself as a hothead, but everything Mom was doing made me feel prickly, tender, frustrated, and angry. Bryan, though, he kept it together and asked, "Why is she leaving? I don't get it. I feel like I'm missing part of the story here. I feel like Jen and I have been missing a big part of the story for a while now—since the beginning maybe. It's been, what? A year? Two years?"

"Your mother thinks going to Doctors Without Borders will help her. Bryan, you're right. You don't have all the facts, but it's not my story to tell. I hope your mom will eventually tell you everything." Dad stopped talking and rubbed his forehead. For a moment, it seemed like he'd forgotten we were in the room. Then he looked at each of us in turn. "I'll tell you this, and please remember it: There is no place in the world, no person in the world who can fix you. You are the only person who can fix you. You have to trust professionals enough to guide you through what's a dark, dark place. You just can't plunk yourself down in a different part of the world and expect that to fix all the mess in your head."

"You think?" I asked, sarcasm heavy in my comment. "She's a mom. Your mom isn't supposed to reject you, yet my mom is rejecting me. I constantly wonder if I did something wrong." Dad shook his head to disagree, but he didn't get to try to sugar-coat the situation.

"Yeah, you know, I don't know. All I can tell you is maybe she'll work things out and get the help she needs, and maybe she won't. It's up to her."

"Well, she fucking sucks. I don't understand, and I think whatever her problem is, she's burned her bridge with me. We are not children, and we aren't stupid," I said, acid in my voice.

Bryan said, "We need her, too. Well, we needed her before she sucked. I thought we needed a mom. I don't know anymore what we need. I know Jen needs something, though." Bryan looked at me. He always knew. As soon as something good or bad happened, it was like he had an electrode on his skull connected to mine, and he always knew how I felt and when I needed an extra push or shove to return to the center of my lane. Bryan and I knew I wasn't in any lane right now. I was going off-road in a hot pink dune buggy with big yellow smiley face antennae.

"I wish I had answers, and I wish I could tell you how everything was going to play out, but I don't," Dad said somberly. "Your mother and I haven't discussed how often she's going to call, email, or even come home to visit, but I imagine she will communicate while she's gone…" he trailed off, and by the way Dad was talking (which was pure fantasy), I think he was trying to convince himself as much as he was trying to convince us. On some level, we wanted to believe him, and so, for a while we did. Then after a while, none of us, including Dad, believed him. But looking back on those weeks before Mom left, I don't think he ever thought she was going to come through for any of us.

If nothing else, we were pros at going through the motions. I mean, we had been going through the motions for two years. We had a big going away party for her. Our hearts weren't in it, though. Everyone from her office came—they all thought she was some great humanitarian. Dad, Bryan, and I knew she was a coward, running away from us and whatever was troubling her.

All of our family, our friends, some of her patients and their families came. The mayor came. We roasted a hog and a bunch of chickens (which came from a meat locker and not our chicken coop). People brought pies. There were so many pies. And salad. And if I never saw another pot of baked beans again, it would be too soon. The dogs stayed close to the tables where people were eating. They were always happy for table scraps. People asked questions about Mom's decision to go to work with Doctors Without Borders, and she expertly dodged the majority of the questions, and when she couldn't, she would feign seeing someone she needed to talk to before they got away.

Meanwhile, Bryan's and my friends helped entertain the little kids with Rosemary, Sage, Axl, Jolene, Henry, and Jiminy—so many animals. Henry was the biggest hit, though. The little girls wanted to brush his mane, and some of the really little kids were able to sit on his back for a photo. Henry was no fool. He knew his lot in life was to look good for the camera. It would have been a great party if we weren't celebrating Mom.

Eventually, though, Mom got stuck with someone and couldn't make as hasty an escape as she would have liked. One of Mom's friends from medical school, not a close friend, came with her husband, daughter, and baby. "Sara, we're so sad to see you go," Mom's friend said, wrestling a wriggling baby on her hip. "I know you're going to do great things. I always thought the world was a much better place with you in it."

"Thank you," Mom said. I could tell she was trying to get away from her friend, but this woman wasn't picking up on Mom's non-verbal cues.

Mom's friend was clearly struggling as she tried to hold the baby and put food on her plate. She paused a moment, shifting the baby to her other hip, realizing it was futile to do anything that involved holding a plate in one hand and a baby held fast to her other hip with her remaining arm. "Can you hold Mackenzie? That pie looks great," she said absently, handing the baby toward my mother, who had actually put her hands in front of her and was backing away.

"Ordinarily, I would love to, but I can't right now. My hands are dirty. I was just with the kids and the animals, and my hand sanitizer is in the house. I'm so sorry. I'm sure someone else could take the baby for you."

Mom walked away from her friend and Baby Mackenzie like they were on fire. Her face was turning red, and she made a bee line into the house. She didn't come back outside until her friend had left. In fact, most of the party guests had left by the time Mom returned. She was sullen, like she was every night when she came home from work, spent, like she was counting the minutes until she could call a close on the day and go to sleep.

After everyone had left, and our grandparents helped us get things cleaned up, Bryan and I sat down on our front porch steps with our dad. Bryan spoke first, giving a knowing laugh, "Mom. She ditched her own party. Priceless. Just like she's ditching us."

SURPRISES

SARA - AGE 26

If nothing else, Rob and I were planners. But there's this saying: Man plans. God laughs.

In the beginning, when we were planning the wedding and our lives together, we planned when children would enter the picture. We had a decision to make. Honeymoon after medical school graduation or baby? I would have a little time between graduation and when my residency began, and it would have to be enough time to serve as maternity leave without actually being maternity leave. Rob could take paternity leave for up to 12 weeks, but he could work from home, too. If we were going to have two kids, then I wanted them close together. Theoretically, we could be done with diapers in three years if everything went according to plan. I didn't know how long it would take to conceive and thought we could stop all methods of contraception around 18 months before finishing medical school, which came out to 6 months after our wedding.

All the planning was a wonderful exercise but was futile when I pulled a few all-nighters and missed some birth control pills. I resumed the pills when I remembered, but when I got to the placebo week, I didn't have a period. I didn't start the next pack and waited to see if my period would start. And it didn't happen. Jesus, Joseph, and Mary, and all the saints.

"So, honey," I said to Rob. "Contraception."

"My vote is no contraception at all after the wedding," Rob said. "We don't know how long it will take to get pregnant. We can be careful around the fertile window until we're really ready to get pregnant. I can control myself for a few days if you can control yourself." He waggled his brows. I laughed.

"What if I were pregnant before we got married?" I asked.

"It happens. If you were already pregnant, that might be hard on you during clinical rotations when you have long days or are working nights. I can help as much or as little as you need, but I can't carry a baby. It's your call entirely," Rob said.

"Remember those all-nighters I pulled at Terri and Devin's?" I asked. Rob nodded. "Yeah, well, I neglected to take my birth control pills."

"Okay," Rob said, drawing out the last syllable.

I produced a red solo cup and took a Walgreen's bag from under the table, spilling the contents. There were five boxes of pregnancy tests. "I'm going to go in the bathroom and fill up this cup, and then I'm going to dip every test into the urine, and then we're going to wait and see what happens. Okay?" I was nervous and Rob's eyes grew wider and wider while I talked.

"Do you think you're pregnant?" he asked.

I nodded.

"All righty, then. Let's see what happens. Do you need me to do anything, hold anything?"

"Could you hold my purse?" He looked around the room. "I'm kidding. Just sit down. There's nothing for you to do."

He was nervous, too. The unknown was a nerve-racking business.

Ten minutes later, we knew. We were going to be parents. It wasn't according to plan, but there weren't words to describe our elation. We stripped each other's clothes, celebrating with enthusiastic sex. It wasn't like I could get more pregnant than I was already.

Later in the evening, we sat on plastic Adirondack chairs on our back porch. Rob had lit a small fire in our chimenea. The spring air still had a bit of a chill in it. I clutched a blanket tightly around my shoulders. "The wedding is a month away," Rob said. "I think we should tell our parents now for moral support and stuff. I mean, they've been through this before. We're proof of that, and, well, and…that's what I think," he paused. "But I defer to you."

"I think we should tell them, too. I think you're right."

When we told our parents, we decided we would have them over to our rental house for lunch. My dad had to acknowledge his daughter was having sex, and he had to look my sex partner in the eye. Rob's dad was excited for us. Both of our moms were starting to talk about who would stay with us and for how long after the baby was born.

"Mom. Eva. I know you're both excited, but don't get too invested until we're past the first trimester. Things happen," I said, fingers crossed that we would have a smooth pregnancy. "But if everything works out, we're probably going to have a Thanksgiving, Christmas, or New Year's baby. We have our first pre-natal appointment next week, and we'll start getting details."

My mom and Eva looked at each other then at me. "Do you want us to come with you to your appointment?" Eva asked.

"Mom, no," Rob said. "I'm the father. It's the first appointment. I'm going with Sara. We'll fill you in after. For now, let's focus on the wedding and keeping this under wraps. No big pronouncements until after the first trimester. But we need your support. It takes a village and blah, blah, blah."

"In the meantime," I said brightly, "we can celebrate with some delicious sparkling grape juice." Rob brought a tray of plastic champagne flutes out of the kitchen in the first trip, and then brought the bottle of grape juice out in an ice bucket. He poured everyone a glass, and while we were waiting to toast, I stared at the bubbles rising in my flute. Each pocket of air, trying to rise to the top of the liquid to escape into the room surrounding us, going anywhere, somewhere, and maybe nowhere. Maybe just a molecule bouncing around in this room forever bearing witness to our lives.

The Daily Routine: A reflection

Jen

Mom was gone. She didn't call, didn't write. At Dad's urging, we called and wrote, but we eventually stopped. It was pointless. We moved on with our lives. On the even days of the month, my day began with a one hour run on the treadmill. On the odd days, I did yoga or Pilates at the studio down the street from our house. If I felt extra energetic, I went to the gym for a kick-boxing class. After a workout, I would make breakfast and throw something together for lunch, then shower and get ready for school. I thrived on routine, and my dad and brother were part of my everyday. After school, I tried to get in a two or three mile run to clear my head. I didn't make a huge deal about it, though, because I knew Dad and Bryan were watching my activity and food intake. I just really needed the extra run, even when I knew I was in calorie deficit already.

For Dad and Bryan, though, I tried always to be cheery. Each morning, they saw the bright, sunny Jen I thought I had been before Mom decided to desert her family. Mornings with Dad and Bryan rolled out practically the same way every day.

"Good morning!" I announced loudly. "How are my two favorite guys this morning?"

Bryan would usually say something like, "Why always so loud?" Sometimes he would say, "Can't that noise be held until later?" He was not a morning person.

Sara, Mom, whatever...decided her calling was Doctors Without Borders. After the first year in Africa she was somewhere in Asia the second year, and now somewhere in South America. I didn't really care exactly where she was because she didn't care about any of us. She had been back once.

I played it up in my mind how we would be when she came back: we would all put on smiles for one another, act happy. In my visions of her return, we would act like we were so happy an outsider would have thought we were high. We were just so, so very happy. We were helium filled balloons, competing for space to float closer to the ceiling than anyone else in the room. If we were floaty enough, maybe she would love us again and decide to stay. But, the reality of the situation was that ultimately, the helium leaked, and our balloons gravitated toward the floor again, and Mom left. Dad would pick up the broom, and brush away the discarded remnants from the floor, and our lives would go back to what they had been before her visit.

We had Rosemary and Sage. I loved them all the time. Even when they tracked mud into the house, even when they threw up somewhere in the house, I still loved them. And they were dogs. I thought that parents loved their children even more than their pets. I knew I would love my children more than I loved Rosemary and Sage, and I loved our two dogs a lot. Our mom, though? Had she given up on us? We weren't getting any clues from anyone that helped us understand what we had done wrong—if we had done something wrong.

Sara James. I loved her. I hated her. I didn't understand her. I didn't want to understand her. I wanted to give her grace. My grandma always said, "Grace costs you nothing," and on an elemental level, I knew she was right. But Mom dumped us like rotten garbage. She decided she would rather take care of other kids and people, and she left us wounded and alone, without the care we needed to put ourselves back together again.

Dad tried really hard to play the role of both parents, and most of the time he succeeded. Our family unit changed, though, for the better. And even with life and love brimming all around us, it was tempered because Mom was a ghost everywhere, and we could not exorcise her. Over time, the tug of war between love and hate had become indifference. Sometimes I thought it would be better if she were dead, and then I hated myself. Who wishes death on a family member? But from an emotional standpoint, if she were gone forever, I could begin to heal and not feel left behind. We were the detritus of her life.

A Visitor

Rob - age 41

Several months after she left, Sara called to say she was going to sign the divorce papers and email them back to the lawyer. "Well, wow. I don't hear from you for months, and the first thing you're calling to tell me is about the divorce papers. No niceties like, 'how are you?' or maybe 'how are the kids?' I mean, it's been like crickets here with your refusal to check in with us. Your mom even says you're ghosting her, too."

"Look," she said flatly. "You were right in everything you said when you told me to leave our home. I am not okay. You and the kids are not okay. The only way for us to move forward is to end things."

"God!" I exclaimed into the phone. "You just want to decide everything for everyone, don't you? Everything has been on your terms—not telling the kids about the miscarriage for the past two and almost a half years ago, making me keep it a secret, making all of our parents keep it a secret. Doctors Without Borders. And now you finally call and don't give a damn about anything going on in our family. That's just rich, Sara. I don't even know why you're calling about the divorce papers. You've been doing whatever the hell you've wanted for over two years now."

"You told me to get the fuck out," she yelled into the phone. "If I'm recalling correctly, you said you were done. Don't make me the bad guy in this divorce."

"Of course you're the bad guy. You took months to arrange your post with Doctors Without Borders and never clued me in to any part of your plan. I think you decided we were done way before then."

"Fine," she said, resigned. "We can talk again next week."

"I'm going to tell Jen and Bryan about the miscarriage. Jen thinks it's her fault you left, like she wasn't good enough. Bryan thinks he didn't care enough about you and love you enough and you left because we didn't value you while you were here."

"If you tell them about the baby, they're going to think they're nothing. This isn't your story to tell," she begged.

"I'm pretty sure that I'm one half of the story," I said. "I mean, I'm not a doctor, but I know how babies are made, and besides, Jen and Bryan already think they're nothing. You did a great job of reinforcing it throughout the almost-two years before you left." I knew it was a cruel thing to say, and I didn't care. We walked around on tenterhooks after the miscarriage through the time we put her on the plane to Africa, and during the time she was still here, she didn't get help, and she didn't get better, and she withdrew to the point we all felt invisible around her. Hell, Jen was trying to become invisible, and Bryan was falling apart trying to keep his sister from destroying herself.

I hung up on Sara and geared up for how I was going to tell Jen and Bryan.

The next morning, I received an email from Sara with an attachment. It was a letter from her to Jen and Bryan. It was everything the kids needed to know two years ago. Sara gave permission for me to read it to them, and I decided to invite both my and Sara's parents to dinner during the upcoming weekend. Jen, Bryan, and I, and Sara's and my parents would work through the feelings and emotions. We adults would support the kids any way we could.

I was going to take a different job. I received offers all the time for corporate roles, and I had an offer to be the CIO of a large company. If it came through, I would sell the house, and we would move. The kids and I could all get a fresh start. We were not going to continue living somewhere that had become overwhelmed in sadness and bad memories. I had a responsibility to my children. I could not and would not fail them.

Saturday night, we gathered around the table. Jen set a beautiful table every night. Even if we were having spaghetti, she would go the extra mile every single time. She said she didn't just set a table, she 'styled' a table. She would tear out pages from 'Martha Stewart Living' and model our table after whatever intrigued her in the magazine. We were passing around mashed potatoes, glazed baby carrots, and pork tenderloin, the buzz of conversation animating our meal, when we heard the door open and something heavy landing on the floor toward the front of the house. "You all get started eating," I said. "I'll go see who's at the front door."

I made my way to the living room, and there she was. The noise had been a large, stuffed canvas duffel bag. Sara and Jen, physically, were carbon copies of one another. They were both tall, lanky, built like distance runners. When Jen was little, the two of them wore their hair the same way. Where Jen's hair was a shiny chestnut color, Sara's now had gray sparklers threaded through her hair. Where Jen now wore her hair in a high ponytail, Sara had cut her hair into a chin-length bob. What I saw in both their eyes, though, was sadness and anger. Jen's expression, though, had taken on a look of defeat. Tonight, Sara looked exhausted, and still carried around the albatross that was the pregnancy loss. I knew nothing had changed, and it killed me. She hadn't healed while she'd been gone, and now, here she was. "What are you doing here?" I asked. "I was going to read your letter right after dessert."

"No hug? No kiss? No welcome home?" she asked slightly sarcastically, a faint smile gracing her lips.

I remained silent, staring at her. When I met her in Terri and Devin's kitchen, she was lively, quirky, brimming with curiosity about life and love, and the possibilities we could create together. I could never have imagined her turning into this shell of who she had been.

"Frankly, I don't know why I came back. I thought maybe I could read the letter, but I don't think I can," her voice trailed off.

"I don't want you to see the kids," I whispered. "Seeing you will hurt them. Showing up unannounced? You're like a wrecking ball to them. Can you wait in the office? I want to get through dinner and dessert, then read the letter. Do you actually want to see the kids?"

Her mouth opened and closed two or three times, with no sound escaping her lips.

"Don't worry. I'm here to do the heavy lifting, like I always do."

The Letter

Sara - Age 41

Jen and Bryan,

I want to preface this letter by apologizing to you both. I ran away from home, and I ran away from our family. I took the coward's way out, and I think I'm still being a coward since I'm writing a letter instead of sitting down and talking to you in person.

If I had tackled what was happening at the time, things might have turned out differently, or maybe they might not have. However, I could have spared everyone some grief and pain by sharing what was going on and by putting my pride aside and getting help.

What happened? You were both in junior high—seventh and eighth grades. In a nutshell, there was a surprise pregnancy. We were waiting until the end of the first trimester before we told anyone I was expecting. During the first trimester, anything can happen, and that's when things can go wrong. I suppose I should have been a little worried, since I was 39 at the time, but I thought since I ate right and exercised regularly, I had nothing to worry about.

Close to the end of the first trimester, I had a miscarriage. It was devastating to me. I wanted that baby. I needed to be needed. The two of you were growing up, becoming independent, and you didn't need me like you did when you were little. Until I had found out I was expecting, I hadn't realized how much I missed the feeling of someone's being wholly dependent upon me and their total need for me.

What you saw and experienced was me working all the time, and when I was home, I was basically hiding from everyone. Your lives went on. I tuned out all the stuff you were going through, though. You didn't need me like a baby would need me, but you did need me for support in growing up.

I failed you, and I am sorry I wasn't there for you.

Your father went for grief counseling and therapy, and it helped him. I didn't go for counseling, and I still haven't. To be a better human, though, I am going to get help. I can't keep living this way. I don't have close friends, and I feel so isolated from everyone, and I know it's not healthy.

While I was still in the throes of actively running away, about a year after the miscarriage, I looked into Doctors Without Borders. I did phone interviews, virtual interviews, and I went to a couple in-person interviews. I made plans to leave everything and everyone behind because everywhere I looked was a reminder of what I'd lost. I did it all in secret and then dropped the bomb on your dad when I waited until the last minute to tell him what I was doing. I shut everyone out.

I understand your anger, and I don't have a right to ask you for anything, but I am going to ask you for any amount of forgiveness you can muster. I didn't do right by you, but I want to do better.

Love,

Mom

After Dinner Chat

Rob - age 41

"I read your letter to everyone," I said, running my hands through my hair, tugging at the ends. Jen always said when I did that, it made my hair look like Sonic the Hedgehog. I smiled faintly at the thought of my brave girl.

"And...how did it go?" Sara asked. She had a hopeful look on her face, and I felt indignant. How could she think reading her letter would make everything all right? There was no magic eraser to pop out of the sky to make everything better, to make the last two, almost three, years go away.

I stared at her. "How do you think it went? You may have heard some of the loud chatter coming from the dining room—if that's an indication of how it went."

We didn't talk to each other for probably a good minute. My first impulse was to comfort Sara, but why on earth did she need comfort. But, there we were. She was sitting on the sofa where she had slept so many nights after the miscarriage, and I found myself in a wing chair, and I thought oddly, how this reminded me of the setup in my therapist's office.

I wanted to defuse things between us a bit, though, to give us a chance to have a conversation that didn't end with me going crazy and doing a whole bunch of finger-pointing. To move forward, I had to push down my anger and move into a rational headspace. Finally, I said. "What do you think you know about your children? Why don't you start with Jen?"

"Well," Sara said, hemming a bit. "I know that Jen loves to run and likes animals. Good student. Hard worker," she answered.

"And Bryan?" I asked.

"I think Bryan wants to be a doctor. Good listener. He's also a good student and hard worker."

"You have some of the facts. Nice work. Let me tell you what you missed. Jen has an eating disorder. She makes all A's and obsesses over keeping the house clean. She runs for an hour every day. She doesn't even weigh a hundred pounds. She's in therapy. She and I have had to have a contract about her caloric intake and her food and exercise behaviors. Bryan and I watch her like a hawk."

Sara's face turned pink, and the color spread to her face, neck, and, finally, chest. "And what about Bryan," Sara asked breaking the silence between them. "What don't I know about him? What have I missed?"

"For a long time, Bryan cried himself to sleep every night. Not just some nights or once in a while but every night." I looked Sara in the eye.

"His crying jags have tapered off, but Bryan is worried all the time about Jen and me, and even you." I gave a sad smile before adding, "He also makes all A's." I went to my desk and pulled out copies of the kids' most recent grade reports and handed them over to Sara, who looked through everything and, impressed, she nodded. I continued, "They both think if they had been perfect, you wouldn't have left them behind. Bryan is dealing with anxiety. At one point, I was sitting across the dinner table from him, and I noticed he had no eyelashes. He had pulled them out. He says he did it out of boredom, but the therapist says it's an anxiety-related behavior. He's 14. I'm telling you this because this stuff our children are experiencing—it's directly related to you and your actions." Sara looked like I'd punched her in the gut.

"Why are our parents here tonight?" she whispered.

"I knew I would need extra support for the kids, and frankly for myself, when I read your letter. Getting through all of this myself was hard. But trying to help the kids has been the hardest thing I've ever done," I answered, rubbing my hands up and down the sides of my face.

"What's next?" Sara asked me. We had a handful of things to do, and we needed to be strategic about who would tell them what.

I said, "I'm going to tell the kids we are splitting up—which won't be a surprise. I'm going to tell them you're here to take care of some of the legal paperwork. You wait here, then I'll come back and escort you into the dining room, and we'll all sit around the table and talk about grief, post-partum depression, depression in general, and your state of mind having nothing to do with our children. We are going to answer every question the kids have. We are going to reassure them they had nothing to do with your decision to work abroad." I stopped, caught my breath, counted silently from five to zero, took a deep breath.

Sara was quiet. "Fine," she said finally.

"Fine," I replied in agreement.

Facing My Demons

Sara - age 41

I sat on the couch, waiting for Rob to come back for me. I heard what began as the low hum of voices begin to escalate in volume. I heard Bryan's voice, Jen's voice, my parents' voices, Rob's parents' voices. At first, they sounded like they were shocked. Anger definitely followed, and then they were quiet again, and I heard someone say, "It's over?"

To say I was tired from traveling for the past two days was an understatement. I thought about stretching out on the sofa, but I knew I'd fall asleep, and this was not a time to check out of a heartburn-inducing situation. I popped up, pacing the room, picking up some of the little knickknacks on the bookshelves, all the little reminders of the life and family Rob and I had built together. All these little nothings were something. They had become tiny little knives, stabbing my brain and heart, a constant companion whispering to me what a failure, a fantastic failure, I had become.

Rob re-entered the room. He sat heavily in the wing chair and leaned forward, his elbows on his knees, hands cradling his head, fingers clasped behind his neck. "They don't want to see you."

The Lake

Jen - age 15

Puberty. Oh, my god. I keep hearing old age is not for the faint of heart. That's all fine and nice, but being a teenaged girl is no walk in the park either. I began accumulating every kind of acne cream or astringent recommended by this or that celebrity or influencer on social media. I discovered concealer for hiding the acne that didn't mysteriously disappear with the creams and all the other stuff I was buying because some of those social media girls had no idea what they were talking about.

I didn't have a female touchpoint who wasn't a senior citizen. What I did have was an absent mother who decided a surprise visit would make everything better, but she wasn't here to weigh in on puberty. She was here for absolution, I think.

Gram and Grandma made the right call getting us out of the house and going to the lake. I was sitting on the back porch of the lake house, staring out at the lake. The sun was coming up, beginning to burn the mist hovering over the water. Gram came up behind me, placing a gentle kiss on the top of my head. She held a steaming cup of coffee in her hands and took the seat next to me.

"Good morning, honey. Did you get a good night's sleep?" Gram asked quietly, her voice reassuring and smooth. I glanced at her, and her gaze was firmly directed toward the sun slowly climbing through the tree line.

"I did," I answered. "I always sleep great when we come to the lake." I pulled my knees up to rest my chin on them. I angled my head toward her and asked, "What was my mom like when she was my age?"

"Ah, sweetheart, in the teen years, she was a typical teenager. She sure was a neat kid, though, when she was younger. We did a lot of things together as a family. She was a lot like you. She loved to get outside and play, and then she discovered the running club at her middle school, and she took to it like a fish takes to swimming." Gram turned to me, a gleam in her eye and a faint smile on her lips. "She seemed to have a calling to care for people when she was in kindergarten or first grade. She used to carry around the funniest little red purse, and she stocked it with bandages and antibiotic cream, basically creating a mini-doctor's bag." She raised her coffee mug to her lips and laughed just a bit.

"What's funny?" I asked.

"One day, your Grandpa Howard was outside working with some wood. I can't remember what he was doing exactly, but he wound up getting a nasty splinter in his hand. He came into the house making a racket about this splinter that might be the end of him. Your mother came into the room, and she patted him on the head. 'Daddy,' she says. 'Sit right here, and I'll take care of this.' She went to her room and came back with her red doctor bag, which now also contained tweezers and alcohol prep pads." Gram and I smiled at each other. "Your grandpa was sitting in the chair just like she'd instructed, and she starts telling him some story about a moose. The funny part of all this was that the moose story was actually riveting. While she was telling the story, she had cleaned off Grandpa Howard's hand where the splinter was located. She never missed a beat during the story. By the time she finished, she had removed the splinter, put the ointment on it, and topped it off with some gauze and paper tape."

"What did Grandpa Howard say?" I asked.

"He was so surprised. She worked through the whole procedure, and he didn't even register what was going on, and then voila! Everything was better."

"I don't want to be a doctor," I said.

"You don't have be anything you don't want to be. Your mom's mission and journey are her own," Gram said. "In that way, she and Bryan are a lot alike. But you are supposed to be exactly who you are. You're going to have your own mission and journey, and that's a really good thing. I'm going to pass along some advice to you, all right?" She looked at me and waited for me to make eye contact with her. This had to be important.

She said, "You have the rest of your life to figure out what you want to do, and you have the freedom to change your mind at any time. Isn't that great?" She reached over to pat my cheek. "Do me a favor, though," she said. "Don't be someone that isn't you just because you think you need to be someone else to make everyone else or a specific someone happy. You are a fantastic young woman, and anyone worthy of your time will love you exactly as you are. Got that?"

"You and Grandma are the best," I answered. "We got lucky having you two as our grandmothers." I squeezed her hand, and we looked at each other. It seemed we were trying to read one another for any other hidden truths or vulnerabilities.

"Can I tell you something? About my mom?" I asked, and Gram nodded. "Every time I think of her, I get caught up in this spiral of love and hate toward her. Her showing up the other night kind of pushed everything to center stage. I think I wanted to punch her, and I wanted to hug her, and I wanted to ask a bunch of questions, but I didn't want her to think that I wasn't hurt by what she did."

"I know, honey. I feel for you kids."

We sat there for a while, looking onto the lake, fish nipping the water's surface for insects, mourning doves marking the new day.

"Did you like being a mom?" I asked.

"Oh, gosh, yes. It took Grandpa Howard and me five years of trying before we had your mom. We had miscarriages, fertility treatments, you name it. It wasn't a good time, but we kept trying. All that loss is hard on people as individuals, but it's tough on a marriage, too. We did all the counseling, and we became stronger as a couple." Gram took another drink of her coffee, setting the mug down on the little side table between our chairs.

"We had a backup plan, though. We would have adopted if we couldn't have our own biological child. We figured a time frame for how long we would pursue having our own child, and then we would start the adoption process. We had almost reached the end of our time limit when we discovered we were expecting your mom."

"Did you and Grandpa Howard tell her about the miscarriages and your health problems?" I asked.

"We did. We always called her our fantastic girl. She knew she was a miracle, and maybe having to live with that kind of knowledge was too much for her to handle. I don't know." Gram's voice drifted off. "As parents, we always tried to do our best, but we're not perfect. We weren't perfect. We made mistakes. At the time, you know you're going to make mistakes, and you just hope that the after-effects don't wind up somehow being amplified. You hope they just kind of fade away and don't have long-lasting implications, but that isn't always the case."

Decisions

Rob - age 41

I was doing the sudoku in the morning newspaper. I never did the puzzles in the paper. It was something my mom did every morning while I was growing up, and since I was waiting for Sara to wake up, I thought the puzzles would kill some time. A second pot of coffee was brewing, and I had begun to think about lunch. Sara had been asleep for nearly twelve hours. I had a gallon jug filling with water and as I turned off the tap, Sara startled me with a quiet, "Good morning."

A squeak escaped me, and I jumped a little. "Jesus, woman. You scared me," I said. "I think you may have shortened my life by five years just now."

"Sorry about that. What do we have on tap for today?" she asked.

"I'm going to water the plants on the porch. You slept through breakfast, but there's a fresh pot of coffee brewing if you're in the mood for coffee. We can go into town to grab some lunch, if you're hungry," I answered. Sara looked at me expectantly.

"Ah, right," I said. "I need to call the attorney. We can go over there and sign the paperwork for the divorce." I paused, "Or not."

"I think it's for the best," she said. "Don't you?"

"I don't know, Sara," I said. "I keep going back and forth on this. I'll admit I was really angry when you unilaterally decided to leave. Then I kept thinking that maybe Doctors Without Borders was your true calling, and maybe I was just too hasty. But then I would think about the process and the lying by omission, and I think your actions were something very loud and clear that we were over when you finally told me what you were doing."

She turned away from me and rummaged around in the cabinet with the coffee mugs. She filled up her mug, back still facing me, and she took a good pull on her coffee before setting the mug on the table and looking at me. She didn't say anything, and I couldn't read her expression, which was probably the biggest clue we were finished. I had always been able to read her, and now, she was someone I didn't know. She was a shadowy outline of the woman I had known and loved.

"Rob, I think I need to share with you, give you some feedback. You have been giving me all kinds of feedback for the last two years, and I've been too caught up in my own shit to respond, and then you just keep adding more shit to the heap that's been growing and growing," she said.

"Okay, tell me your thoughts. I've been wanting to know what's going on in your head for over two years," I responded.

"Almost immediately after the miscarriage, you went into problem-solving mode. I know the quick response was good for you, but it wasn't something I could do because I had to deal with my grief. When you started going to therapy and feeling sunnier, it made me angry, sad, and jealous."

I was stunned listening to her, but she continued. "I dug in my heels and wanted you to make a miracle happen, and then I realized you couldn't make a miracle for me. You were busy keeping the ship that was our family afloat, which meant there was nothing left for me." She looked at me very earnestly. "It turned out we didn't know each other as well as we thought we did. You didn't know what I needed when I needed it, and you made me feel like a criminal for not fitting into your framework for healing."

She was right. I expected her to do what I was doing and feel like I was feeling the same way and with the same timing.

"There were so many things I wish I would have done differently, but things played out the way they did, and I'm not okay. Someday, I think I will be better, maybe not the girl you met at 22, but a different version of who I am now, banged up with scars, but better than I am today. I'm so sorry for what I dragged you and the kids through, and our parents. You know, I never told anyone at work about the pregnancy and miscarriage, and they were dumbstruck when I announced my resignation. To be honest, I was surprised any of my partners showed up for my going away party," she said with melancholy.

"I wish you would have gone for therapy," I said. "You could have leaned on me, but you didn't. You could have gotten anti-depressants, but you didn't. We could have sold the house, moved anywhere in the world to get away from how you felt being here. You didn't do anything to try to climb out of the hole the miscarriage created, and I tried, Sara. I really tried." We looked at each other intently. "You decided to give up. You gave up on the kids, on me, and you gave up on yourself."

Sara didn't say anything, and her expression was something I couldn't decode, hammering home what we needed to do. She spoke up, "We are different people, Rob. We process our emotions very differently. I think there were times throughout our marriage where I let you bulldoze me into things that I didn't necessarily want to do, but I went along with it anyway. It was my choice, though, and because I made the choice, I have to live with the good and bad outcomes. All the animals? Left to my own devices, I don't think I would have added to the two dogs. We didn't need to move here. We could have stayed in town and been fine, but it's on me that I didn't make any objections. I let you run the show. All the time. But the thing I realized is that you can't run and regulate what's going on in my head and heart."

"I get it. We're done. As angry and hurt as I was and am, I kept holding out hope," I said.

She paced back and forth in front of the kitchen table, taking her time to measure her next words. "I kept wondering what our marriage would look like if I were gone one year, two years, indefinitely. It doesn't make sense for either of us. We aren't the same anymore. Let's be frank, Rob. We haven't been partners for over two years. I haven't been any kind of co-parent for over two years. Be very honest with yourself. That's not something either of us wants as a future. I can't be a good partner if my partner is constantly keeping score. I can't get onto an even playing field with you—ever. As much as you want me to get better, you're not allowing me the freedom to figure out what I need."

"That's all I want for you, Sara," I want you to feel better.

"No, I don't think so. You want me to fulfill my family roles first and foremost. Getting better is secondary. What I'm telling you is you don't know me like you thought you did, and I don't know you. We'd never faced anything like this before, and when we had this tragedy, we were two people who shouldn't be together."

She was right, and we both knew it. I knew it way before now, but hope is a funny thing, and giving up hope feels like failure, and no one aims to fail. I left the room to call the attorney to see if they could produce hard copies of the divorce documents for our signatures since Sara was here in person to sign everything.

I had been seeing myself as a martyr by being married to her through this dark time, thinking I was taking the high ground, and it was a bitter pill to know I hadn't been a great partner to her—but she was right. I hadn't been a good partner. We fell apart in the face of a setback. She was doing the brave thing, though, following through with the divorce. If it hadn't been the miscarriage, it would have been something at some other time in the future. I never thought we'd fail as a couple.

We left the house, stopped at a café we used to love when the kids were little. Sara ordered a patty melt—one of her trademarks from our early days. I ordered a BLT with avocado. This place put nearly a third of a pound of bacon on their BLTs, and I always joked about the bacon and mayo on the sandwich, "If you hear a loud noise while I'm eating this sandwich, it's my arteries snapping shut."

We were going through the motions today, not even trying to make small talk. I broke the silence, "You stop being my wife, but you won't ever stop being Jen and Bryan's mother. You need to figure out if you're going to have any kind of relationship with them, and you're going to have to commit to holding up your end of whatever the relationship is—if there is one. Can you get therapy at all, even telehealth?" I asked.

She deflected my question but said very slowly and soberly, "Yeah. I've looked into it. I'm going to do it. I'm not exactly ready yet, but I'm going to do it. I am so tired of feeling like shit and like a failure. I know what I did to you, to the kids, and I am cognizant of the fact that I ran away, okay? What happened, for me, was like a category five hurricane. I, uh, just didn't know how to, um, restore everything that was knocked out in the storm, and I wasn't prepared for a storm in the first place."

"Well, your hurricane sure fucked the rest of us," I said, then thought better of it. "Okay. I'm at turns numb, angry, or hopeful, and that was the anger coming out. I wasn't a great partner for you, and for that I am sorry. I want nothing but the best for you."

I took a large bite of my sandwich, stared at Sara, who was 100% focused on her patty melt. I subtly shook my head in frustration at the whole situation and this ridiculous lunch. I broke the silence, "I want to give you something to think about. What role do you want to play in Jen and Bryan's lives? What do you think you're going to be able to give them? I don't want you to promise more than you can deliver. If you don't think you can be the mother they want and deserve, then I don't think you should make that one of their expectations. Just think on it tonight. We can talk again in the morning."

She set her patty melt down on her plate, wiped her fingers on her napkin, and looked up at me. There was sadness and fury in her gaze. "Look. I know what I did. I feel awful for what I did. I also felt awful while it was all happening, but I'm not alone in this. We were a team. I don't remember you ever sitting down with me just to ask what I needed," she said in a chillingly quiet voice. "You were always insistent on telling me what you thought I needed, and you were always playing the martyr. 'Oh, Sara. I'll do this. I'll do that if only you'd get better.'" She paused while it sank in. "You beat me over the head *all the time* with your ideas, and it was never a comfort. It was always a yardstick for how I was lacking in every way." She picked at her napkin then wiped her mouth and dabbed at her eyes. "You made it easy for me to pull away." She settled her napkin on her plate and stood. "I'll wait for you in the car."

We went to the attorney's office, signed the paperwork, and they told us they would file everything with the courts for us. The attorney told us we were one of the easiest divorces they'd ever handled. Sara asked if we won a prize. The attorney, a pretty stoic older guy, had grey bushy eyebrows, and his response to Sara's quip was raising the two brows, which seemed to turn them into a very mobile-looking caterpillar just above his drooping eyelids.

That night, I went to bed but stayed up. I knew I wouldn't be able to sleep and turned on the TV. I hunted around all of the streaming services to see if there was anything I'd want to watch before finally settling on an old movie with Stan Tucci and Oliver Platt. I would call the movie a madcap comedy. The Sara of the old days would have asked what century I was born in, and I would have said something like, "The twentieth century, my dear," in an affected English accent, and the old Sara would have laughed herself into a coughing fit.

Eventually I drifted off, waking to the sun's earliest light peeping through the windows, almost gingerly. I took a moment to sit up, stretched my neck in different directions, waiting for the satisfying pop, finally making my way to the kitchen for a cup of coffee. Sara was already seated at the table, a mug held tightly in her hands, staring out one of the windows, a far-off look in her eyes. She registered my presence, briefly making eye contact before returning to whatever held her attention outside our home.

"I was up a long time last night," she said. "I thought about what you asked me. You know, the role I want to have in everyone's lives. I don't want to be anything to anyone. I want to be a doctor, and I want to go back to Africa. I think I can't do or be more than that, at least not right now."

"Okay," I responded, more as a question than anything. "What does that look like for you? What is it you want from me, from the kids?"

Sara fidgeted with her coffee mug. Her face contorted, and her pupils raced back and forth. She was putting my question through whatever process she had for decision-making, trying to think through a solution. She was struggling with saying what she wanted to say. "At first, I thought I didn't deserve anything from any of you because. Because I left. I saddled you with everything, and I didn't even give the kids a reason for anything. But I do deserve something. I am their mother, and I know I'm not acting like a mother at all right now, but I won't be like this forever. I don't want to be like this forever, but I don't know how to go back, and I don't know what I'm going to be like in the future." She was crying now, full-on ugly crying, her voice thick with tears. "Maybe in the future, I think I will want to be in their lives. I don't know what it will look like, but I know I can't keep going on this way." She wiped her eyes and nose. "But see, here's the thing: I'm finding my own way to the other side. I'm figuring out what I need to do for me. I've been really lonely, Rob. Not just in Africa, but I was lonely here, too. It was partly a monster of my own making, bad luck, and the two of us not talking, or you doing all the problem-solving. But I've hit a wall, and I know something needs to change. Doctors Without Borders seemed like a pathway for me to pull the focus away from us." She pointed back and forth between us.

I felt the hairs on the back of my neck raised in alarm. "What do you mean when you say you 'can't keep going on this way?' Do you mean being absent? Persona non grata? Deeply depressed? I don't know what you mean. Do you?" She looked at me quizzically. I had lost the ability to get inside her head and read her. "Listen, whatever you decide, if you promise something, please follow through on your promises. Don't break their hearts over and over."

I stood there a moment longer, looking at her, and I couldn't see *my* Sara. Her body was shaking from her own crying, but I didn't have it in me to offer her any sort of comfort. By the way she was looking at me, though, I realized I still didn't understand what she was trying to say, and I didn't have the energy to try to figure it out. But I knew one thing. She wasn't the only architect in the demise of our marriage, and I would have to learn to live with and understand where I had failed Sara...and me.

LOVE AND STUFF

SARA - AGE 23

It was a Saturday in the summer, right between my first and second years in medical school. My last free summer. Clinical rotations would start between years two and three. My apartment complex had a nice quiet swimming pool. We brought a cooler full of beer and soft drinks to the pool, called for pizza delivery around lunch time, and lay next to the pool for a couple hours. Rob and I were gloriously in love.

"You're starting to look a little pink," he said. "Do you want me to put more sunscreen on you?"

"I think I'm going to jump in the pool to cool off for a few. You can slather some stuff on me when I get out, okay?"

He raised his brows lasciviously, saying, "I'll slather some stuff on you, if you know what I mean."

"I always know what you mean," I said, smiling warmly at him.

I swam a few leisurely lengths of the pool free style, then ended with a length on my back, and Jesus, Joseph, Mary, and all the saints, the sun felt so good on my face. I didn't think I had ever felt this degree of contentment. I toweled off and went back to my deck chair, dropping my hand off to the side for Rob to take, but he didn't grab it right away. He was fiddling around in his duffel bag, digging around for something. "Babe, the sunscreen is under your chair, if that's what you're looking for," I said.

"No. I'm trying to find—ah. There it is," he said. He lurched from his deck chair, grabbed a towel, and laid it down on the ground next to my chair, then he sort of crumpled onto the towel.

"Are you ok?" I asked. "I'm very worried about your gross motor skills."

"Ha, ha," he said nervously. "No. I'm fine. I'm having some feelings. You know how much I love you, right?"

"Yes," I said, "and I love you, too."

"See. When two people love each other, it's so great. You know, you come together as a unit, and the love you share can get you through anything. I feel like we're a team. We can face anything together. Don't you think so?"

"I do," I said, and it seemed like he was winding up a pitch, and I had best pay attention to the words now coming out of his mouth. I gave him all of my focus and truly noticed he wasn't simply crouched on the towel. He was getting into a squat, almost like he was trying to get into the starting blocks before a race.

He went on, "You give me strength I didn't even know I was missing, and it kind of makes me sad to think I almost didn't meet you. I almost didn't go to Devin and Terri's the night we met, but they begged me to come over and make some food for the party. And I did, and it was the best night of my life," he said.

He was no longer crumpled, crouched, or ready to race. He was on one knee next to my lounge chair, and he was holding a small jewelry box. "I spoke with your parents the other day, and they gave me their blessing. I want you to marry me. I want to marry you. I guess I'm asking, would you do me the honor of marrying me and making me the happiest man in the world?"

I looked at the ring, nestled in the box, and it took my breath away. The center stone was an emerald cut diamond. The side stones were emerald cut sapphires. The ring was the most dazzling, sparkly thing I had ever seen, and this man, my man, my Rob, wanted to put the ring on my finger. He wanted to spend his life with me, and I couldn't imagine a time where I wouldn't want him in my life. I looked deeply into his dear face, full of feeling and bottomless love he had for me. I felt the tears running down my face before I even registered I was crying.

"Yes! Yes! I want to marry you. I want to spend my life with you. Yes! Oh, my gosh," I responded. "I love you!" And I loved him so much, and I didn't think anything could ever tear us apart. In my mind, I was already starting to form the picture of what a life and family with Rob would look like, and, to me, it would be babies, puppies, kittens, rainbows, white picket fences, happiness, and sheer joy.

I knew, deep down, nothing good ever comes without some bumps, but our love could withstand everything thrown our way. Rob's mettle, my determination, and this thing between us would galvanize us.

We began pre-marital counseling within a month of our engagement, which only solidified what I already knew: Rob was my bedrock and my best friend. As long as we communicated, shared, loved, respected each other, truly listened to each other, we'd be happy, and we'd be able to get through whatever was thrown in our path.

Part Two

Moving Forward at a Run: A reflection

Jen

After Mom's visit, Bryan decided (if there were any future visits) he would put on a happy face. I didn't know what kind of face I would wear, but I would not and could not give her any more mental or emotional real estate. She didn't care about us enough to get the help she needed. Fine. I didn't care about her either. My priorities were the three of us. Bryan, Dad, and I had become poster children for the healing art of psychotherapy. I had a lot of work to do balancing calories and exercise.

Rewiring my thinking, though, took time, meditation, and visualization, and a physiological obstacle. I didn't have enough caloric intake to fuel my running. Dad had found a therapist for me who dealt with teenagers with eating disorders who were also athletes. Victoria Ross was the right person at the right time. My whole life, for a while, revolved around seeing Dr. Ross several times a week initially.

"Tell me something, Jen," she said during one of our earlier sessions. "Tell me about what a good run feels like. Take me through every part of your routine before you walk out the door."

"I run at different times of day. If I run earlier in the day, I seem to have more energy. On the days I get started early, I set my alarm. I always get up without hitting snooze and go through some yoga poses to get stretched out. Is this the kind of stuff you want to hear about?" I asked.

Dr. Ross nodded. "I'd like to hear everything. Nothing is too trivial. Go on."

"I always brush my teeth before I go downstairs. I get dressed. Usually shorts and a sports bra, socks, and running shoes, and put on my watch. If it's raining, I run on the treadmill. If it's decent outside, I go outside. If it's sunny, I put a little sunscreen on my face. I fill up my water bottle if I think I'm going for more than a five mile run. If not, then I drink a couple glasses of water before I leave the house."

"Where do you like to run? Do you have different routes? How do you decide where you're going to run when you walk out the door?"

"It depends on the amount of energy I have. Lately, my runs have been shorter because I've either been too tired in the morning or I'm just worn out at the end of the day," I answered.

"Why do you think you're worn out or tired?" Dr. Ross asked.

"I know it's because I'm not eating enough or I'm not eating the right things. I know that. But I can't turn off the math in my head."

"Tell me about the math," she said, and she had the good grace to look like this was something new she was hearing, but in her line of work, it couldn't have been novel.

"I look at calories in and calories out, surplus and deficit. It's a seesaw. Sometimes I win, and sometimes I lose. Winning and losing are difficult to define and often a moving target. I know my weight is low, and in my brain I lose when I'm in calorie surplus and win when I'm in calorie deficit. And what I'm seeing now is that I'm losing when I'm calorie neutral or in calorie deficit because I don't have enough fuel to run as far, fast, or as long as I want."

She nodded.

"Why are you still running? Your mom is in Africa. You mentioned before that you wanted to compete with her college times and records.

"I know. She's not here now, and she probably doesn't care about her old stats and records. When I first began running, it was something that tied me to my mom. She ran. I ran. She didn't notice that I ran."

I paused, raising my voice, "Like she never even acknowledged what I was doing. It was weird. I kept ratcheting up my activity level, but she didn't seem to be aware of anything outside her immediate sphere. At first, I was so frustrated." I was wringing my hands, recalling the feeling of being invisible to my own mother.

"I knew she had run track and cross country in college. I found her old times and records, and I focused on beating her times when I ran. What I learned was being tall was something in my favor. I had the mechanics for distance running, just as she had. Over time, though, I gave up on competing with her. And I started really enjoying what I was doing. Her stats gave me a benchmark, and it became a goal I could work toward."

I paused, and I smiled, looking the doctor in the eye. "You know what I discovered? I am a girl who loves a goal, and I learned I loved to compete."

It was during this visit that I *started* to realize I didn't need to tie my personhood and my self-value to my mother. I still had so much damage she had left, but running was a good, pure thing for me, and I wasn't going to let her ruin it. There was still so much re-wiring I needed to do in my own brain. Months later, I asked Dr. Ross if she would be willing to meet jointly with my dad and me to discuss sports psychology. She felt I had made progress by just adding on seven pounds to my weight, and she agreed. The session with her, my dad, and me was pivotal. It helped me become more serious about my sport, We continued down the path of looking at food as more than fuel and that it could be an enjoyable experience, which was and is still something I consciously grapple with daily.

PHYSICALLY MOVING ON: A REFLECTION

BRYAN

I knew Jen sometimes went through my phone, and being just a little passive aggressive, I intentionally left it unattended. She could be a meddling older sister from time to time, but I wanted her to see the reminders I entered:

Weekly check-in with Dad and Jen – update journal.

I had a journal and kept records on Dad and Jen. I was charting on them. Knowing she was invading my privacy, I wanted her to know I was watching and documenting, and what was going on wasn't something she could later say was fiction when I had a record of my observations. She had to know I knew she was snooping, and it just meant she couldn't get away with falling apart without anyone knowing. I knew. I always knew.

When Mom and Dad's divorce was final, we all moved on—we physically moved. Dad sold the house. The new owners kept all the animals, but we kept Rosemary and Sage. Our lives were on an upward trend: new house, new school. Mom took a second post in Asia after her first year. Dad took a new job, which he said he enjoyed, but Jen and I could tell he didn't enjoy the added responsibility, and he missed working from his home office every day. It made me happy to see him going to an actual office in an office building, though. He needed to be around people and being cooped up all day, every day, was not going to help him heal from the breakup of his marriage.

The grandmas were around a lot more, and they did everything they could to provide us with some adult female guidance and supervision since Dad's job was more demanding and required him to work in an actual office. Having the grandmas around was mostly nice, but sometimes a pain. We couldn't get anything past them.

Dad's new job came with a big pay bump. Our new house was lovely. He hired a decorator and gave her instructions to make it look like home. The decorator, Maggie, was in her forties, and she spent time with Jen and me individually to get a handle on our aesthetics. It was funny, because three years ago, I don't think I had a clue what my aesthetic was, but I wanted bookshelves. I had been buying books, tons of self-help, medical and psychology textbooks, eventually working my way into neuroscience.

One day, Jen looked at the stacks of books in my room. "You're a star," she said. "And you're a sap." I looked back at her.

"That's a weird compliment and insult," I said. "I don't know whether to be embarrassed or annoyed."

"You're brilliant. You could be like a robot, but you're a teddy bear. You wear your heart on your sleeve with the love and care you have for Dad and me. Maybe don't worry so much. Okay?" Jen said, and she gave me a little flick on the side of my head. She pulled back some, and grabbed me by the shoulders, shaking me just a little. "I hate seeing the constant worry behind your eyes, in the tense set of your jaw, in the way you run your fingers through his hair, the defeated slump in your posture when you think no one is looking."

I knew I was observing everyone else, but it never occurred to me that they were watching me, too. Jen told me to journal for my own benefit, not just charting her and Dad. She had been journaling based on the recommendation of one of her therapists. There were more than one therapist now, and journaling seemed to be something important her therapists wanted Jen to do, and she admitted it was something that had been helping her.

Jen and I had both become people-pleasers after Mom left us. Not sycophants, but definitely wanted everyone to be happy. Jen was more bent on making sure everyone was satisfied, beaming, and practically clapping their approval her direction for whatever task she had performed. I was less desperate when it came to making everyone happy all the time, but we were both driven to be the best.

Jen snooped on me. I snooped on her. In her journal, our lives were a succession of bullet points on a checklist. She checked them off, one after another on the lists she created. Her record keeping was different than mine. She caught me looking at her journal.

"Hey, nosey," she said.

I felt my face heat up. "Your journal is kind of a lot. It's way different than mine. I wasn't sure what I should be putting into a journal, and I just kind of write down random and rambling thoughts. Your journal, though...whew! It's mind-blowing."

"I wasn't sure what to put into a journal either. I didn't know if it needed to be a diary or a series of letters or a recap of my day or what. Then I just started making lists of things I needed to do, or things I had completed. Every time I check any item off my list, I feel so empowered. Most of the things on the list are things I've added on a prospective basis. After a while, I started to add things that just popped up. I put them on the list and immediately crossed them out as soon as they were complete, and some of the stuff was already complete." Her eyes widened before she went on, "I don't know ahead of time all the points I'm going to check off and add them as they occur. Working through the list, completing tasks—it's all very therapeutic for me."

Her lists looked neurotic to me, but if the crazy record-keeping would bring her back to the center of her lane, then so be it.

Eventually, Jen's journals became project plans and action plans, and they looked like something from some corporate management meeting. Eventually, she put some of her data points into a spreadsheet and created color graphs. I had no idea why it was so important to her to keep up this level of organization, though. It seemed like as her eating improved, she was spiraling into hyper-organization and problem-solving.

I snooped around in Jen's journal again, thinking maybe it might give me clues and insights into how she was dealing with her own demons. I thought maybe her journal would be something I could emulate myself. Did I think I was being an invasive dickhead of a brother? Probably, but worry for my sister superseded thinking I was a dick.

Jen's journal had taken on a life of its own, and I realized my sister had become a highly organized and complex thinker. Her journal was technical but still retained some of the hallmarks of a teenage girl. The pages had become full of project plans with estimated completion dates and all the sub-steps needed to execute the deliverables, and it all blew my mind. Her lists and plans were covered in highlighter, colored ink, stickers, little doodles in the margins, every step in a plan or bullet from a list drawn in with the flourishes, flowers, curlicues, meandering lines, curves, patterns going nowhere but looking beautiful in their pursuit of flowing together into a cohesive picture. One of her big post-move goals looked like a movie marquee and simply said: Make new friends. After our mom's sendoff party, we had both withdrawn, but Jen's friend group had become much smaller. In a smaller font, Jen had written in bubble letters: Have a social life.

New Friends

Jen - age 15

New school year. New friends. New everything. I worried a little that all the kids at our new school would already have established friend groups, and it might be difficult to be the new girl as a sophomore, but I was wrong. Before the fall term began, I quickly made a new friend, Darcy. She lived not far from our new house, and she introduced herself to me one morning while I was on my morning run.

She came from an intact family. Darcy already had her driver's license and had invited me to have dinner with her and her family before going to see a movie. She had stick straight white-blonde hair cut into a pageboy cut. She was the rare girl who could wear bangs. She had two younger brothers who were identical twins. They, too, shared the white-blonde hair. They were in fifth grade, and they were a lot. They couldn't keep their hands off each other. They would punch each other in the arm, smack each other on the back of the head, twist each other's arms behind their backs. They were loud. When Darcy's dad came home from work, the expectation was that Darcy's mom had dinner ready to go.

Darcy's parents were beautiful people, too. When we walked through the front of the house to the kitchen, every family photo looked like it had come from a catalog shoot. Darcy's mom, a tall willowy woman with the build of a tennis player, had a thick head of golden hair that looked like the sun was constantly kissing the top of her head. Her dad had light brown hair that picked up glints of red when the light hit it just right. They both had startlingly blue eyes, and cheek bones as perfect as cut glass.

We took our places around their kitchen table. Darcy's mom took a casserole dish out of the oven and carefully placed it on a trivet on the table. The trivet had some motivational saying about the power of family. Darcy's dad was hungry, and no sooner than the casserole dish made contact with the table, he pulled off the aluminum foil covering.

"Gwen," he said like he was talking to a small child. "Tuna casserole, really?" His voice started to increase in volume. "You really expect me to eat this fucking shit? You must think I'm some kind of asshole to serve this to me. You did this on purpose, which makes you a goddamned fucking cunt. This is just the type of fucked up sneakiness you like, isn't it? You're itching to set me off." I think I heard him say under his breath something to the effect of, "This is completely fucked up bullshit."

Darcy's mom picked up her empty plate and slammed it down on the table and spoke very loudly, "Well, fuck you. Everyone else in this family loves tuna casserole. And, yes. I do think you're some kind of asshole." Darcy's face had turned red, and the twins both seemed to be trying to fade into the background. I felt about 2 inches tall. I didn't know Darcy's parents. This was my first time meeting them, and I wanted to leave but Darcy had driven, and she seemed frozen throughout her parents' exchange.

Her dad whispered, "This is bullshit," then picked up the hot casserole dish with a potholder, calmly walked from the table, opened the sliding glass door, finally standing on the deck and flinging the dish like a discus thrower into the backyard. He turned around, a serene look on his face, making eye contact with Darcy's mom. He returned to the table, saying very conversationally, "No. Fuck you, Gwen. Now. What are we going to eat for dinner?"

Darcy abruptly rose from her seat, screaming at her parents. "I can't believe you. I never have friends over, and you know why? You are horrible. You're an embarrassment. Look at the boys. They're afraid of you. Is that what you want? You," she turned her head toward each parent, making eye contact with them, and issuing almost in a growl, "are awful parents!" She looked at me. "I can't do this." Less than 30 seconds later, we were in Darcy's car, heading away from her house. "Would it be all right if I stayed at your house tonight?" she asked, angry tears leaving tracks down her cheeks.

After witnessing the scene at her house, I could hardly refuse her. I called my dad to let him know we'd be having an overnight guest, and he was cool with it. Darcy stayed with us through the weekend. Her mom dropped by to leave some clothes for Darcy. They spoke little during the handoff, ending with a stiff hug. Maybe a month or two later, Darcy's parents separated. What had become more apparent after their separation was how Darcy seemed to have a weight lifted from her shoulders once she didn't feel like she had to referee her parents' fights or flee the family home.

"They've been at each other's throats ever since I can remember," Darcy said to me one day while we were shopping for homecoming dresses. "I think my brothers act the way they do as a diversionary tactic. If my parents are trying to wrangle them, at least they aren't screaming at each other. That's my theory, anyway."

"I hate to ask, but what made them finally decide to end things?" I didn't really hate asking all that much because I really wanted to know. My parents' situation was so different.

"I called my grandma and said I wanted to come live with her and my grandpa to get away from my parents. I told her the boys would need to come, too, because our home life was toxic. She asked me what was going on, and I told her. She was shocked."

"Really?" I asked. "She had no idea?"

"My parents put on a really good show outside the house. Anyone who didn't spend time inside the four walls of our house thought we were like a TV family. But Grandma and Grandpa invited my parents over to their house for dinner, without us kids, and they asked them to think very hard and very sincerely about whether or not they still loved each other, were still in love with each other, and if they brought out the best in each other. Were they behaving toward one another in a loving and respectful way? The thing that got me the most, though, was when they asked my parents if their relationship was what they wanted their kids to use as a model for what a healthy relationship between a man and woman should be."

"I think your grandparents could have a talk show. I wish they could have talked to my parents after my mom's miscarriage. My parents quit talking. My mom retreated, and my dad was walking around trying to figure out how to solve her problem, and she wouldn't let him into her head," I said.

Darcy nodded, and I think we both were trying to make sense of who had it worse. "Well, after the grandparent showdown," she said, "things seemed to take on a life of their own. Our parents sat us down and apologized to us for all the bad behavior we had to witness for nearly our whole lives. They said being terrible to one another wasn't anything they wanted us to think was good or normal. They said married people do fight, argue, but they do it with love, and their fights didn't have anything to do with love anymore. They were unhappy and took it out on each other, and we kids were sitting in the fallout zone." Darcy seemed resigned while she talked. "It's been good, though. Dad has a condo, and Mom hired a lawn service to handle the yard, and we spend quality time with our parents separately, and it's a lot better. Definitely more peaceful. I still get hives when they're in the same room, though. Dad has been coming back to the house to get more of his stuff to take to his condo, and it still makes everyone go onto hyper-alert for possible nuclear annihilation." She mimicked an explosion, shuddering. "I hope someday we can all be civil. I mean, I don't want there to be two opposing camps when I eventually get married. I don't want to think we're always going to be on the verge of a Chernobyl-type of disaster."

Darcy's parents did divorce by the end of first semester of our sophomore year, and it was mostly amicable in the way where they didn't live together, were out of each other's hair, and weren't fighting over 'things' or money. Her parents were both present and active in everyone's lives, and they got on well enough in public. There was still a lot of tension hovering about any time they were together, and there was the continued threat of someone losing their cool and a loose 'cunt' or 'fucker' being unleashed. Years later, they learned to be arms-length friends. They were never going to be friends who invited each other to barbecue or anything good or close friends would do, but they did get to a point where the whole room wasn't going to take bets on who said 'fuck you,' first.

But I think I was a little envious Darcy and her brothers had two parents who wanted to be part of their lives. My dad was doing double duty between Bryan and me, and our grandparents were doing their best to fill in the gaps our mom left behind. It still rankled that our own mother didn't want to be part of our lives. I knew there were people who didn't want to be parents, but our mom had been a great mom up until she wasn't.

SOMETHING UNEXPECTED

ROB - AGE 41

My mother, Jen, Bryan, and I hit the mall. My closet was the maw of a beast, filled with outdated clothes, concert tees, ratty jeans, sneakers. When we sold the house, Sara's clothes went to her parents' house. The new closet in the new house was seemingly put together by a team of Swedes. Optimized storage made everything look clean and logical, and it seemed like I was profaning the closet with my shitty, old, work-from-home clothes. "Dad, no offense, but you need to step up your wardrobe. Maybe it's a tech thing, but I'm surprised no one has gifted you clothes or department store gift cards. You're the Chief Information Officer, not a guy programming apps in our basement," Jen said. She pulled a double-breasted suit away from where it was hanging. "This is awful. Did you wear it in high school?"

"Oh, my gosh," Bryan said. "I want to wear this for 90's day during spirit week. It's so bad." I looked at my son who was holding up a shiny, silk shirt. I had loved that thing, and now it was being mocked. Fashion, much like time, marches on.

"Fine. You guys win. I think I've been too comfortable working from home all these years. It just kills me to admit that I might need grownup clothes." I called my mom, and she was happy to make a day of it with us. We'd shop for clothes for everyone, have lunch somewhere nice, get home and hang everything in our closets, and do our own Iron Chef competition for dinner.

With the move, the kids would be starting at a new school. We had a family meeting and decided private school would be better than public, just because they didn't want to be overwhelmed in a large school, and their old school had been smaller in size.

The kids wore uniforms in their new school, and we had to make sure we had locked down all the accessories. I wanted them to start on the right foot, and I wanted them to have decent after-school clothes. It was important to me that we were all starting fresh, and to that end, clothes seemed like a very good idea. The best idea. My mom seemed to be filled with glee and treated us all like her personal dolls she got to dress up. We didn't take my dad. I could picture the look of torture on his face, and I thought about forcing him to come with us just for the entertainment value.

We hit a bunch of the teeny-bopper stores in the mall, eventually making our way to Nordstrom. We went directly to the office, and I asked if there were any personal shoppers available to help us with everything we needed. I knew I'd need to peel off from the kids for a bit. The double-breasted suit was abominable and a terrible, shiny, thin polyester. I could admit it was bad, and a new suit was in my future. I wouldn't be wearing a suit frequently, but I think I knew there were meetings I would have to attend, and Jen was right: I needed to dress more appropriately for the role. There had to be a way I could be mature and still embrace my programmer style.

The four of us sat quietly in customer service, and the personal shopper was someone we all knew. It was Maggie the Decorator. "Fancy seeing you here," I said.

"I have a part-time job here. I pick up a couple weekend days every month and love having the discount." She smiled.

"Mom, this is Maggie. She decorated the new house. Maggie, this is my mom, Eva James," I said, introducing them.

"Maggie, you did a lovely job making the new house into a home for Rob and the kids. It's very warm and inviting, and I think they're all enjoying it." We looked over to the kids to see if they were going to engage and join the conversation, but they were glued to their phones.

"Kids? Kids?" I cleared my throat. "Kids," I repeated in a higher volume. They finally looked up startled. "You know Maggie. She also works for Nordstrom. She's going to help us with everything we still think we need. Sound good?

I think I could have been asking them if they wanted to colonize Mars, and I would have witnessed similar looks on their faces. Jen made eye contact with me. A slow, knowing smile broke across her face. "Would you like to join us for dinner? We're doing our own Iron Chef thing. We compete. It doesn't matter what food you make. It has to be tasty. Grandma and Grandpa will be the judges. Bryan and I can be a team, and you and Dad can be a team, or we can mix it up. Girls against boys." Jen was trying so hard to find someone for me. I applauded her, but I didn't think a hard sell and weird dinner invitation were going to yield results. Jen appealed to me, "Dad? Maggie already knows the layout of the house and kitchen. It'll be fun. Maggie, what do you think?"

We all stood there, looking at each other. I felt weird putting Maggie into a high pressure situation, and I wondered how she would navigate her way in or out. Maggie turned a little pink and was the first to speak. "Can I bring my husband, son, and daughter? Can they be on a team, too?" Jen hadn't figured a husband into the mix, but she was undaunted. When Maggie was meeting with me to get the details for decorating the house, I had noticed her wedding and engagement rings. Since the divorce, this was my new normal—looking at women's ring fingers. Clearly, my daughter was not doing the ring finger check. However, Jen wanted to bring the fun into our new home, and if it meant we were expanding our social circle, then why not?

"Sure," Jen said. "How old are your kids? Do they like to cook?"

"My daughter likes to cook, and my son and husband like to eat. Maybe one of them could be a judge with your grandparents. In fact, it might be good for you and Bryan to meet my son. He goes to the school you two are going to be starting. He's going to be a junior this year. His name is Trent. He's a good kid. You guys would like him."

Maggie's husband, Tom, was a bear of a man. He stood around six foot two, and he was solid as an oak. His hair was brown with glints of auburn throughout, and the guy had the smile of your oldest, best friend, and the minute I met Tom, I pictured going fishing. I am not a fisherman, but I thought, 'I could go fishing with this man. We'd have the best time. I'll take Bryan and my dad, and we'll catch fish, clean them, then cook them for our families." I knew it was completely irrational, but sometimes you get a feeling about people. The O'Briens, Tom, Maggie, Trent, and Bridgette, became our family's closest friends.

Our dinner contest became part of our family lore. Some of the food we made was okay, some was terrible, and there were a few dishes I would deem better than okay. One of the kids started a small fire which was easily contained, and Rosemary ate the chicken right off of Bridgette's plate. Bridgette, was ten at the time, and she was probably going to feed her food to the dogs anyway. It turned out she was going through a vegetarian phase, and the chicken was a superfluous blob of flesh on her plate.

While we were tossing lo mein in the wok, Tom asked if I had started dating yet. "I haven't," I replied. "I'm not sure how to meet people anymore. It seems like the dating landscape has totally changed."

Tom said, "It has. It's all apps and sliding left and right and hoping the person you think you might like isn't catfishing you. You know where I met Maggie?" I shook my head. "I met her at a 5K for breast cancer. We were both in the same corral, started talking, and we decided to walk the 5K instead of running, and we talked the whole way. By the time we finished, we made plans for dinner later that night, and we've been together ever since." He paused just a moment before saying, "I've never set anyone up before, but my sister's best friend has been single, by choice, for about around eight years or something. I've known her since we were kids. She's terrific, and I think you'd get along. She's 34, no kids, and works in HR for a consulting company or software company or something like that. But my sister says Erin is ready to start dating again and would like to meet someone nice. What do you think?"

Sara and my divorce hadn't been final for very long, but our marriage had been over for two years, and it had been so long since I had felt any kind of companionship with an adult female, not just a physical relationship, but feeling like I was part of a partnership involving dialogue, shared interests, and the desire to spend time together. "Okay, sure. Why not? Would you and Maggie want to double with us?"

"I am going to give you the best advice for your first date with Erin. Don't double with us on the first date. Maybe the second or third or something. She has a dog, and you have two dogs. You and Erin and the dogs should go to a dog park for a while, then take all of them for a walk. You can also grab lunch someplace outside with the dogs. You'll have a nice time. See how it goes. I think you're going to hit it off, and I wouldn't be surprised if you'd decide to have her meet Jen and Bryan by the third date. That's my prediction anyway."

Tom called his sister, and her squeals of delight were loud enough for me to hear from five feet away. I laughed. After ending the call with his sister, Tom said, "She's actually out with Erin right now and is casually going to see if it's all right to pass along her number. I texted some of the photos from tonight for Tess (my sister) to share with Erin."

I nodded. Tom's phone began to vibrate, and he picked up, smiling, chatting with his sister. "You're not going to believe this. Tess, her partner Carlotta, and Erin are close by right now. She wants to know if it's all right for them to stop by. No pressure, though."

"Sure," I said. "We can see how they like the egg rolls Jen and Maggie made." I grimaced because what they made was not an egg roll. Jen was ordinarily a good cook, but Maggie's cooking was unknown to me, thus blaming her for the fried mystery seemed appropriate. Tom commented the same, but with the focus on Jen. Could it be the two of them paired together could only make questionable-looking food? No one could make heads or tails of what it was they had made. It was revolting to view, but the inside was good. It was a mystery how their egg rolls turned out to be so strange. We all saw the picture from the recipe on Jen's phone, and what they cooked wasn't close to looking like the picture.

Our house was filled with life. Tom, Maggie, Trent, Bridgette, Tess, Carlotta, Erin, my parents, my children, and I were assembled for a rousing game of charades, then karaoke, which turned into a dance party when the kids paired their phones to our portable speakers and started the most outstanding playlist on Spotify. I think Tom's setup idea was going to be sidelined by the impromptu turn the night was taking, and I would just see how the chemistry worked with

Erin. If there wasn't any chemistry, no harm, no foul. This night was taking on a life of its own, and we were going to see where it took us. It was a good night for the James family.

WORK

SARA - AGE 41

I don't think anything could have adequately prepared me for Doctors Without Borders, and Africa was something else that no amount of preparation, videos, or self-study would have ever been able to capture. The sights, sounds, people, food, foliage, fauna. It was so much bigger than my worldview had been. My parents and I had traveled when I was growing up. We had been all over America, and we had been to Europe and Asia, but we had never ventured to Africa.

The first couple weeks, I was in a city, and it seemed like any other cosmopolitan city anywhere else in the world. The hustle and bustle, noises, people in a hurry to go wherever it was they needed to go. Mostly those weeks involved completing paperwork, various assessments, meetings, and then we came to my last day in the concrete jungle. I had always thought of Africa as being full of rain forests and like the jungle from *Jungle Book*, and as a rational adult, I understood a cartoon wouldn't be an accurate representation of real life.

The heat was something. I sweated all the time. Once I arrived at my clinic, I was startled that the photos I'd seen of the clinics were very good facsimiles of my new reality. Each morning, I arrived early to go over every surface in the exam rooms to ensure they were as clean as they could be. I made sure we had plenty of supplies in every drawer and cabinet and none of the sterile seals on any of the supplies had been breached. Each evening, I went through the same routine. I cleaned every exam table myself. It wasn't that I didn't trust the clinic staff to clean the equipment, but more along the lines of wanting everything to be clean according to my own standards. These patients weren't getting enough medical care, and many came from miles away, sometimes on foot, sometimes by motorized vehicle, and the vehicles varied widely.

My very first day, my first patients were a family with an infant. More specifically, it was a mother and four small children and an infant. The children were small, underfed, but happy. Their mother was concerned about the baby. She spoke English, which was a relief to me that I'd be able to communicate with my first patient myself. The mother said she had found out she had been infected with HIV by the baby's father. She was concerned the baby, too, had HIV and wanted to have the child tested.

The nurse and I took the baby's blood, and he howled after the initial surprise of having the needle inserted. "Do you want to have your other children tested?" I asked.

"Oh, no. That's not necessary," she said.

"Are you sure? Since you're here and you traveled over four hours to get here…"

She answered by shaking her head.

"Okay. Do the other children need vaccines or anything?"

"Oh, no. They are fine. Look at them," she said, beaming at her other youngsters.

"And you're managing your HIV all right?" I asked.

"I have medication, and I am fine. I will be fine until I'm not fine," she said.

The nurse and I had taken all of the woman's demographic information, and we had all of her contact information as well.

"Today is my first day in this clinic," I said. "I don't know how long the turnaround will be on the baby's bloodwork. Will it be all right if I call you with the results?"

"That would be just fine," she answered. She looked at her brood. "Are you ready to go back home?" she asked them. There were some eager faces, and some who knew they were going to be strapped into seats in a bus without air conditioning for a good chunk of the day.

Each day, I worked, my day filled with diseases I had read about in medical school and knew how to treat but had never encountered in my suburban practice in the States. Each night, I returned to my rooms and fell into bed, exhausted. The other doctors in the clinic had brought their families with them, and on occasion, they would invite me for dinner, but I felt like an interloper.

I kept to myself mostly and after around six months, I contacted Doctors Without Borders to see what other countries had a need for a primary care doctor. I made the decision not because I hated Africa or my patients, but I was lonely, and almost every waking minute of my existence was tending to these people. I didn't have friends. There was no time to make friends. I worked almost fourteen hours a day, seven days a week.

These patients needed me, though. If they didn't need me, personally, they needed someone like me to tend to their health and physical wellbeing, and I hadn't realized I was taking this post and not setting any personal boundaries for myself or my time. If someone came in at 6:30, right as we might have been closing up for the day, I opted to stay, evaluate, and treat the person.

Overall, the work was gratifying, but the feeling was swallowed up in my exhaustion and pervasive feelings of loneliness. And the damnedest thing, I still felt the sting of the pregnancy loss. I couldn't outrun it if I tried, not even if I traveled half-way around the world. I would have to face it head-on if I wanted to get past it, and with being so isolated, I didn't want the miscarriage to continue hanging over me.

I saw a very elderly patient one afternoon for a skin abscess on her leg. She said, "Doctor. There is a sadness around you." I was stunned because I'd had a smile plastered on my face the entire time I'd been with the patient.

"I do?" I asked, surprised.

"You do. I sense you're lonely and alone. If you want to be happy, truly happy, you need to allow yourself to feel happy. And if you're happy being alone, so be it; but I sense you aren't happy being alone."

And she was right. The only person who could do something about it was me.

Dealing with Stuff

Jen – age 15

Someone told me that we have to be open to possibility, and if we're open, then the universe will provide. It sounded weird and new agey, but the gist of it seemed reasonable. None of us would turn ourselves off to possibility, to the idea that good things would come to us. My dad was getting reacquainted with himself, and his self-rediscovery invited a whole new cast of characters into our lives. Granted, it all stemmed from running into our decorator who had a part-time job at Nordstrom. And this particular happenstance, well, it changed things for our family.

Had we not had a run-in with her, Dad wouldn't have started his bromance with Tom, and we wouldn't have started having the wacky themed dinner parties with the O'Briens, Tess, Carlotta, Erin, all of our grandparents, and whoever else trickled in on the heels of any of the people who had become regulars in our lives.

Trent O'Brien went to our school, and it was a relief to meet someone before the school year started who could show Bryan and me around a little. It was going to be nerve-racking enough to be the new kids. Trent was going to start his junior year. He also ran cross country, and we immediately connected over running. I wasn't sure if Bryan would do any sports in high school, but I knew he might be open to football. He was tall, lanky, and broad-shouldered like our dad. Maybe he'd swim or play tennis. Or maybe he would decide to get involved in theater or debate or get a part-time job or something else entirely. It was exciting to see everything opening up in front of Bryan, and I desperately wanted him to quit worrying about me as much as he did.

He read and studied a lot, like a hobby. Bryan wanted to understand Dad and me, especially me, like on a cellular level. Why was I bent on perfection? Why was I running, watching everything I put in my mouth? What was I trying to achieve? What was going on in my head? Were neurotransmitters going crazy or not firing like they should? He was the strangest guy, but the coolest, too. I knew that while I was running, my head was clear. My thoughts blew along beside me, like they were sweet scents carried on a breeze. And, thank you therapy, I was getting a better handle on food, but it was really about control. So many things had happened outside of my control, and what I put in my body was something over which I had dominion, and it gave me a sense of power.

Bryan poked his head into my room one afternoon, gently knocking his knuckles on the doorframe without trying to seem nervous, but I could tell he was nervous. "Hey. You up for a heart to heart?"

"Okay," I drew it out into about eight syllables. "Shoot."

"I wanted to touch base with you to see how your therapy was going. How you're doing balancing your running and maintaining a diet that doesn't put you into calorie deficit."

The subject took me by surprise. It shouldn't have been a shock to know Bryan was watching me like a hawk. And the upheaval of our family had changed me. I had been seriously depressed, and therapy had helped. I was still going to therapy because I knew I needed continued help and support. I knew the concern and status check were coming from a good place, which helped me not to react in an explosive way.

Dad worried about how much I ran every day. I didn't think running for an hour was excessive. Eventually, though, we saw a sports psychologist, and we also saw a running coach. They helped me learn how to train effectively, not excessively, and how to process my feelings without channeling every feeling I had into spending more time running. Dad had a nutritionist talk to me about how to eat while training without losing stamina or feeling sluggish. I had to learn to cope because landing myself in a hospital, or worse, would be abandoning them in a different way than Mom had. But, I would be abandoning them nonetheless.

I decided I would let Bryan go through all the materials I had received from my coach, psychologist, and nutritionist. Bryan wanted to be part of the team, and it made sense. He was the only person under our roof who hadn't been included in the team initially, and it didn't seem right to exclude him, especially given his interest in neuroscience and psychology. The two of us looked at all the new information as tools I could use to form a workable, healthy regimen, and control myself and my future.

Even though I was angry at Mom, hurt, and scarred, I started to gain perspective after learning about the miscarriage. I had to be able feel my own feelings and process everything so long after the fact and had come to the conclusion there was nothing any of us could do. We weren't able to provide Mom with any emotional support or just hold her hand or hug her because she made the decision not to let us in. I pictured us as nanobots with tiny tubes of super glue, working diligently in Mom's brain to rejoin all the broken pieces of her.

We went to the art museum on a field trip during eighth grade, and one of the exhibits was in the Asian gallery. There were bowls and other things called kintsugi. The premise was pretty interesting. The pottery had been broken, but instead of throwing it out, it was repaired, and the joining compound was usually gold or a powder with gold in it. I had heard the repaired bowl became stronger than before it was broken, but I'm not willing to put money on it. However, one of the things I learned was not to throw something if there was a way to fix it. The other thing I learned was how there could be beauty even in something broken. Our family was broken, and my dad was doing his darnedest to shore up the gaps as best he could with gold from his own heart.

That Girl

Bryan - age 14

Jen had this friend, Darcy. She was a year ahead of me in school, but the first time Jen had her over, I think I knew she was "the one." According to Jen, Darcy's parents were a shit show—a lot of yelling, screaming, name calling. She and Jen were together a lot while her parents' marriage was breaking up. One afternoon, she came by to see Jen, but Jen had just left for a run and would be gone for an hour.

"Do you want to hang out and wait?" I asked her, hoping she would.

"Are you sure I won't be in the way?" she answered. "You don't have homework or somewhere else you need to be?"

"Nah," I said. I tried to be casual and play it off that I had everything under control. I had a little homework, but it was less than an hour's work and could wait until later. Geometry was simple. I could crush proofs in my sleep.

"Cool," she said. She put her keys on the console table in our entryway and followed me through to the family room.

"You know," she said, looking me in the eye, "I know you're younger and stuff, but you seem like you're a lot older. Why? Why do I sense you're an old soul?"

I mulled over my answer. At 14, I didn't feel old. My body didn't ache in the mornings, but at night, I went to bed thinking and thinking, and sometimes, it felt like my brain would never turn off. Dad. Jen. School. So much to toss around in my head. By the time sleep would take over, mental exhaustion acted like an overheated circuit and powered down. "I think, with everything with our mom, it forced me to grow up. I wanted to be a peacemaker and make everything better for everyone, but our mom's version of 'better' was to leave. Initially, we didn't have a clue why she fell apart, and we blamed ourselves. After we understood she was probably having some kind of major depressive episode and post-partum depression, and she wanted no help getting through it, we started to heal. Jen's still got a ways to go, though."

"Geez. I don't know what's worse. My parents when they're screaming, or the dead silence." We both sat there quietly for a beat, and it was weird in a way. We were bonding over our parents' marriages and the dysfunction, and we stewed in it a moment. But I didn't want their wrecked relationships tainting this moment, and I had to think quickly.

"Do you want to play a game?" I asked. "We have this deck of cards. Jen and I made them. They have people, places, things, ideas, movies, books. All kinds of things on them. You draw a card without looking at it and hold it above your forehead. It's like 20 Questions. You ask me yes or no questions and try to figure out what's on the card." Darcy smiled. Her teeth were perfectly white and actually gleamed. I like to think the smile she wore was just for me. She took a card, careful not to look at what was written on the bottom, and held it over her bangs. Her brows furrowed minutely at the sensation of her bangs being mashed down on her forehead. She was beautiful.

"Sure. Why not?" We sat on the couch looking at each other with the card deck between us. We played a few rounds before Darcy said, "You have the greenest eyes I think I've ever seen."

"You have the bluest eyes I've ever seen," I responded.

"Have you ever kissed a girl?" she asked, and I nodded. "Do you want to kiss me?" she asked, and I nodded.

We both leaned forward, our lips touching lightly at first, and there was some kind of electricity. We moved closer to each other, and I cupped the side of her face as gently as I could. She was warm to the touch, and she responded by putting her arms around my neck, and then we were full on making out. We stopped after a few minutes, and I was breathless. She was breathless.

"Wow," she said. "I think you kissed me senseless."

"I think you kissed me senseless. You may have ruined me for all other women," I said lightly. "If you aren't too scandalized by my being a lowly freshman, I would like to put it out there, though. I would very much like to kiss you again."

"I think I'm on board with your suggestion. I like the idea of having a younger man," she said, giggling. And her giggle got me. I don't think I had ever made anyone giggle, and it felt like I imagined drinking pink champagne might feel, all light and bubbly, and something only a girl could share with me at that particular moment in time. Maybe it was something only Darcy could share with me. "Just so you know," she said. "I did tell Jen a while back how I kind of had a thing for you. She asked me if I wanted her to put in a good word, to feel you out, but I told her I would figure it out on my own and in my own time. I don't want you to feel weird about kissing your sister's friend." Her dazzling smile faltered just a little. It was obvious from the lowered volume of her voice and down-turned gaze she had thought about this. Her rosy cheeks brightened.

"Wow," I said. "You're a planner, aren't you?"

"I don't know about planning per se, but I do know I think you're different, cool, smart, and very cute."

And Darcy became my girlfriend. Her relationship with Jen changed somewhat. She came over to hang out with both of us, but she always ended her time with me. Eventually, Trent entered the picture. He and Jen were two sides of the same coin. Life is funny. Our parents didn't meet until after college, and it seemed like Jen and I were meeting these people who were congruent with us, while we were in high school. Jen would never cop to the fact Trent might be her person. She was so scared of putting herself out there and being left, not being enough. She was kind of like Henry the miniature horse when we first brought him home. He was timid, unsure, scared of us and being in a wholly different environment. We found so many different ways to show him love. Feeding, watering, brushing, braiding his mane, spending time with him, walking him. Eventually he knew we would never harm him, and he trusted us. When Dad sold our house and kept the animals with the house, I think I missed Henry most of all. Not that my sister is a horse, but her mistrust of people reminded me of Henry's initial mistrust of us until we had proven otherwise.

I picked up Darcy's hand and asked, "Would you like to walk the dogs with me?"

"Sounds good," she said.

When we rounded the corner, returning to the house, we saw Jen slowing her run and approaching us. She saw our linked hands and smirked knowingly. "Can't say I didn't see this brewing. Who made the first move. Wait. Let me guess." She paused, eyeing me, then eyeing Darcy. I tried to keep my face neutral, but Darcy blushed. "Darcy!"

I clutched my chest, "You wound me. But, yeah, you're right. I had no idea. I just thought she was your smart, hot friend who tolerated my presence. I thought my heart would languish in silence." We all laughed, going back into the house.

Jen, Darcy, and I put dinner together. When we sat down for dinner, Darcy and I held hands and placed them on the table. "I sense a disturbance in The Force," Dad said. "Something going on there?" Dad pointed to our joined hands with his fork. Darcy and I smiled at each other, and I looked at my father.

"Dad, I have news. Darcy and I are a thing."

"OK. Well, I'm happy to hear that. We are going to have some rules about overnights since there's been a status change to your relationship."

"Geez, Dad," Jen said. "I'm not pimping anyone out. Relax. If Darcy stays over, she's staying with me. There will be no teenage sexy time happening under your roof."

"Great," Dad said, doing an exaggerated brow mop. "I am far too young to be a grandfather."

I gave a cough. "You had to go there, didn't you?" I said, and I knew my face was turning red.

After dinner, Darcy said she needed to go home to do homework. I walked her to her car and held her against me. She leaned against the driver's side of the car. Our foreheads were pressed together, and from being so close, it looked like she had a single eye when I looked at her. I told her she had a cyclops eye, and we both laughed.

"I'm so glad you said something about your feelings," I told her. "I really had no idea and always felt fortunate Jen's gorgeous friend didn't mind having me around when she came over." She blushed. This girl blushed a lot, which was surprising because she had more swagger than I was ever going to have. I continued. "I'm not sure I would have felt sure enough to say something to you about my feelings. Maybe eventually Jen might have said something to me about making a move, but I am just so happy you said something. I'm perceptive about a lot of things, but apparently not the opposite sex."

"I don't know when it hit me how much I liked you," Darcy said. "I mean, I knew you were cute. A lot of the girls talk about you, and I had the inside track. But you're more than cute, and I liked your, I don't know, dimensionality. I guess dimensionality sounds right." Our heads turned toward each other, and we shared our first goodnight kiss. I will never forget that night. I knew it was the beginning of something very important.

Boys

Jen - age 15

Our new house, as it turned out, wasn't very far from the O'Briens. Some mornings, I would run to Trent's and we would go on a morning run together. Other times, he ran to our house, and we left from there. His training schedule bolstered what my coach and psychologist were teaching me. I learned perspective and moderation. Trent and I made plans to go to a store for runners, Runners Gotta Run (we called it Runners for short), where they analyzed your gait with video, and based on your gait and style, they were able to recommend the right shoe. Trent drove, and I think it may have been the first time I had been in a car with him by myself. I felt a little giddy and became very intent in observing the scenery and trying to be as chill as possible. I could and would be a cool girl. Cute boys hung out with me all the time. Ha! Oh, my god. Who was I fooling, and why hadn't I thought this through before now?

"I was thinking," he said, maybe a little nervously. "Do you want to make a day of it today after we get our shoes? Grab some lunch or something, maybe go rent pedal boats at the park? Catch a movie? I don't have anything going on today and didn't know what your day looked like, and I thought it would be nice to do something together." He rambled, and it was cute. His face gently reddened, and if I hadn't noticed the blush, I never would have thought his intentions were more than platonic. I was struck by the realization. This cute boy liked me. Oh, my god. What? I mean, I knew I liked him and had an innocent little crush on him, but wow. I think he liked me back. All this time, I thought he thought of me as his running bud. I needed to reboot my brain.

My mouth, however, didn't need my brain to reboot, and the next thing I heard was my own voice, very calmly saying, "I don't have anything going on today either, and I'm open to whatever you want to do. Maybe we can start with lunch after we get our shoes. Who knows? Once we have some food in us, we may figure out how to spend the afternoon. I'm notorious for falling asleep in movie theaters, though. Be warned." I smiled as I warned him, and with the smile, my nerves relaxed. This was Trent. We talked about everything, and we had never been awkward around each other at all this summer.

"Noted," he said.

We continued to Runners in companionable silence, stealing looks at each other and flashing shy grins now and again. This was a version of Trent I didn't know, and it was cute. He hadn't been timid or reserved around me from the moment I met him--until now. I grabbed his hand, interlocking our fingers and jostling it to loosen up the tension. "Trent. Relax. It's still me. I'm the Jen of yesterday, last week, and last month. I'm still the Jen who fell over the uneven concrete on the sidewalk in front of my house." I took a deep breath before saying, "And I'm happy you want to explore a different side of our relationship because...I'm interested, too." Then I blew out all the air in my lungs. We were quiet, the only sound in the car was the clicking of the turn signal as Trent turned into the store parking lot. Had I said too much? Was I reading him wrong? I didn't think so, but he was quiet.

Trent pulled into a parking space, turned off the car, and looked down to where our hands were still joined. "This," he said raising our hands a little, "makes me happy. Getting to know you has made me happy." He raised our hands up toward his lips, turning the back of my hand toward his lips and placed a short, sweet kiss on my knuckles. "I don't want to leave any room for speculation, Jen. I would like to date you." His gaze met mine, and I got it. No speculation.

Julius Caesar – The Dinner

Rob – age 42

We saw the O'Briens a lot, and it wasn't unusual for Tom or me to drop in on each other, maybe hang out and have a beer. Weekends had become a social renaissance for me. We started hosting theme dinners. The theme for my 42nd birthday dinner was Julius Caesar—I only hoped no one at dinner tried to kill me. My parents and Sara's parents rented costumes and appeared at our front door as members of the Roman Senate. The kids wore bed sheets and carried scrolls with Shakespeare's soliloquies from "Julius Caesar" printed. They each read a section in lieu of a toast when we sat down to dine.

The food was Caesar salad and homemade pasta carbonara. When Bryan saw the peas in the sauce, he exclaimed, "Et tu, Brute?" The kid hated peas. The signature drink of the night was our best reproduction of the Orange Julius. We took ridiculous photos. One of my favorites was Tom reclining on the couch, and Maggie standing over him, feeding him grapes. Tom's sister, Tess, and her partner, Carlotta, had recently moved in together, and the two of them had made a chariot out of the large box from their new refrigerator. The best part of the chariot, though, was how it was hitched to the tiny little plastic toy horses with dental floss. Erin, who I liked and had not asked on a date yet, had decided to come to dinner as the Roman goddess Minerva because she wanted to have a stuffed owl perched on her shoulder. We were all very grateful she didn't show up with a taxidermy owl. I channeled Tim Matheson from the toga party scene in "Animal House," and wore a necktie with my toga.

We did a theme dinner every month. We did our own take on one of the black/white parties. Everyone had to wear black, but all the food had to be white. Tess and Carlotta dressed as nuns. Tom and I were "Men in Black," Bridgette, Jen, and Jen's friend, Darcy were Goth girls, Erin and Maggie were witches, and Bryan and Trent were vampires. All of the grandparents plus Tom and Maggie's parents were the Supreme Court justices. The salad was some kind of raw cauliflower salad with bacon in it. We agreed bacon was allowed because everyone knew: Bacon makes life worth living. The main entrée was chicken breast in a Mornay sauce. The sauce had the perfect bite to it, and if a bowl had been placed in front of me, I would have drunk it all and licked the bowl clean. There was a choice between the two sides: spaetzle noodles or fingerling potatoes. The plates looked bland when the food selected and served all looked the same, sad and unoriginal, even though, the dishes were getting a second life because of our dinner party. Dessert, however, turned out to be a master stroke: vanilla ice cream, sugar cookies, and baked Alaska. The cherries in the baked Alaska were white Queen Anne cherries. The ice cream and cookies quickly morphed into ice cream sandwiches.

The evening's entertainment was karaoke, but the songs had to have black, white, or a reference to magic. Erin sang "Witchcraft," and I couldn't take my eyes off her. There she was, singing a stripped down version of the song and wearing the pointy witch hat. Her skin, dark as midnight, shone under the lights in our family room. She was luminous, and this is so stupid-sounding what with the witch outfit, but I was completely under her spell.

As the night came to a close, Erin, Jen, and Darcy were deep in conversation, and Jen said, "Dad, Erin is taking Darcy and me tomorrow to do some shopping for some girl-type things." Erin made eye contact with me, and I knew she was taking them to get fitted for new bras, and I couldn't have been more thankful to have Erin volunteer to go with the girls. It would have been weird for me, and sure, I could drop them off at the bra place, but it's not the same without someone taking on the female authority role.

The next day, Tom dropped by while I was doing the edging along the sidewalk in front of the house. Erin, Jen, and Darcy were at the bra place,.

"I saw you and Erin making some meaningful eye contact last night," he said, waggling his brows.

"Yeah. Remember the first time you and I met? You and Maggie said I would like Erin? I think you're right," I responded. "What is it you want to tell me about her? I know you, Tom, and I can see it all over your face."

"Ah. Fine. She married her college sweetheart right out of college, and he was a cheater. They were married two years, and she divorced him when she discovered he had crabs. Her words were, 'I draw the line at pubic lice.'"

"Gross," I acknowledged.

"She's dated here and there, but, for the most part, she has stayed single. She's 34, and she'd like to meet someone nice, remarry, and I think she'd like to have some kids of her own. She and Tess have been friends since they were little. When Tess came out, a lot of her friends disappeared, but not Erin. Who Tess loved made no difference to Erin." Tom paused, his voice breaking a little when he talked about his sister. "I think it was Erin who helped our parents accept Tess's sexuality. Erin helped us all, and our entire family loves her, and I think Tess's life would have been very different had Erin not been so present and accepting."

We were quiet for a time before I abruptly said, "I'm going to ask her out." My declaration was followed by silence.

"Tom. You're supposed to react. You're supposed to be supportive, or you're supposed to warn me and threaten my man parts if I hurt Erin," I said.

"Nah. You're doing it all on your own," Tom laughed before turning serious. "Listen, man, I know you've been hurt, and I know it's been a difficult few years for you. Why didn't you ever do the dog walking date I told you to do the first night we met?"

"First off, it was the first time I'd ever met you. Then when Tess, Erin, and Carlotta came over that same night...well, I wanted to see if I felt anything. I wanted to get to know her a little before asking her out. It's different with having my own kids, and then even more intense because she knows my kids. I don't want to blow up anything. You know?" I dropped eye contact. This was 'talking about our feelings' territory, which I usually reserved for therapy.

Tom gave my shoulder a gentle cuffing. "I don't envy you, man. Not to rub it in your face, but I am so fucking happy to be happily married."

"Yeah, I hear you."

RELATIONSHIP PERSPECTIVE
BRYAN - AGE 14

My girlfriend can drive. She is my *older woman*, and I think her being older AND mobile adds to her mystique. We go places. We can escape together. Not that I have much to escape lately, but Darcy's situation is different with her parents' marriage disintegrating and the two of them bickering, trying to decide who got what, which kids would visit which parent and when, and what if one or all of the kids decided they want to live with one parent instead of the other, and a whole lot of other stuff, details--minutiae intended to make people even more dissatisfied with the person they had once selected as a life partner.

I've met Darcy's family, and her parents are great as long as they aren't in the same room with one another. When they're together, they bring out the worst in each other. They push each other's buttons on purpose. I imagine I'm watching a movie, and I can talk to the characters. If it's a horror movie, I know the killer is right around the corner. I stop the movie, step into the frame and tell the character, "Hey, if you turn the corner, there's a guy there with a knife, and he's going to gut you like a fish. You will most certainly die, and it will be truly unpleasant." Then the moron goes ahead and turns the corner, and just like I predicted, the bad guy cuts him into sushi grade prime human meat. Even with a warning, the threat was too tempting.

Darcy and I rode back and forth to school together, and mornings in Darcy's car may have been my favorite part of the day. She was always fresh-faced, smiling, and, no joke, I think she smelled like sunshine. Even with all the crazy happening in her home life, she had learned to leave it behind every morning.

She didn't bother coming inside to hunt me down or make small talk with Jen or Dad. Jen had been hitching rides with Trent most days, and Dad was getting out of the house usually before we left for school.

I tossed my backpack into the backseat of Darcy's car, put on my seatbelt, and leaned over to kiss Darcy good morning.

"Guess what?" she asked brightly.

"Lottery?" I answered her question with a question. She nodded. "No clue. What?"

"Dad bought a condo, and the movers are coming on Saturday to get all of his stuff."

"I'm surprised he has enough stuff to merit having movers," I said.

"I think he likes the idea of people disrupting the regular flow of weekend activity in the house. Maybe one last fuck-you to my mom. I don't know." Darcy stared out the windshield a moment, then turned to me. "Can *you* promise me something, Bryan?"

"I can try. What am I promising?" I asked, taking her hand in mine.

"If we start making each other miserable, we end things. We don't wind up hating each other. We either work through it, and if we can't, then we part as friends...or something like that. I don't think I could handle hating you."

"Same," I said. "I can certainly try to honor your request. Can *you* promise me something?"

"Shoot," she said.

"Let's communicate, be thoughtful and mature and stuff. Okay?" I may have sounded like I was begging, but between her folks and my own, I felt like I knew what I was talking about.

"Yeah," she said, leaning over the console to give me a sweet, quick buss on the cheek.

Last First Date

Rob - age 42

I made a reservation for dinner at a nice place. Great ambiance, music, lighting, nice menu. I could do this. We knew each other and had hung out together with our friends and families. She had been around Jen and Bryan. Everyone knew each other and liked each other, and I *liked* her. Erin. She had an indomitable spirit and was free with her emotions. She, I think, liked me back. My last first date was with Sara. Our first date had been a good one. It led to marriage, Jen, Bryan, and for a long time, a happy family and life together.

Jen, Bryan, and I were in new territory now, and we were all feeling our way around blindly it felt like sometimes. I parked the car in front of Erin's house and picked up the bouquet of flowers resting in the passenger seat—red roses and blue hydrangeas. I thought they were beautiful together and unexpected, but just looking at them—I don't know. It all came together, and they worked.

She answered the door before I rang the doorbell. "Hi," she said. "I'm a little nervous. I'm not going to kid you and try to come off all self-assured. I am nervous." She laughed self-consciously.

"Great ice breaker," I said. "For the record, I'm nervous, too." I paused. "You look beautiful, and these are for you," I said, handing her the flowers. And she did look beautiful. She wore an aqua linen sleeveless sheath dress, a few inches above the knee, and the pale color starkly contrasted with her hair and skin. She seemed to glow, and her gaze met mine over the flowers as she took them and ushered me inside.

"Rob, these are gorgeous. Let me get them into some water, and we can go."

An obese orange and white cat made its way into her family room while I waited for Erin. He sidled up to me, rubbing his chin against my leg. Erin had slipped back into the room, "Chuck likes you. He's marking you."

"Not to be a fat shamer, but how much does this cat weigh? He's like Jaba the Cat."

"He is big, and he's on a diet. I adopted him from a shelter two months ago. The vet thinks he's around 13 or so, and we're working on his diet. He'll have a lot more good years if we can get his weight into a healthier range. His hips aren't great, and he can't really jump up onto the furniture or anything, and he is heavy. But he's incredibly sweet." She bent down to pet Chuck, and her fingers came away with a nice coating of cat hair. "He's shedding like it's his job right now. I have to be better about brushing him." Chuck flopped on the floor and rolled onto his back. A moment later we were treated to an unholy stench.

I coughed and covered my nose and mouth. "Oh, my god. Wow. I know that's not a human smell."

Erin covered her nose and started laughing. "Yeah. Chuck here enjoys pina coladas, long walks on the beach, and filling my house with his odoriferous stylings." Erin looked down at Chuck lovingly. "I think he would run away from the smell if he could get himself off the floor easier." He rolled back and forth on the floor. I couldn't tell if he was trying to get up or if he was attempting to scratch his own back or stretching.

Dinner was outstanding. We went to a tapas restaurant, ordered a bunch of things, shared everything, and it was so easy. We talked and laughed, and it felt like we had known each other for years. We clicked. We talked about our marriages and divorces and the pain that accompanied the breakups. Her situation was different because her husband decided he wanted to play the field and have a wife. "I never would have known he was a cheater until he brought home crabs. I'm so lucky he didn't give me syphilis or something. It was so gross. I threw him out immediately, and then I stripped the bed and threw out all of our bedding. The next morning, I called a realtor and listed the house. I didn't want to live anywhere that reminded me of the pubic lice...or him. I think I was angrier about the lice than the cheating, and I realized our marriage wasn't strong enough for me to give him a second chance. My second phone call after contacting the realtor was to my doctor. I had every STD test under the sun, and miraculously, I didn't have any diseases. For that reason, and that reason alone, I forgave him. But, as a couple, we were done."

We talked about Sara, the miscarriage, Jen and Bryan, and how we were moving on with our lives. "I'm committed to getting things right with the kids. For almost two years, they thought it was their fault Sara fell apart and then left. And, I have to take the blame. I should have told them what was going on. I could've told them in a way they could understand. Sara had just checked out. We're all in therapy, and we are healing."

"They're great kids," Erin said. "Would you ever consider having another child if you remarried?"

"I would," I said, "if it were important to my wife. It would be like starting over again, but I think entering into a new marriage would be like starting over again, too. It would be building something brand new. I love kids, and I think Jen and Bryan would be on board with having a little brother or sister. Do you want children?"

"I do," Erin said. "I don't need to create a whole tribe of children, but I would like to have at least one."

After dinner, we walked for a while, and I took her hand in mine. It felt completely natural. We seemed to have burned through our nerves from earlier and had settled into easy conversation and companionable silence. When I took her home, I walked her to her front door. "I'm going to kiss you," I said. "This evening has been so perfect and easy, and I have to know if kissing is going to be as incredible." She nodded and looked up at me.

I bent down, and our lips met, fitting together easily, and our connection was strong, instantaneous, and magnetic. This was the kind of kiss, in my mind, to inspire a song, poetry, all kinds of odes or whatever, and I knew. I think she knew, too. I think I felt my toes curl. When we finally broke apart, we stared at each other, stunned. "Wow," I said.

"Wow, indeed," she said.

"I think life has a funny way of working out," I mused. "Do you have big plans tomorrow?"

"I'm having brunch with Tess and Carlotta, but after that I'm free."

"Debriefing the date?" I asked.

She nodded.

"I hope you give me high marks," I said.

She nipped my lip and smiled. "Very high marks, Mr. James."

"Come to our place for dinner tomorrow. It'll be you, me, the kids, and maybe Trent and Darcy."

When I finally got home, I lay back on my bed, staring up at the ceiling, I knew Erin and I would get serious, and I knew it would be fast. I knew we would have a future together, and I knew she would love my kids, and I knew we would have children or adopt or whatever she wanted. And as all of this unfolded in my mind, I knew I would have to talk to Sara at some point. I didn't need her blessing, but I did feel she had a right to know, since this would impact our children. I'd wait a month and see how things were going with Erin and me and the kids, but I knew Erin, the kids, and I were going to move forward in life together, as a family. When I knew everyone was on the same page, then I would talk to Sara.

COMMIT TO CHARTING A NEW COURSE
SARA - AGE 42

I pursued a new posting with Doctors Without Borders. After I found out I would be going to Asia, I decided I was going to make some goals for myself.

- Set boundaries. I was going to have reasonable start and end times to my day.

- Go on vacation. I needed to have a break. Now that I knew just how much I was needed, I had to be able to recharge to continue being a strong clinician and get through the day-to-day.

- Explore my surroundings. Again, if I'm going to be somewhere and heavily in demand, I would need to recharge, and knowing something more about where I am, besides my patient load, would be stimulating.

- Make new friends. Connect with staff and colleagues.

- Accept invitations (i.e. make new friends!).

- Find a therapist and start therapy.

- Exercise.

Once everything was in writing, I knew if I didn't achieve my goals, it was my own fault. I would make this year a year of healing and achieving. It was in writing, for God's sake.

Asia was going to be so much different than Africa for me. Different continent, different people, climate, food. Different me.

I was so committed to having a different experience, I had begun emailing one of the doctors in the clinic, Claire. She was from France. She had finished her residency and opted to go right into Doctors Without Borders. She had been in Asia already for ten years. She had met and married her husband in medical school, also a physician, and they had decided to dedicate their lives to serving. They had two children and were homeschooling them as best they could. After several email exchanges, Claire and I decided to have video calls once a week.

"Luc and I made a very conscious decision to wait until we had truly acclimated to being abroad before starting our family. Everything we have done with our children has been very carefully thought out and planned. There will come a time when we won't be able to homeschool them. We will either return to France, or we will send the children to an international school in Japan. We hate the idea of sending them to boarding school, but we have some time, and, more importantly, the children have some time before we need to make those kinds of decisions."

"Wow," I said very inarticulately. "You really are planners. My daughter was a surprise, and our son followed not too far after."

"You mentioned before your children aren't here. How do you feel about that? Do you miss them?" Claire asked.

"I do miss them but not like you would miss your children. I really short-changed my kids, and I think I'm probably going to spend the rest of my life either trying to make it up to them or push myself out of the framework of their lives and be more like a distant relative," I said truthfully. I wasn't sure just how open I could be, but it was my desire to forge authentic relationships, which meant exposing all the warts, bruises, and scars—all the ugliness.

Claire looked at me across the miles and the universe as our signal bounced here there and everywhere. I saw what was her characteristic shrug, and she said, "I will hug you, hold you close in my heart, and we will explore together. You will tell me everything, and I will listen. I will hold your hand, and you will find your way.

Okay?" She placed a kiss in her palm and blew it toward her computer screen. I believed what she said, and I knew I could tell her anything and feel safe.

Claire and I finally met in person when I arrived. She picked me up at the airport. We shared a hotel for the first few days after I had reached the nearest large city with a Doctors Without Borders administrative office. This time the paperwork was only slightly quicker to complete, but it was still a lot. I had to have blood taken to ensure I wasn't bringing any disease with me from Africa. We had dinner and too many drinks the first night we met in person. We had an opportunity to become friends since we weren't up to our elbows in taking care of people who needed care—patients, husbands, children. We were simply two women who had a lot in common, and I found Claire to be non-judgmental when I told her my entire story, which she followed with her hands covering her mouth and a low, "Mon Dieu!"

After finishing all the official Doctors Without Borders business, Claire drove us back to where I'd be spending at least the next year. It was tiny—not like a 'tiny house' on television but a really small house, maybe suitable for a couple. It was clean, furnished, and for as small as it was, the space was very efficient. If I'd been a realtor, I would say my house was 'well-appointed.' I'd been traveling light since leaving the US, and there was no danger that the storage would be a problem.

My situation in Asia was very different. We weren't operating a clinic like the one where I'd been in Africa. We were working in a small hospital. There were, of course, primary care physicians here, but there was a healthy amount of specialty care as well. Some things never changed. I delivered babies in Africa, and I delivered babies in Asia. I saw so many women who hadn't received prenatal care due to distance or circumstance. I saw very young mothers, young mothers, and mothers of advanced maternal age. Not every baby was wanted. Some went home with their mothers, and others went directly to adoption agencies. Seeing all the babies didn't get easier for me, though, and I made a mental division when I was in the moment to focus on being a physician and birthing all of these new humans and not going into a self-flagellating spiral where I perseverated on my own loss. As a coping mechanism, it wasn't the best. I scrutinized my goal list daily, and it was apparent that I had to get my head on straight to be able to function in any environment where I would be delivering babies.

I found a running trail but very quickly learned there was a yoga class that met in the hospital every morning. With the monsoon season, running wasn't going to be practical for me year round. The hospital yoga class turned into a form of healing for me. I was more centered and had begun to find some peace. Even with my angst, sadness, and conscious dissociation for all the mothers and their babies who were or weren't wanted that I was bringing into the world, after six weeks or so, I took the plunge. I found a therapist, and I committed to working through the goals on my list. I added a few, in vain, that were contingent on how I made it through therapy and unearthing some courage and bravery I had forgotten existed for me.

Coping Mechanisms

Jen - age 16

Happy sweet sixteen to me. Just about three and a half years or so since Mom's miscarriage. I felt kind of battle-weary. The scale had started to tip in a positive direction, and I wasn't complaining. I went through my calendars and journals to get a read on just how much had changed: new house, new school, new friends, boyfriend. Dad had a special someone. Bryan had a special someone. Mom was out of the picture. It was a lot of stuff. And so much therapy.

I felt like I had been to enough soul scorching appointments that I should have been able to lay claim to a free book, tank of gas, or even a coupon for a free ice cream cone. Dad, Bryan, and I all spoke to one another with a very pronounced "I've-been-to-therapy" approach: A lot of 'I feel,' or 'How does that make you feel,' or 'Have you considered,' or 'I'm thinking out loud, but how about.' Of course, being human didn't prevent us from exploding on occasion, but when we hit the larger land mines, we were sensitive to one another and modulated our responses, and I realized reducing the intensity of my responses didn't change me as a person, but it stressed me out a lot less. The realization worked its way into my running, too. It changed my perspective, and I shared all of this with my coach and psychologist.

I had transitioned from Dr. Ross to a sports psychologist. Dr. Ross was so instrumental in getting me into a healthier frame of mind when it came to exercise and food, and when it was time for me to move to the next level for keeping my head on straight and focusing on my sport, she referred me to another doctor who dealt with elite athletes. It was the first time anyone had mentioned the word 'elite' when it came to running and me. It was this thing I did that gave me peace of mind, that I enjoyed, and that I was good at. I knew I was the best girl runner at my school, but 'elite' was something I hadn't heard until Dr. Ross said it.

But my time spent running was sacred to me. It was nearly magical. My runs became filled with more creative thoughts and were less self-defeating. My times improved. A switch flipped where I was running toward and not away from something. Trent and I discussed this when we went on our runs together.

"What do you visualize you're running toward?" he asked.

"Sometimes it's you, college, a test or paper that I'm working on, the general future. It varies, but it's usually something positive or a challenge I can prob-lem-solve." We continued running at a comfortable pace which Trent moderated to accommodate me. "I do a lot of self-talk. The more self-talk, the more real things become. But I truly believe what I'm telling myself."

"Walk me through the process later. I want to try it," he said.

Later that night we were lying side by side on the floor in my bedroom after I had shown Trent my journal and how I documented my thoughts and goals and dreams. While we lay on the floor, I spoke softly about what was on my mind and began to imagine what success would look like and how it would feel. I whispered the negative things I wanted to shake off, and then I talked about how it would feel not carrying that stuff around, I always thought of an anthropomorphized pack mule carrying all my burdens up a hill, and I saw myself taking this or that pack off the mule, giving him a carrot, and saying, "It's ok. I'm going to keep taking stuff off of you. This trek can be fun, the adventure of a lifetime." And as the pack mule shucked off the various packs, he smiled at me, and we were both lighter.

Trent started following my process, and his times improved. I discussed all of this with my psychologist, and he took note of my performance changes. My coach had noticed the improvement in my time and pace. He noted the change in Trent's, too. "I don't want to drug test the two of you, but I rarely see improvement like I've witnessed with the two of you. I have to drug test you, though, to remain above scrutiny, but I want to know more about how you two have ratcheted up your performances." I described everything. Trent talked about how he incorporated the journaling and meditation into his daily routine.

"Would you two be willing to do a workshop for the rest of the team?" he asked. We nodded.

"If I gathered some colleagues, would you be willing to do a workshop for them, too?" he asked.

We agreed. My thought was simple. As teenagers, we had an inclination toward negative self-talk. My coping mechanism had helped me physically and psychologically. It had done something wonderful for Trent, too. Was what I was doing groundbreaking? Probably not, but as a teenager, it did give me a lot of insight into myself and helped me stop a lot of negativity.

During dinner that night, I talked through my day with Dad, Bryan, and Erin. Erin's face lit up while I spoke, and she had so many questions. She worked in human resources, and she felt what Trent and I were doing had sound implications in the workplace. After dinner, I went through the process with her. We were quiet for a while after I went through my journaling and meditation routine and how my self-talk and visualization worked. I made her lie on my bedroom floor to get into the right headspace (and I knew, at first, she thought something weird was about to happen). "Sometimes I get so comfortable I fall asleep," I admitted. We both giggled a little. We both looked up at my ceiling, like it had answers or something; but it was just a ceiling. Again, we were quiet, and for me, it was a pregnant pause. Finally, I just asked her, "How do you feel about my dad? The two of you are one of my self-talk focuses."

"Oh, yeah?" she whispered.

"Yeah," I replied.

"It's only been two months, but I love him," she said simply. "Your dad makes me happier than I knew I could be with another person."

"We've been getting to know you, and you've been getting to know us for a few months before you and Dad ever started dating. Bryan and I love you, Erin," I said. "We want you in our lives. We haven't asked Dad outright what's happening, but we see it all over his face. I write about and visualize us being a family." We were quiet for a time. She took my hand and squeezed it. "Have you told him you love him?"

"The other day." I could hear the smile in her voice. I rolled over and hugged her. She put her arms around me, hugging me back. "And you need to know that I love you, too. I love Bryan. I love the four of us together."

My breath hitched, and I was crying. "Hey," Erin said, stroking my hair. "I hope those are happy tears."

"I never thought I would have a strong female presence in my life again. I hoped, journaled, visualized, talked to myself about it over and over again. And here you are," I said through all the emotion, and I squeezed her. We stayed on my floor like that for a while, until I broke the silence. "Are you ready for dessert?"

Erin laughed. "I am. I saw what you made in the fridge. You're going to have to teach me how you make the things you make."

"Well..." I said, trailing off. "It all starts with a nutritionist. I'm working on getting better about eating and food, in general. The past few years have been hard, but I'm working on being healthy, and I can't give up on dessert."

Everything Old is New Again
Rob - age 42

After a four-month courtship, Erin and I, my parents, her mom, and the kids went to the courthouse, and we made it official. Erin became Erin James. She moved into the house, and shortly after the new year, she told me we were having a baby. We were trying, and it didn't take long. She was worried it would take a while since she was almost 35, and fertility drops off the older women get, but we were lucky. We opted to share everything with Jen and Bryan. They knew Erin wanted a child, and our first attempt would be trying to have a biological child. If it didn't work, we weren't going to pursue IVF or anything. We were going to adopt. We might adopt anyway. We wanted our child to have a sibling to grow up with, and we loved the relationship between Jen and Bryan. Since the baby would be so much younger than the two of them, it would be like an only child, and we both thought it might be lonely.

Advanced maternal age is what the doctor called Erin's pregnancy. It was also a 'geriatric pregnancy.'

"I know I'm no shrinking violet," she said, "but I'm not 75 either. Geriatric, my ass."

"You're a delicate rose," I said absently stroking her neck while we sat on the couch binge watching 'Arrested Development.'

The upside of the advanced maternal age business was that we went to a high risk specialist, and we had several early ultrasounds, and we also had a lot of genetic testing. During the first ultrasound, I was a little stunned when I saw the wand that was going to be surfing around in my wife's uterus. I expected an external approach. Erin took it all in stride.

The tech took measurements to try to date the pregnancy and see how things were progressing. We heard her muttering under her breath while she was typing into the computer. "Erin and Rob, the doctor is going to come in to go over the ultrasound results with you, but don't worry. Things look good so far. The doctor will give you the official results, though."

Dr. Annabelle Childress entered the room shortly after the ultrasound tech left. "Erin! Rob! I'm so happy to see you." We both knew Annabelle through different channels, and she knew our story and was a friend.

"We weren't going to trust this baby to just anyone!" Erin said, beaming.

"Well. I hope you're going to trust me with more than one baby," Annabelle said. "Sometimes, your ovaries, especially when you get older—and you're not old—but sometimes they release more than one egg. Maybe each ovary will ovulate, or maybe more than one follicle will mature and multiple eggs will be released. Your ultrasound showed two heartbeats and two separate fetuses. It's too early to see the gender of the babies, but it looks like you're having twins, and as a high risk pregnancy, I would like to manage you and deliver the babies when it's time."

I passed out, completely slumped over in the chair I was sitting in, and since it had no arms, I slid out of it, hitting the floor. When I awoke, I was still on the floor, but there was a small pillow under my head. Erin and Annabelle were looking at me like I was something interesting they had found under a microscope. Amusement danced in their eyes along with a small measure of concern.

"Erin," I said. "Are we having two babies?"

"Right now," she said, "we're having two. Sometimes one of the twins is absorbed by the other, but it appears there are two babies on the way." She smiled and leaned down to kiss me tenderly. I sighed and smiled and thought about going back to sleep but realized I was on the floor in the doctor's office.

"Well, fantastic news!" I said, slowly sitting up and rubbing the back of my head. "We'll need to come up with two names, and I think Erin, you should drive us home. I cannot be trusted."

Erin patted my hand, giving me a loving look, laced with concern for my reaction, then spoke to the doctor, "He has a very delicate constitution." She turned to me, "Honey, are you going to be all right? I know this is a surprise to both of us."

Annabelle said, "You're not the first father-to-be to faint. I promise you." We all laughed, and Erin's face just had a glow. If she was beautiful before, she was simply radiant now.

I smiled, feeling tears running down my face. "I feel great. It's a shock. I mean, two babies, but we have an amazing support system. I mean, wow." I wiped my eyes and face. "Okay. I've had my moment. Let's focus on you and getting home. Holy shit. *Two babies.* We can do it," I rambled, knowing I sounded like an idiot who didn't know how babies were made. And we were intentional about making these babies.

We both took the rest of the day off. I texted the kids to come right home after school. They came through the door in a whirlwind of books, backpacks, coats, gloves, and boots. "Where is Erin?" Jen asked when she saw me in the family room on the couch, concern etched across her brow.

"She had to get the ultrasound pictures to show you. We have a video, too."

Bryan sat in one of the wing chairs. "Why do you have black eyes?" he asked.

"Well, that's a funny thing. I sort of hit my head today when I passed out."

"What?" both kids said in complete incredulity.

"It's not as bad as it sounds. We'll give you all the details in a sec."

Erin came into the room with the ultrasound photos and gave them to Jen and Bryan. They flipped through them.

Jen asked, "Why do these say Baby A and Baby B?"

Bryan answered, "I think it means there are two babies in Erin's uterus. Am I right?"

Erin and I nodded.

Erin said, "It's early days. Things happen. You guys know that better than anyone. But, if the pregnancy is without incident, the twins will be delivered four weeks early. We do know they're fraternal, but we won't know gender for a while. We will go through all the genetic testing to make sure they're healthy."

"We also decided we were going to have a theme dinner next week with the O'Briens, all of the grandparents, Trent and Darcy. It's going to be 'pairs.' We want to tell our closest friends what's going on," I said.

"What about Mom? Are you going to tell her? It would suck for her to find out from someone other than you. Not that I'm all that concerned for her feelings, but I think it's probably a courteous gesture," Bryan said. Jen nodded her agreement.

"Good idea," I said, looking at Erin, and she nodded in assent.

I emailed Sara later in the evening to schedule a phone call. She was quick to respond, which was a surprise. She said she had time to chat first thing in the morning for me, which would be evening for her. She said she also had news.

In the morning, true to her word, Sara called. I wanted Sara and Erin to lay eyes on each other before Erin and I married. I tried to put myself in Sara's shoes, and if I were the mother of two children, then I would want to be able to see, hear, and speak to the person who would be living under the same roof with my children. We had a stilted conversation, and Sara seemed pretty disconnected, but I felt I had done my duty. The pregnancy, though, might be an easy conversation, if her previous calls served as examples of what to expect; or it might be a horribly tough conversation if it brought back everything that reminded her of the miscarriage. Still, though, I wanted her to know her children would have half-siblings in the relatively near future. She'd been gone a year and a half and had only been back to visit once.

When my phone rang, I answered as I would normally answer any call. Sara's voice sounded bright, happy. She was nearing the midpoint of her second year with Doctors Without Borders and was in Asia.

"Rob, I'm jumping in to tell you I started therapy. It's been via telemedicine, but it's been good, and it has helped me so much."

"Um, well, that's great. We're all big fans of therapy here in this house. Sometimes I feel like I live with two therapists."

"I have some news," she said.

I wondered what her news might be. Maybe she was coming back to the States, maybe she was getting married, having a baby...I had no idea what she had to share.

"I have news, and you have news," I said. "Why don't you go first."

"Well, you know how I was in Africa for my first year with Doctors Without Borders? Then this year, I've been in Asia. Asia has been amazing, but I began looking for something where I had fluency with the native language, which brought me back to the US. I'm not ready for the US yet. It's still a little too close to home."

"I guess I can understand your need to separate yourself from a particularly tough time in your life," I said, even though I couldn't understand abandoning my home, job, and family.

"Well, there's an initiative in South America next year, and I've been offered the opportunity to take on the lead role with getting a clinic started and staffed. We are so understaffed to be able to serve everywhere in the world where there's a shortage of healthcare professionals, and I have an opportunity to bring something acutely needed to South America."

"Is this something you want to do?" I asked.

"I really do," she answered.

"How long do you think you'll be in South America, and when would you be leaving Asia?"

"Well," Sara said. "That's the thing. I would finish out my twelve months here in Asia, then I would leave for South America. I'm not sure yet exactly where they would be putting me. Details are still being worked out, but I'm really excited about the opportunity."

"It all sounds great," I said, maybe a little too brightly. Silence followed. It felt so lengthy, I wondered if the call had dropped. "Hello? You there?"

"Yeah. I'm here," Sara said, some of the excitement gone from her voice. "What was your news?"

"Before I get to my news, do you want to know about the kids? How they're doing? You haven't called, written, or emailed like we agreed. Before I get to my news, I want to talk about what you had promised."

"I know. I'm sorry. It's just so hard to talk to them. I feel guilty that I'm a terrible mother. I don't know what to say to them. The last time I talked to them, it seemed like they didn't know what to say to me, and it's like we're all walking on eggshells. And then when I hang up, I feel sad and bad, and I don't want to feel those feelings, and then I think, 'Well, Sara, if you don't want to feel awful, just don't call. Easy peasy.' And I know it's the shittiest excuse in the world. I am selfish. I didn't know I was such a selfish   person." At least she had the decency to sound contrite, which made me not feel like she was a complete shit. And therapy! That was a win, for sure.

"I think," I said, "if you don't mind my offering some suggestions, I have some ideas how you can start to build some bridges with them."

"Rob, I would do almost anything short of leaving my job." I wasn't sure if she really meant what she said. She had told me before that her first priority was her job, but I had to think there were other things taking precedence over her kids, and we weren't spouses or even friends anymore. We were co-parents, and she wasn't any kind of co-parent. There was no way she believed what she was saying, and I certainly didn't believe it; but we were having a civil conversation, and I didn't want to rock the boat.

"I'm going to send you some prompts. You're going to answer the prompts in writing sometimes, and verbally other times. We've been doing a lot of these kinds of exercises in our therapy sessions. Probably what we've all enjoyed the most is bringing good memories back to life and acknowledging the hard things and making some sort of peace with them. Sometimes it's an uneasy peace, but we have taken some hard roads to get to where each of us is now." I took a beat before adding, "Do you think you would be on board with something like this? I would start with prompts that are easy, and we could work toward some of the things that have been tough, but we wouldn't hit any of those until way later."

"I can try. I want to try," she said, ending on a deep sigh. And, again, I don't know that she truly wanted to try. But, whatever…I wasn't going to beat a dead or dying horse.

"Okay. My news. Erin and I are expecting. We found out the other day we were having twins. We are seeing a high-risk OB/GYN because of Erin's age, and it turns out there are a few other health concerns we didn't know about until recently. Jen and Bryan are going to have some much younger siblings in about five months. We're through the first trimester, and the plan is to induce at 36 weeks."

"Wow," Sara said. "Two babies. How are Jen and Bryan taking it?

"We decided to tell them the day after the positive home pregnancy tests. We had a confirmatory blood test, just to be sure there weren't any false positives. They are excited and know big changes are coming, and we are all talking about what the changes may be. Erin and I were very clear to communicate to them that we wouldn't be using them as built-in babysitters. If there are times they want to watch the babies, great. If not, that's fine, too."

"Did you tell my parents?" she asked. Her voice became quieter and serious, and knowing she was in therapy bolstered me somewhat because she had someone to talk to. She had someone who could help her process all of this. I knew it was going to be heavy news for her to take, and hearing it from me directly had to be better than hearing it second- or third-hand. I heard her breathing heavily on the other end of the call, almost like the wind had been knocked out of her.

"We're planning to tell all the parents at the same time this weekend. Your mom and dad are part of the family we have cobbled together. We have big family get-togethers every month, and they haven't missed a single one. We all love them. They want to be part of a family unit, and Jen and Bryan are their grandchildren. Since these babies are going to be part of Jen's and Bryan's lives, your mom and dad are going to want to be part of everything. They have accepted Erin and my marriage, and they're very supportive." There was a good fifteen seconds of silence, but I heard her breathing, and I decided not to fill the space.

"Oh, my god," Sara whispered. "What have I done? What have I done to everyone?" I heard the thickness in her voice and the sniffles. "Rob, I am so sorry. I'm sorry I didn't get help. I'm sorry I just left. I didn't know what to do or how to feel better, and I felt trapped by this thing I felt had happened to me—only me." Her crying stopped her from continuing to talk.

"I'm not going to tell you what you did was all right, but I've noticed during this call how you're actually starting to sound like your old self, and I think, if you can find your way back to something akin to the person you used to be, then you could chalk it up to a win. Start to stack up the wins, you know? Work on building the bridges."

"I'll try," she said between hitching breaths. She was crying hard, and it might have been a breakthrough or a wakeup call, I thought, perhaps a little too optimistically.

"Your first prompt: talk or write about the first time we met. Easy, right?" I said as upbeat as I could. "Maybe you could write four or five questions you want to ask the kids. It might help you ease into conversation with them."

"Okay. I think I can do that. I really will try. Congratulations on the pregnancy. Sincerely. I am happy for you and Erin."

News of the World

Sara - age 42

Rob had news. He wanted to talk. I had an idea, but I didn't want to guess wrong. As promised, I called Rob in the morning. I was working on follow-through.

"Sara. Good morning," Rob said when the call had gone through and our computer cameras were catching up with beaming our images from earth to outer space and back to earth. "So...I have some news."

"I have news, too. Do you want to go first, or should I?" I asked. For the first time in a long time, I felt breezy and light for this conversation with Rob. I was excited and it was nice to have positive news of my own to share.

"You go first. You sound like you have something big going on. I hope it's good stuff," he said, and he sounded sincere.

"Rob, I started therapy. It's been via telemedicine, but it's been good, and it has helped me so much."

"Um, well, that's great. We're all big fans of therapy here in this house. Sometimes I feel like I live with two therapists."

"I have more news," I said.

"Go on," he said, and I heard a smile in his voice along with something else. Was it trepidation? The look on his face gave nothing away.

"Well, you know how I was in Africa for my first year with Doctors Without Borders? Then this year, I've been in Asia. Asia has been amazing, but I began looking for something where I had fluency with the native language, which brought me back to the US. I'm not ready for the US yet. It's still a little too close to home."

"I guess I can understand your need to separate yourself from a particularly tough time in your life," he said, and I knew him well enough to know he couldn't understand abandoning his home, job, and family.

"Well, there's an initiative in South America next year, and I've been offered the opportunity to take on the lead role with getting a clinic started and staffed. We are so understaffed to be able to serve everywhere in the world where there's a shortage of healthcare professionals, and I have an opportunity to bring something acutely needed to South America."

"Is this something you want to do?" he asked.

"I really do," I answered.

"How long do you think you'll be in South America, and when would you be leaving Asia?"

I said. "That's the thing. I would finish out my twelve months here in Asia, then I would leave for South America. I'm not sure yet exactly where they would be putting me. Details are still being worked out, but I'm really excited about the opportunity."

"It all sounds great," he said, maybe a little too brightly. Silence followed. He legitimately looked pleased for me. On the screen, his image wasn't moving. I waved my hand in front of my screen. "You still there?" I asked.

"Yeah. I'm here," he said, waving back at me.

"Tell me. What's your news?"

"Before I get to my news, do you want to know about the kids? How they're doing? You haven't called, written, or emailed like we agreed. Before I get to my news, I want to talk about what you had promised."

"I know. I'm sorry. It's just so hard to talk to them. I feel guilty. I'm a terrible mother. I don't know what to say to them. The last time I talked to them, it seemed like they didn't know what to say to me, and it's like we're all walking on eggshells. And then when I hang up, I feel sad and bad, and I don't want to feel those feelings, and then I think, 'Well, Sara, if you don't want to feel awful, just don't call. Easy peasy.' And I know it's the shittiest excuse in the world. I am selfish. I didn't know I was such a selfish person."

I had to assume accountability for the situation. The miscarriage wasn't my fault, but my response, running away, all of it...I had to own it. I knew I wasn't a horrible human being, but I owed my whole family so much more than a simple apology, and I needed to be 100% sure about what I was able to do. Sara James is no superhero, but I'm not a villain, either.

"Sara," Rob said, "Therapy! That's a big win for you. It's incredible. I think, if you don't mind my offering some suggestions, I have some ideas how you can start to build some bridges with the kids."

"Rob, I would do almost anything short of leaving my job." I wasn't sure if I really meant what I said, at least not yet. I had told Rob before that my first priority was my job. What else took precedence over my kids? Rob and I weren't spouses anymore, and to say we were friends would be a stretch. We were co-parents, and I wasn't any kind of co-parent—I was an absentee. I knew Rob didn't believe a single thing I had just said, and being the kind of person he was, he wouldn't call me out, especially since we were having a civil conversation, and there was no way he would want to rock the boat.

"I'm going to send you some prompts. You're going to answer the prompts in writing sometimes, and verbally other times. We've been doing a lot of these kinds of exercises in our therapy sessions. Probably what we've all enjoyed the most is bringing good memories back to life and acknowledging the hard things and making some sort of peace with them. Sometimes it's an uneasy peace, but we have taken some hard roads to get to where each of us is now." He took a beat before adding, "Do you think you would be on board with something like this? I would start with prompts that are easy, and we could work toward some of the things that have been tough, but we wouldn't hit any of those until way later."

"I can try. I want to try," I said, ending on a deep sigh.

"Okay. My news. Erin and I are expecting. We found out the other day we were having twins. We are seeing a high-risk OB/GYN because of Erin's age, and it turns out there are a few other health concerns we didn't know about until recently. Jen and Bryan are going to have some much younger siblings in about five months. We're through the first trimester, and the plan is to induce at 36 weeks."

"Wow," I said. "Two babies. How are Jen and Bryan taking it?

"We decided to tell them the day after the positive home pregnancy tests. We had a confirmatory blood test, just to be sure there weren't any false positives. They are excited and know big changes are coming, and we are all talking about what the changes may be. Erin and I were very clear to communicate to them that we wouldn't be using them as built-in babysitters. If there are times they want to watch the babies, great. If not, that's fine, too."

"Did you tell my parents?" I asked. To say his news was a surprise was an understatement of the highest order. My voice became quieter and serious, and I'd be sure to schedule an extra session with my therapist right after this call. He was having two babies. I heard and felt my own breathing getting heavy, like the wind had been knocked out of me.

"We're planning to tell all the parents at the same time this weekend. Your mom and dad are part of the family we have cobbled together. We have big family get-togethers every month, and they haven't missed a single one. We all love them. They want to be part of a family unit, and Jen and Bryan are their grandchildren. Since these babies are going to be part of Jen's and Bryan's lives, your mom and dad are going to want to be part of everything. They have accepted Erin and my marriage, and they're very supportive." There was a good fifteen seconds of silence.

Rob sounded so happy and excited, and all I could do was try to look happy for him. I was happy for him, but it seemed unfair that he was going to get what I had so desperately wanted. I knew my smile was weak, and Rob looked concerned, too.

"Oh, my god," I whispered. "What have I done? What have I done to every-one?" I was going to cry, and I knew in my bones this wasn't about me, humans, by nature, are a selfish lot. "Rob, I am so sorry. I'm sorry I didn't get help. I'm sorry I just left. I didn't know what to do or how to feel better, and I felt trapped by this thing I felt had happened to me—only me." I cried hard enough that I couldn't talk through it, and it was humiliating that Rob was watching me fall apart, but he was good and kind enough not to end our video call.

"I'm not going to tell you what you did was all right, but I've noticed during this call how you're actually starting to sound like your old self, and I think, if you can find your way back to something akin to the person you used to be, then you could chalk it up to a win. Start to stack up the wins, you know? Work on building the bridges."

"I'll try," I said between hitching breaths. "But I want you to know I am really, sincerely, so very happy for you, Erin, and the kids. Those babies are going to be incredibly lucky little people."

I'd been feeling optimistic, and I would continue to feel optimistic. South America would be great. I was going to give my new clinic my best effort, and I would take a little bit of each day into planning how I might be able to strike a balance I could live with when it came to my kids.

I think Rob had told me before, "Don't promise what you can't deliver." This is where I needed to gauge what I could deliver, and then if I could do it, I'd back it up with a promise.

"Your first prompt: talk or write about the first time we met. Easy, right?" he said, a brilliant smile on his face. "Maybe you could write four or five questions you want to ask the kids. It might help you ease into conversation with them."

"Okay. I think I can do that. I really will try. Congratulations on the pregnancy. I am happy for you," I said trying to force my own smile and knowing I was failing in an epic way. I wanted to add, "I hope everything goes more smoothly for all of you than my last pregnancy," but I kept that to myself, and I was legitimately proud I had held my tongue.

Procrastination

Jen – age 16

I sat quietly in the nook in my bedroom overlooking the front yard. There was a paper due for my AP English class. We had to choose a painting and a poem we felt described the painting and expound on why we had made the choice and detail the reasons the poem and painting complemented one another. A gentle rain was coming down, water lightly streaking the windows, making trails down the panes. For a while, I wondered if the trails were the same every time water hit the glass. Then I started thinking about all the outside factors that could impact how the water came in contact with the window, and I figured there were probably no identical instances where the conditions allowed the trails to be the same. Then I wondered if there could be some kind of predictive equation that took every possible condition into consideration that might forecast exactly how the water would trail down the windows. Then I thought, 'Well, duh. Of course there was,' but who would want to be bothered to figure this out. And then I realized I was spiraling into a rabbit hole and not focusing on my paper.

Sighing, I opened the poetry anthology. Some of the poems were very obviously inspired by works of art, and conversely, there were works of art inspired by some of the poems. I could take a traditional approach and go with a classic poem, or I could try something entirely different and look for some contemporary poetry and pair it with something fresh, or fresh to me, at any rate. I remembered there were two paintings. I must have been eleven or twelve at the time when my mom showed them to me in an art book she had. Neither painting was contemporary, but my mom had once said these two always made her 'feel.' One was The Potato Eaters by Vincent Van Gogh, and the other was The Gleaners by Jean-Francois Millet. I pulled them up on my laptop. They didn't make me feel anything, and then I remembered a bigger than life painting I had seen inside the Biltmore Estate called The Waltz. At the time, I thought it would be cool to get a reproduction or a poster of the painting, but the posters never captured the vibrant yellow from the painting correctly, and I decided it would be best to remember the painting in my mind than see the image every day and be disappointed it wasn't the real thing. What it all boiled down to was this: I wasn't being productive with my time. I texted Darcy to see what she was doing.

Darcy: I'm in your basement watching a movie with your brother. What's up?

Jen: I think I have the blahs. Trying to work on a paper and can't get started.

Darcy: Come watch this movie with us.

Jen: Maybe. I'm going to see what Erin's doing.

Darcy: She's down here with us.

Jen: Hmm. Maybe I'll come down there. Might see what Trent's doing.

I thought about making cookies or brownies. Since it was raining, I didn't feel like going outside to run, but the treadmill wasn't high on my list either. I had already journaled for the day, flipped through the scrapbook I was making for Erin and the babies, chronicling the pregnancy, and I wondered how our mom was doing with the knowledge. I cared about her as a human being, but she was so foreign to me now. We rarely heard from her. She was just this person, out there in the world, doing her own thing, as if she had no strings tying her to anyone anywhere. She had become Pandora's Box to me. I decided to email her. Who knew if my message would unleash something. She'd been so uncommunicative in the time she'd been gone; she would probably never read the message. I thought I could maybe ask some questions, clear my head. I had no clear goal or plan for what I wanted to get out of sending a message. I didn't expect anything. Bryan and I had been trained not to expect a damned thing when it came to our mother. She was a cautionary tale to us, more fable than flesh. I realized I was equating my mother to something like an imaginary friend, but so be it. So, yeah, I was emailing her out of boredom, procrastination, and a pinch of need.

Mom,

Hi. It's Jen—your daughter. You once told me about The Potato Eaters and The Gleaners. What made you like them so much? You said they made you 'feel.' Why? What else makes you feel? Can you tell me about when I was born and what went through your mind the first time you held me? What about Bryan? How did Dad handle becoming a dad for the first time? We're getting very excited about the twins. Things seem to be going smoothly, and Erin is feeling good. Her belly is rapidly expanding. She's all baby, though. She and Dad decided not to find out the gender of the babies. We have a lot of yellow and green around here until we see those little people.

Bryan and I are so excited to be the big brother and sister. Dad and Erin said we could babysit if we wanted, but they would never force us or make it an expectation. It was thoughtful of them to say that, but I want to see, hold, and care for the babies. I probably won't be able to do it on my own, though. Two completely dependent little beings are probably overwhelming.

Don't know if Dad told you, but I have a boyfriend, and Bryan has a girlfriend. Bryan's girlfriend is also my best friend—which is funny because Bryan is also my best friend. My boyfriend started out as my running buddy, and it turned into something different. He's a year older and a grade ahead of me in school. He's super nice, smart, and he gets me...AND he's cute, too. I think if things don't work out for us as a couple, we'll always be friends. It's how we started, and we talk about everything all the time. He's great, though.

I've been thinking about college. It's too soon to visit schools, but I think I might like to be a sports psychologist. I'd like to be able to help athletes keep a healthy perspective on their bodies and how they perform athletically and psychologically. My coach thinks I might be able to run at a division 1 school, but I still have very high academic standards for myself and professional goals. I don't have any delusions that I'm an elite athlete, but every single parent with a child who has above average athletic talent seems to think the child will be an elite athlete, and then you've got unrealistic expectations being put on a kid who is a good, strong athlete, but NOT an elite athlete. I'm a good runner, but I'm not Olympics material. It would be nice, though, to get a big scholarship to run for a big school. When it quits being fun, though, I'm going to be done. I'll always run. It gives me so much mental clarity, but when the competition stops giving me joy, then right there—I'll finish the season, and simply run for fitness. But athletes need coping skills, and they need to be realistic. At the end of the day, we're all just humans and subject to the human condition. Anyway, that's my take on sports psychology and where I might be able to help athletes.

I realize you're busy and stuff. You can answer, or you don't have to answer. I'm not even sure you'll read my message, but I've decided I'm going to write you like I would a diary. You can choose to get to know me or not. It's up to you. I'd like to think, at some point, you will want to get to know me. I'll want to get to know you, too, but I know so little of your back story because I was still pretty young when your headspace changed. I know what Gram tells us, but I'd love to hear it directly from you. I do want to know you because you're still my mom.

--Jen

Adults

Bryan - Age 15

"Dad, do you want to go for a bike ride?" I hovered outside his home office. He was opening mail with a disgusted look on his face.

"I would love it. These are bills, and they'll still be here when we get back. Let me change clothes, and I'll meet you in the garage in five."

I made my way to the garage to take our bikes off the hooks where our bikes hung on the wall of the garage. I had a mountain bike, Dad had a road bike, Jen had some kind of crazy retro-looking pink bike with a rattan basket on the front and a bell on the handlebars, and Erin, funny enough, had the same bike as Jen only in lavender. Also, Erin's basket had a giant daisy. They rode their bikes to get ice cream around once a week during the spring and summer. Erin's belly continued to swell, and we all continued to spur her on with love and hope. We all talked to her stomach daily because we wanted the babies to know our voices as soon as they came into the world.

There were two things I learned from Erin's pregnancy: 1) I couldn't wait to see my little siblings; and 2) I was going to practice safe sex when I started having sex—which hadn't happened yet.

I was adding air to our bikes' tires when Dad came to the garage, ready to go for a ride. "Is there something you want to tell me, Bryan?" Dad asked, eyeing me carefully.

"There is," I admitted. "Let's hit the road, though, and I'll fill you in."

"Do I need to be worried?" Dad asked.

"I don't think so," I said. "I think I need to talk some things out. You probably already know, so I think I might need some words of wisdom, if that's okay."

"Oh. Sure. I'm not sure how much wisdom I have to dole out, but you're welcome to as much as you want or need." Dad smiled, giving a small laugh.

We cruised down the street, a light breeze brushing against our faces. I pulled up next to Dad's bike. "Okay. Not beating around the bush. Jen has been emailing Mom. She sends something to her daily. Sometimes the messages are long, and sometimes they're short. Sometimes it's a complete download of her feelings and lots of questions, and sometimes it's just about her day and maybe only a sentence or two. I'm not sure how I feel about it all. I don't know if this is healthy for Jen. I mean, what if Mom never responds to her? Won't that hurt Jen? I don't know if I can handle it if Mom rejects Jen again because it would be her rejecting both of us all over again. Once was enough."

We reached an intersection and came to a stop. Once we were back on our bikes, Dad said, "I know your sister has been emailing your mom. She said she had no expectations your mom would even read her messages and was sending the messages as kind of like an online diary. I think it's all right so far. Jen is facing what has been a demon—her mother's abandonment. Jen is totally in control of the situation. She tells me when she sends something to your mother, though. I've also spoken to your mom about what your sister is doing."

We rode along in silence punctuated by one of the neighbors' dogs barking, kids playing, sprinklers watering lawns. It was so normal, so average, and our mom was such an outlier. "Your mother is going to respond—to both of you. She and I discussed this, and we are happy Jen started her emails. Your mom wasn't sure how to reach out to you kids in a way that wasn't going to seem forced. I can tell you this, though. You're both probably going to learn a lot about your mom. She's been working on pulling together some stories about how we met, fell in love, got married, had you kids, and had a life together. It was a good life for a long time."

"Geez, Dad. When were you going to tell us? Have you told Jen already?" I asked. These adults loved to ration information. I was going crazy worrying about my sister, and Mom and Dad had had a dialogue and, again, they discussed what we did or didn't need to know. The last time they decided to keep information from us, we had no idea why our family was falling apart, and we thought it was our fault. "So. Huh. Hmm. I have some thoughts," I said.

"Great. I'd love to hear them," Dad said.

"Why can't you just be upfront with us? I don't think it's a wise play for you to decide what we can or can't handle. I think you need to tell us what's going on with you, with Mom…with whatever. We are teenagers, and we have reasoning skills. I mean, God, Dad! Did you even think for a minute that we can be rational and sane human beings? " I paused a moment, getting my breath and pedaling harder up a small hill. When I reached the top of the hill, I walked my bike to the side of the road, leaning it against a large boulder. I sat on the ground next to my bike. Dad joined me.

"You're right. I think I worry you two are fragile because of what you've already had to deal with, but you both have proven to be resilient. Especially you, Bryan. The role you've taken on isn't one I would have put on a child. You were ten years old when the miscarriage happened and sheltering you backfired in a really negative way for all of us. Heck, everything backfired for everyone." Dad leaned forward and pulled a couple of wrapped granola bars out of his back pocket. "Want one?" He held it toward me as a peace offering.

"Sure," I said.

"I have to tell you, when you said you wanted to talk, I thought this was going to be a sex talk. I know you and Darcy have been dating for a while now. I was a teenager, too, you know. Things get hot and heavy, and I want you to be careful. I know you both are very intelligent people. Just remember, in the heat of the moment, accidents can happen. Make sure you're prepared."

"Oh, my god, Dad. Um. Thank you?" I was mortified and continued eating the granola bar. We were quiet for a time. I folded the granola bar wrapper into a long cylinder, held it to my eye, and pretended it was a telescope. It was entirely too narrow to see anything, but I still pointed it toward my father, studying him over the top of the wrapper. He looked happy and relaxed. "You ready to head back?" I asked.

"Sure," he said. "You fooled me, kiddo. I really thought this was going to be a sex talk, not a 'Jen-Sara-talk.' You know, your mom is going to do better. I'm not just saying things. When I told her about the twins, I thought she might go off the deep end, but she's in therapy now, and she has someone who can help her process the news and her relationship with the two of you. I check in on her if I don't hear from her, and I'm aware she isn't doing much to reach out to either of you, but I do know she's improving. She's starting to sound like her old self a little bit. I don't know. It's been a long time since she sounded anything like the woman I used to know, and the last time we spoke, I think I heard her again."

"Maybe I'll email her, too. Do you think it would mean anything to her?"

"Hard to say, kiddo. If I've learned anything, I've learned I cannot predict your mom's behavior."

ANYTHING BUT A LAZY DINNER
ROB - AGE 42

It was a stroke of genius. We were 34 weeks along in the pregnancy. The doctor wanted to induce labor at 36 weeks, but she said the babies could come some time sooner. They were on their own timetable. We still didn't know the gender and wanted them to be a surprise. We had names picked out, though.

Since Erin's maiden name was Walker, we figured Walker would be fine for a boy or girl. I was thinking it would be a better middle name for a girl, but I wasn't the one carrying these babies. If she wanted to name them Arnold, then she could name them Arnold. We asked Jen and Bryan if they had any suggestions. One was Tessa, giving a nod to Erin's best friend Tess, who was the reason we had met. The other was Bryn, which was Bryan without the 'A.' It was still a really nice name. The boy name we all seemed to like was Walter, but we'd call him Walt. Of course, if the babies came out and they looked like William and Bart or Claire and Margo, then we'd go with whatever seemed to fit their little faces best.

The stroke of genius, though, was the dry run for getting to the hospital in case Erin went into labor earlier than the scheduled induction. We all had jobs. There were lists printed and lying around the house. There were instructions—even a set in the console in the car. No one wanted to leave anything to chance. I also made a diagram. It had the layout of the house and where shoes, coats, car keys, wallet, and of course the Go Bag. The car seat bases were already set into both Erin and my cars, and the car seats/baby carriers were next to the Go Bag, which was another stroke of genius. My thought was simple: Whoever was driving Erin to the hospital (Jen now had her driver's license), would grab the car seats and the Go Bag on the way out the door. In theory, everything would go off without a hitch. Also, there were fail safes to the plan. If we screwed up anything, someone could always come home and grab whatever we had forgotten.

In the 'Hospital Run' rehearsals, we were doing great. I felt confident. Erin felt confident. Jen and Bryan felt competent. They also felt like I was a lot. I knew I was. I knew the feeling of waiting for a baby to enter the world. It was the same way I felt before Jen and Bryan were born, and there was nothing like the adrenaline rush of excitement for a baby, and nothing worse than the lace of fear along the edge of the excitement. When Bryan was born, he was quiet and blue. There was a lot of slapping his bottom, and, at the time, I don't think I had ever been more scared. The nurses were rubbing him, and then he began to cry, and his tiny, perfect face filled with the anger and shock of being removed from the warm womb (I told Sara to say 'warm womb' fast five times) he had inhabited for the prior nine months. There are things in life that can't ever be forgotten, and the birth of children is one of them.

Jen and Erin had become very close. They had their own routines and had developed some rituals. Jen learned to braid Erin's hair, and the two of them did their nails on Sundays, or sometimes they did facials. They shopped, cooked, baked. Jen was still obsessed with laying out, I mean 'styling,' the perfect table for family meals. Jen and Erin announced they were going to host a special dinner on the 34 week mark of the pregnancy, the weekend after Labor Day. Erin was very tired, and the dinner was going to be themed: The Lazy Dinner.

As usual, everyone would bring something, but the rule was it couldn't take more than 25 minutes to cook, including prep time. We gathered around the table, champagne bottles littered here and there, and sparkling cider filling in the gaps for the non-drinkers and under-21 set. We were cleaning up dessert and getting ready to play Two Truths and a Lie using the dictionary. Erin was coming back into the room and stopped abruptly, grabbing the door frame. "Oh, shit," she said, looking down. "I really liked this dress." She started crying. Water gushed for about 10 seconds. "Dammit," she said through her tears. "I love this rug. Rob, you're going to have to call the carpet cleaners."

Jen sprang into action, giving orders, ticking this off a list like she had done this a hundred times before. "Erin, go into the bathroom right now. I will meet you there in one minute. I'm going to get you a change of clothes." The only thing unplanned was Erin's water spontaneously breaking in the middle of a dinner party. Jen ran into our bedroom, quickly grabbing clean underwear and a fresh dress for Erin, then dashed to the hall bathroom where Erin was waiting for her.

I saw the door open, and Erin grabbed Jen by the shoulders, pulling her to her fiercely and holding her against her in a loving embrace, I would say, of nuclear proportion. As soon as they left the bathroom, Jen was on the phone with the doctor. She had been timing Erin's contractions from the moment Erin's water had broken. Everyone was doing what they were supposed to be doing. I was handed my keys and wallet, and I had all the stuff I thought I was supposed to have. I was on auto-pilot. This was happening. We were having babies.

We met Annabelle, our doctor, at the hospital. She said, "If you had been dilated too much more, you wouldn't have had the choice on the epidural. Good thing you arrived when you did." She said things looked good and said she would check back with us in about 30 minutes. Jen turned on the Spotify playlist she and Erin had put together for the birth. It was spa music—very soothing and ambient.

Erin said, "Hey, Jen, can you switch to the other playlist? The one with all the party songs?"

"Sure," Jen said. The next thing I heard was the intro to *You Shook Me All Night Long*. I don't think I could have loved the two of them more than I did at that moment. Erin's contractions were awful, and the anesthesia helped some, but there's only so much the drug can do when the patient was expected to push out a couple of babies.

Annabelle came back in during *Purple Haze*. She checked Erin and said, "Folks, I think we're ready to push." And then I fainted. This time, though, I wasn't sitting in a chair. I had been standing and hit the floor. As everything went dark, I heard Jen calling for Bryan, asking him to move me to a chair and to check me for a concussion.

I don't think I was out for too long. When I woke up, I had a headache. Jen and Erin's mom were each holding one of Erin's legs, and Erin's face was sweaty and contorted. There was a lot of breathing, and I knew how the breathing worked. I was supposed to be there, holding Erin's hand and counting with her through the breaths. "Honey, I'm good. We're going to breathe together."

Annabelle looked at me from between my wife's legs. "Rob, can you look at the mirror? Baby A is crowning. He or she will be out soon. We need to focus all of the breathing and pushing on bringing this little darling into the world."

"Got it," I said. I took Erin's hand, and we looked at each other. Then we both looked up at the mirror. "Ready to get these babies out of your body?"

"More than ready," she said. Jen gave us both a watery smile, and Erin's mom took my elbow and squeezed it.

Both babies were small, I thought, but Annabelle said they were good sizes for twins. They were born screaming and crying during *Thunderstruck*, and they looked so much alike. I couldn't tell them apart, except for the fact that one was a boy, and one was a girl. I mean, babies look like babies. I'd be hard pressed to tell Jen and Bryan apart from their baby photos. Babies. But these babies had Erin's black hair and, so far, my green eyes. After Erin and the babies were cleaned up, we were moved to a regular room. Friends and family started taking turns coming in to see Walker Reed James and Bryn Rose James. Erin's mom's name is Rose, and we thought it sounded good with Bryn. It was surreal. We had been having a dinner party less than three hours ago.

I pulled Jen aside later, "Honey, I think you'd be an amazing CEO, Military General, or ER doctor." She just looked at me. "I think what I'm saying is this: The way you marshalled us all into action...I think you can do anything you set your mind to doing with your life."

She smiled and hugged me, her eyes shining. "I think right now, I want to focus on being a big sister."

Later that evening, I sent an email to Sara to let her know the twins had been born, everyone was healthy, and a photo of Jen, Bryan, Erin, Walker, Bryn, and me. I thought it would be important to Sara to get information from me personally, not via x degrees of separation. I was also very aware of how difficult it might be for her to stomach the existence of the altered family unit in light of the baby she and I had lost. It was my desire to be as compassionate as possible without rubbing salt into a wound that may or may not have healed. She would never say much on the subject of how she was doing from a mental health perspective. Granted, I couldn't imagine how such a conversation would go.

EMAIL

SARA - AGE 42

*J*en and Bryan,

I read every email you two send me. Thank you for each message. Sometimes your messages are the pick-me-up I need to get through the day, and sometimes they're the first thing I see before I start work. Your words, and just the fact that you take the time to write me...it's everything.

I know I don't write back frequently, but I want to do better, and I will do better. Asia has been a wonderful experience and a big change for me. Your father has probably already shared with you that I'm going to be moving on to South America after I finish my year in Asia. I've learned so much here about medicine, people, and about myself. I made the decision to get the professional help I should have gotten four years ago, but I'm just a person, and, apparently, I'm not great at doing what's best for myself. My therapist is wonderful, and she has helped me, and I made a friend here, Claire. She and her husband are from France. They have younger kids and have been in Asia working for around ten years. She has been a tremendous support to me, and she has no qualms calling me out on my, um, baloney.

If there's anything I can pass along to you, it's this: If you're going down a path where you just feel helpless and hopeless, listen to your friends or family or the people who know you as well as you think you know yourself. Really listen to them. Then get out of your own way. Do the hard thing, even if you think your loved ones don't know what they're talking about. Really listen.

I love you both and never stopped loving you. If it seems like I did, what was happening was that I had quit loving myself, and I'm working on repairing that relationship.

Love,
Mom

PART THREE

SATCH

JEN - AGE 16

Walker and Bryn. I could stare at them all day. Mostly, they ate, slept, and pooped. There were periods of time when they were awake, and they seemed to take in their surroundings. Eventually, they started tracking things visually. We had these black and white cards with different designs on them. They were intended to be visually stimulating to infants when they were a few weeks old. Bryan, Darcy, Trent, and I would take turns holding up a card and moving it side to side and up and down. Sure enough, they followed the cards, moving their tiny heads, or training their eyes. All the stuff in the baby book, (I called it the owner's manual) was pretty much on the mark.

Erin was nursing the twins, and she was exhausted. She started pumping breast milk right away to get her milk supply to increase quickly, but it was wearing her out. She seemed relatively content when she was nursing one of the babies. "The pump," she said, "makes me feel very utilitarian. I know how the dairy cows feel on a dairy farm when they have to get hooked up to one of the milking machines." Originally, Erin's goal was to nurse Walker and Bryn for the first year of life. After the first month, though, she decided she would try to make it to the end of her maternity leave. "I'm so exhausted, I don't know if I'd be able to make the drive to work without falling asleep," she said. And right there, the exhaustion: that was my birth control. Jesus, Joseph, and Mary, and all the saints. I could not do everything I wanted to do and be that tired.

I continued writing to my mom. She was almost like an imaginary friend or some kind of pen pal I would never meet, and going through all the effort of writing my messages was freeing because there really weren't any repercussions. Writing to my mom was therapeutic. I think just getting some of my thoughts out of my brain was big. There were things I put in the emails that I didn't put in my journal, and if my mom was reading everything I sent, then that was great. If she wasn't reading my messages, that was okay, too, because the act of putting words to what was going on in my head was a huge help to me, Jen, the teenager. Once in a while, she'd ask a question or offer advice, but, largely, she was ether.

Dad and I were walking Rosemary and Sage one afternoon. The two of them were getting up there in dog years, but they were so happy to get outside with us on a walk. I walked Sage, who was smaller and easier for me to control. In their excitement, they pulled on their leashes, leading Dad and me by the scents they uncovered along our route.

"You know," Dad said. "One of the ultimate tests of trust in your dog is to allow the dog to walk you. You keep the dog on a leash, but you let the dog direct the walk. If the dog leads you into someone's yard for a time, then you go in the yard, too. Of course, if the dog sees a rabbit or squirrel, you chase the rabbit or squirrel with the dog. There are inherent flaws, but the gist is trusting your dog enough to give him or her the authority to go wherever, and they know you're content to follow them."

"Have you ever done that?" I asked.

"I have," he said. "I don't recommend deciding to do it for the first time in a state park. You'll wind up chasing God knows what through the woods." We laughed.

"Is that what happened to you?"

"I had a dog when I was your age, a boxer named Satch. He wasn't the smartest, but he was a sweet boy and fierce. We went to a park one weekend, and I learned my lesson when Satch chased a chipmunk or something—I never got a glimpse of what set him off—but before I knew it, we were running wild through the woods. My arms and legs were scratched and scraped by fallen branches and low-hanging limbs. I was a mess." He smiled at the memory. "Anyway, we finally stopped chasing whatever it was Satch had seen, but I had no idea how to get back to the trail. We wandered around for a while, and I can tell you this: My trust in Satch had waned, but it had waned only insofar as our current setting. I had chosen wrong. I set us up for failure." Dad shook his head before going on. "We eventually came to a different trail, and I followed the trail. We would either find the end or the trail head. Wherever we wound up, we wouldn't be lost."

We continued walking, watching Rosemary and Sage pause here and there. "I learned I couldn't be angry with Satch. He was being a dog, doing what dogs do. If I expected him to do something different, then I wasn't being fair because I was expecting him to be something different than a dog. Of the two of us, I was in the wrong. I made the bad call that day. It was the wrong place to put Satch at the helm."

When we got home, Erin had Bryn and Walker down for their naps, and she met Dad's gaze. Dad reached into his back pocket and produced a twenty dollar bill. "Hey, kiddo. Why don't you stop by the O'Briens' and see what Trent and Bridgette are doing. Go get some ice cream or something. I think I'm going to grab a little nap."

"Gotcha," I said, glancing at Erin. "I hope your 'nap' doesn't result in more babies."

Erin guffawed. "Oh, my sweet, sweet girl. Birth control is my middle name, and so is fun, and caution, and crazy, sexy, happy...I have a lot of middle names, but birth control is right at the top."

I grabbed my laptop, stuffed it into my backpack. Erin came into my room while I was gathering everything. "Hey, do you have a second before you head out?"

"Sure," I answered.

"You know, motherhood has given me a lot to think about. I have these two people hanging off my boobs every two hours, and then there's the pump, which is a thing all on its own. But, I have a lot of time to think about things."

"I can't imagine how you're still standing at the end of the day," I said. "I'm just a bystander, and it seems like *a lot*."

"It is," she said. "But I wouldn't trade it. Every day, I look at those two babies, and I look at you and Bryan, and I pray not to drop any balls, not to screw anything up. With the babies, it's easy. If I screw up, they're never going to remember it."

"Okay," I said. "Makes sense."

"I think what I'm driving at is that the older they get, the more aware they are, the screwups have wider significance. They're going to remember, and they're going to form impressions. I know I'm going to blunder, okay?"

I nodded, and Erin continued. "I know I'm going to make mistakes with you and Bryan, too. I hope they're not showstoppers, but I know with 100% certainty, I will say or do the wrong thing at some point in your lives. What I'm driving at is forgiveness and grace."

"Erin, I can't imagine a scenario where I couldn't forgive you," I said, putting my backpack on my bed and looking her in the eye.

Her gaze penetrated, "I'm not just talking about me. You're growing up, and--if you can find it in your heart--think about your mom. What kind of grace can you grant her? It costs you nothing. Isn't that what the grandmas say?"

"But," I started to say, and Erin cut me off. She knew I had been writing to my mom, and she was totally supportive of all of us getting to a point where we could forgive, where we were whole again, and I loved her for it.

"If I can pass on a morsel of truth: Life is unpredictable."

"Yeah," I responded.

"All right. I'm getting off my soapbox. I just felt like I needed to talk about this with you because I know you've struggled with how your mom fits or doesn't fit into your life and your feelings toward her." She clapped her hands together then clasped them. "Okay. Good talk. See you later." She turned to leave the room, then turned back to me again and hugged me, holding me tight.

I picked up my backpack and car keys and drove to a coffee shop. Trent joined me a little later, and while I waited, I thought about Dad's story and what Erin said. I kept sending emails to my mom and didn't expect anything from her. I did like and appreciate when Mom would respond with a question for me to think over because her questions or thoughts were relevant to the emailed 'diary' entry

I had directed to her. It was gratifying, I guess, to know she was reading my notes and putting thought into what she sent me.

Mom,

Hi. It's Jen—your daughter. Did Dad ever tell you about his dog Satch and the day they were lost in the woods? I'm wondering if I'm expecting you to be something more than human, something more than perfect—able to leap tall buildings and heal yourself perfectly. If that's the case, then I think I might be being unfair to you. By the same token, I think you've been unfair to Bryan and me by not thinking of us as humans with more capability and capacity for thought, compassion, and understanding. There's a possibility, I think, where I might owe you the tiniest apology for expecting more from you than you could give or be. And, I think maybe I need to forgive you, too, because living through the human condition is a big thing, and you may not have been strong enough to brave everything the human condition can throw at you.

I'm switching my focus from humans here. Enter the turtles, stage right. I'm going to use them as a metaphor, and, yes, they are anthropomorphized turtles.

Maybe you decided to be a turtle and shelter inside your shell until you thought it was okay enough outside to rejoin the rest of the turtles. But you didn't hang a sign outside your shell to say you were sheltering. The other turtles thought maybe you were dead or looking for another shell or...heck...the other turtles just didn't know, and since you were sheltering, they couldn't ask questions or try to make you feel better. Eventually, the other turtles left, and all that remained was you and your shell and the quiet and solitude. At some point, you'll poke your head out of your shell, though, and maybe you'll find an empty landscape, or maybe there will be new turtles. I hope you find new turtles.

--Jen

MOTHERHOOD: A REFLECTION

SARA

Throughout each of my pregnancies, I felt, at times, beautiful, bloated, tired, thrilled, scared, worried, hopeful, and a lot of other things. What I think I felt most, though, was an all-consuming love for the little ball of cells growing inside of me. Every week, I looked at a pre-natal calendar to see how big my baby was: a grain of rice, a peanut, a golf ball, a grapefruit, and eventually, what felt like the transmission of a car. We watched all the videos from the ultrasounds, and, quickly, we realized these were only interesting to Rob and me. When we showed more than 30 seconds to anyone, their eyes would glaze over, and they would begin looking for the door. After my mom started to nod off when we showed her our latest video, we decided we would limit the viewing to the ultrasound photos.

Early in my first pregnancy, I played classical music in the car on the way to work. Each week, I would change up the music to introduce different rhythms. I knew the baby would hear the rhythm of my heartbeat, but I had read that exposing a baby to different types of beats made him or her calmer. By the time we reached the middle of the pregnancy, Vampire Weekend was on my list, and I made my way through their discography over the course of a couple weeks because I just really liked their music. Once the third trimester started, I made a party playlist, and decided there were so many rhythms in life, and my child was going to hear so much more than what I had been so careful to curate. I talked to my belly one Saturday afternoon, "You know what, little man or lady? You are going to get to hear all of my favorite songs for the rest of this pregnancy. Then after you're born, you'll have to keep listening to my songs until you can tell me to put on something you want to hear instead."

During my second pregnancy, I started with classical music during the first week, then switched over to Vampire Weekend (because, duh, they were so great!), and then all my favorite songs. Since Jen was only four months old when I got pregnant with Bryan, she didn't really have a lot of input into what kind of music she wanted to hear in the car. By the time Bryan was born, though, she was 13 months old, and she had opinions, and there is no reasoning with toddlers.

With two baby seats occupying the back of my car, facing backward (which sounds horribly boring to stare at the car's upholstery for the duration of the drive) I started playing the little-kid-music, songs like *Old MacDonald*. I had a whole bunch of songs saved that I didn't think had been part of my listening experience since I had been around five years old. Hearing them again, though, was so easy, and my little boy and girl loved all the silly voices I did when I sang along as the farmer or the train conductor or the mama duck or whatever.

In the evenings, Rob and I took turns reading board books that had no stories in them. We made up a story or rhyme or something simple to go along with the picture. There was one book with an armadillo on the page, and Rob said, "Hmmm. What does the armadillo say? He says, 'Hi! I'm an armadillo.'" I laughed so hard every time we reached the armadillo page in the book, which I think was called, "Baby Animals," but all the animals were made with fresh vegetables. Surprisingly, they were easily identifiable. The lamb was a piece of cauliflower with black olives for eyes and apple stems for tiny, spindly legs. I know the eyes had pupils, but I cannot recall what the white dot was that served as a pupil. We saved the book in a plastic bin because I thought I would definitely want to read it to my grandchildren someday.

Yes, Jen and Bryan were only thirteen months apart, nearly Irish twins. I felt lucky we were going to be in and out of diapers with both kids in a few short years. And I think I must have been crazy to think Bryan would see Jen sitting on the potty chair and decide to potty train himself. Toddler logic is not a thing. Toddlers do things on their own timetables. I knew boys took longer to potty train than girls. When I thought Bryan wasn't going to get out of diapers ever, my mom said, "I don't know any adults who failed potty training." She was right. He was going to figure it out whenever he wanted to figure it out. With Jen being a year older, she was already wearing big girl underwear, and we made a big production of Jen and her underwear. I bought Bryan some big boy underwear and let him hold it and look at it, and he said, "I don't like it!" and threw it down on the floor.

Rob said, "Maybe he wants to go commando." It was a good suggestion. I had heard from several of the people in my office that a commando weekend usually ended with positive results. For us, it ended with a steamer vacuum. The takeaway was this: We'd try again in a few months to see if Bryan had changed his mind on the potty chair situation.

When Bryan turned two, Jen had already been potty trained for a year. What I noticed each morning when I changed Bryan's diaper was that he was staying dry through the night. I ran into our bedroom, jumping on top of Rob. "You are never going to believe this," I said excitedly, straddling his dozing form.

"Can you please give me about five minutes to rouse and then get aroused?" he said sluggishly.

"I'm not here for sex! Gah! Our son has had a dry diaper every morning for the past week! I think tomorrow, after I take off his diaper, I'm going to sit him on the potty chair and see what happens. Isn't that amazing?" I may have been crying with joy. "I need you to think of something to give him as a reward. We have to reinforce the good behavior."

Rob said, "Mmmm. Ice cream."

"Sure. Whatever. Will you figure it out?"

"I'm on it," Rob said. "Are you just teasing me by sitting on my crotch?"

"Oh, yeah. I am. Sorry. I have to get the kids dressed. You'll take them to daycare today?"

"If it's Thursday, then, yes, I am taking them to daycare."

I leaned down and kissed Rob on the mouth, then pulling back, I licked the tip of his nose.

"Did you just lick my nose?" he asked.

"Yes, I did. You need to get out of bed.

SMALL NEW LIVES
SARA - AGE 42

Now, knowing there were two little ones in Rob and Erin's care, joining the two bigger ones, it was a balance. I would lapse into the "Poor me," spiral, and then I would start writing, addressing the prompts Rob would send me. Then I would think about the great work I was doing for my patients, and I would think about all the progress I had made with my therapist.

When Rob told me I was starting to sound like the 'old' Sara, it was a sign of how far I had come, and the journey couldn't have happened without my job but also my determination to get help with a very wise therapist who challenged me every time we met. I knew at some point I would be able to look at how much my family's lives had changed, and I could be happy for them down to my marrow. And when I had those feelings, then I knew I was going to be as well as I was ever going to be. BIG goal. It was going on my list.

This time, when I read Jen's most recent email, I responded.

Jen,

I found some turtles. I thought you'd want to know.

Love,

Mom

Kid Duty

Bryan – age 16

Dad and I were in charge of Bryn and Walker for the weekend. For Jen's birthday, she and Erin were going on a girls' weekend. They were headed to Florida to check out a college with a strong running program and to meet with some coaches. Every female we knew thought Dad and I were going to do something idiotic or monumental without Erin and Jen around to supervise. Darcy was going to stop by to check on us and give us some moral support. We weren't going to need it, though. We had Baby Duty down to a science. Maggie O'Brien and Bridgette were also going to check on us, and all three of the grandmas were going to be stopping throughout the weekend.

"Do you find it just the tiniest bit insulting that we are being checked up on by so many of the women in our lives this weekend?" I asked my dad.

"I'm looking at this a couple different ways. Erin needs a break, and your sister wants to go visit a college with a strong running program located near a beach. We have an opportunity to prove we are completely capable of taking care of these children," he said.

"Right. We are up to the challenge. Definitely," I agreed.

"The other approach is to show how much help we need from all the ladies in our lives in an effort to demonstrate how we're just a couple men who can never do the job as well as they can," Dad said, holding his hands out like the pans on a balance scale.

"But if we're incompetent, Erin will never feel like she can get away from the babies. Right?" I asked.

"Right. I think we are better off doing our best and asking for help if and when we need it and having a lovely weekend with the ladies checking up on us. We're not going to do anything foolish like cook. We're definitely ordering for delivery or pickup or something."

"Dad," I said, "they're toddlers now, aren't they? I mean they're over a year old. Maybe we shouldn't pretend they're still little human blobs."

"Yeah, but I love them being little. They're tiny for such a short time," he said a little wistfully.

"Get a puppy," I answered. "Rosemary and Sage are getting up there in years."

"Maybe," he said. "I'll have to run it by Erin. See what she says. She's the boss. I am not doing anything to upset the balance of power in this house." He laughed.

While the kids napped, Dad and I watched a documentary on the creation of the microchip. "Why are we watching this?" I asked.

"I have no idea," Dad said. "I think I was too lazy to reach for the remote to find something else."

"What do you feel like watching?"

"Something mindless," he said.

"Cartoons? Old Scooby Doo?" I asked.

"Old Scooby Doo," he answered.

The theme song came on, and I heard one of the kids stirring, and I wanted to grab whoever was waking before both of them were awake. Between leaving the room to go pick up Walker and coming back to the family room, Dad had fallen asleep. I left a note for Dad, put the baby monitor next to him on the couch, and decided to take a short walk. With all the possible baby accoutrements in the stroller, Walker and I set out. The outdoors seemed to calm him, and I would stop every so often to look at his face. He was going to be a fantastically handsome son of a gun when he got older. He had Dad's green eyes and this café au lait skin that looked like the perfect suntan. If he wound up with Dad's build, he was going to be a heartbreaker. And Bryn. Dad and Erin were going to have to fight off the boys who would be chasing her. Of course I was biased, but they were both the most beautiful children I had ever seen. Not that I had seen a lot of babies and toddlers, but I was pretty certain.

When we returned, Dad and Bryn were still asleep. Grandma and Gram had arrived and were taking pictures of Dad asleep on the couch. I had no illusions that the two of them had no shame in writing on his face with a Sharpie while he slept, and I chalked it up as a win that we had arrived before they could mess with him. I motioned for the two of them to join Walker and me on the back patio.

"Why do I sense you two are up to mischief?" I asked with a joking tone, not wanting them to think I was interrogating them.

"We would never," Gram said, trying to sound insulted. "We were waiting for Rose to arrive before we got into mischief."

"Wow," I said. "Don't you want Erin to know it's all right to take some time to go on a college visit with her stepdaughter? Give us a chance to do right. We all deserve a chance, don't we?"

"Fine," Grandma said. "You're right. We'll be good."

"We're going to order pizza or something for dinner. You could have the grandpas join us, and we can all hang with Walker and Bryn, and you can all be amazed at how competent Dad and I can be." I paused and leaned toward them like I had a secret. "I'm going to let you in on a little something very closely held by Jen and Erin. They left us the owner's manual."

"What?" Grandma said.

"The owner's manual," I repeated.

"The owner's manual to what?" Gram asked.

"Bryn and Walker," I said. "This thing is comprehensive. It even has an FAQ section in it. Jen and Erin started writing everything as soon as Jen booked the airfare to make this college visit. Dad and I don't want them to worry that we're going to mess anything up. We have read through the major stuff we have to handle, like feeding, bathing, diaper changing, sleep, play, napping--which is different than sleep because napping can be a daytime sleeping habit, and sleep is a nighttime activity." I glanced at my phone. Dad had been asleep for about an hour. "Could one of you hold Walker for a little bit? I need to wake Dad. If he naps too long, he'll be up all night."

The grandmas did rock, paper, scissors to see who would get to hold my little brother. I went back into the house to wake Dad. The front door quietly opened, and Rose came in. "Hi," I whispered. "Gram and Grandma are on the back patio with Walker. They're expecting you."

"Thanks," Rose stage whispered. "Bryn's napping?"

"Yes. Do you want to wake her? They're both going to be hungry pretty soon. I'm going to get Dad up, and we'll get sippy cups and food ready for both of them."

When it was all said and done, I think the grandmas wanted all of us to be gone for the weekend, and they wanted the twins for themselves. They fussed over them, taking turns holding one or the other of them. They made the most idiotic faces at the kids and the noises they made...I wish I had recorded some of this stuff. Excellent blackmail material.

While the grandmas were occupying themselves with Bryn and Walker, I sidelined my dad. "Hey, I wanted to ask you about something," I said. "I'm sixteen and driving, and I'd like to pick up a part-time job on the weekends. I've talked to the partners from Mom's old practice and asked if they would let me work in the urgent care clinic on the weekends, and they said yes, but with the caveat that I had to have your approval."

Dad was silent for a second, his eyes growing wider. Then he smiled. "I think that sounds great. Are you going to email your mom?"

"I think I will. I send her messages sometimes, and I don't know if she's reading them or not. She doesn't really respond. I know she sometimes responds to Jen's messages. They're usually very short with a question or something, but nothing that would tell us what's going on in *her* life or asking about what's going on in our lives. It's so weird," I admitted.

"I think at some point, your mom is going to have a bunch of stuff to share with the two of you. I don't know how or when, but I know she's been working on getting some things together. Initially, I thought she would dole it out a little at a time so you wouldn't be overwhelmed, but she's pretty good at choosing the nuclear option."

I took out my phone and pulled up my email and quickly sent Mom a message to let her know my plans for a part-time job. After dinner, I checked my email and saw my mother's response.

Bryan,

Would you be interested in spending the summer working in South America in my clinic?

--Mom

"Dad!" I called, stunned. "What *the* hell?" I showed him the email. He was very quiet and stood behind me looking at my computer screen. He gripped my shoulder, and I could feel the slight shake in his hand. I turned to look up at him, seriousness marked his entire face, and his eyes were hard. He cleared his throat.

In a shaky voice Dad asked, "How do you feel about this? It's kind of huge, and, to be completely frank, I'm flabbergasted and miffed your mom hasn't made a similar offer to your sister."

"I'm going to speak completely off the cuff. Okay? I'm only thinking out loud. Got it?"

He nodded.

"I want to go to med school eventually. Spending the summer in Mom's clinic in South America would be amazing, and it would look phenomenal on my college applications. By the same token, working here in the urgent care center would also look good on my applications, and I would earn money. I don't speak Spanish. I've been taking Japanese, so there's a language barrier. I know what my role would be in the job here. I don't know what I'd be doing in Mom's clinic and would need to get more information. I would be away from Darcy, and before you say anything, I know it's just for the summer. We can cope with three months of distance. But maybe one of the biggest things is this: I don't know Mom. She's a stranger, and if I go all that way, I don't think I'm going to know how to feel. Is she my boss, my mom, my family friend, my weird aunt? I don't know how to navigate the relationship because I don't know what the relationship even is. I worry about being stuck there with her, and what if I decide I really don't like her?"

"Bryan. All valid points. It might be an olive branch, and it might be the only thing she has to offer. I'm still a bit mystified, though, that she hasn't made the same invitation to your sister. And, I'm being completely candid here. I love this for you, but I hate it for Jen." Dad began pacing behind me. "I'm kind of pissed at your mom's lack of tact or concern for your sister. I'm also a little pissed she didn't bother to discuss the idea with me."

He left the room, and I heard him slam the back door. I looked out the window and saw him pulling at the ends of his hair. He had his cell phone out, and I knew he had to be trying to reach Mom. It looked like he wanted to throw the phone on the ground. He was angry. His face was red, and his hair was now standing on end. He sat down on one of the patio chairs, leaning forward, elbows on his knees, hands clasped behind his neck. I joined him, sitting in one of the chairs next to him.

Dad looked over at me. "I don't know what to tell you, Bryan. It's your decision. There's no right or wrong answer, but there are right and wrong ways to handle your decision. Maybe make a list of questions for your mother. I don't think you should make a final decision without having all the facts first. I also think you should schedule a phone call or video call with your mother and interview her. If there's anything that gives you pause, you can get it out in the open. Discuss all of this with Jen and Darcy. They are both going to have opinions and might have some valuable insights or might come up with more questions for you to ask your mother. Thoughts?" he asked.

"Sounds reasonable," I said. In my heart of hearts, though, I knew I wouldn't go to South America. What I wanted was counsel on how to broach the subject with my sister.

A Second Chance

Sara - Age 43

During my time in Asia, I took some time to go to Japan. I had never been and had some time off. I probably should have arranged to come home to see my parents and children, but I couldn't face them. How I failed them burned deeply. So, yeah, after the miscarriage and grief, then I had to deal with being a complete fuck-up as a human being. I stuck to my goals and continued checking things off my list. My friend Claire was incredible, encouraging, and never judged me. She commented on how my general affect had improved throughout my first months in Asia, and I was actually feeling better.

I started writing my stories from the prompts Rob supplied. I hadn't given them to the kids yet, but eventually, I would. I wanted them to know me, but I think I wanted them to have everything all at once and not some kind of "Getting to Know Sara: The Serial." I hadn't informed Rob I was putting things together and wanted to give everything to the kids in a bolus. After a long day in clinic, Claire came to my place for a quick cocktail.

"Sara, you should tell your kids what you're planning. Tell them what you've been working on. They will appreciate all your thoughts and your work in telling the story of who you are, where you've been, what you've been doing, and where you're going. It doesn't take the place of them getting to know you, not as you are now, and not as they are now, but it's a starting point. You should tell them," Claire said. She ran her finger down the condensation on her glass and glanced at her watch.

"Go. Fix dinner. Give everyone a good night kiss from me," I said.

She gave me a kiss on each cheek, and before I closed the door, I called to her, "I've booked a vacation."

She returned her incredible French shrug that asked everything.

"Japan. I'm leaving a week from tomorrow. What do you think?" I said.

She answered with a double thumbs up.

***

I flew into Tokyo, arriving in the evening. It was a Friday night. There were people on their ways to here and there. They were dressed for going out, maybe for dinner, maybe for dates, maybe for a wild night in a club. I liked to imagine where they were going. I noticed a striking man who boarded one or two stops after me. He had an athletic frame and looked like maybe some kind of academic. The train was crowded, and I didn't get a good look at his face, but I started noticing details. He carried a worn, leather messenger bag with papers poking out of the top. His suit was off the rack, a little shiny from wear, nothing special. He turned to face the same door I was facing, and for a few stops, all I could see was his back side. From behind, I could see he had a full head of beautifully cut shiny black hair, artfully mussed. Though his suit was a bit rumpled (leading me to think he might be an academic), he wore the hell out of it. The train's monitors showed which doors would be opening at the next stop. He turned to re-orient himself on the train, and when I saw his face, I think I swooned. I was holding onto the suspended handle, and thank Jesus, Joseph, Mary, and all the saints. If I hadn't been holding onto the handle, I might have fainted. My face must have had a very odd look because he said in perfect, unaccented English, "Are you all right?"

I said, "I'm perfectly fine, thanks. You reminded me of someone."

"I hope it's someone good," he responded, smiling, and there was a glint in his dark eyes. "What brings you to Japan?"

"Well," I whispered, because the train was very quiet, "I'm on vacation for a little bit, and I've never been here...in Japan. I've been in Asia working for the last six months, and I got a great deal on airfare."

"Good for you," he whispered. "Where are you staying? I mean, what part of town?" He eyed my suitcase and backpack.

I told him where I was staying and asked, "Do you live here or are you on vacation or..."

"I'm here to give a talk at a conference, and then I'm going back to California," he said.

"What kind of talk?" I asked. I wanted to keep him talking to me, and I was afraid if I stopped asking questions or pushing forward for a conversation, this short interview would be over, we would go our separate ways, and I would never see this beautiful man again.

"This is going to sound kind of boring, but I'm a gastroenterologist, and I'm here to talk about advances in gastroenterology. It's fascinating stuff," he said, throwing in a bit of a sarcastic tone toward the end.

"I would love to come to your talk," I whispered back enthusiastically, but it felt like I was yelling.

"You would?" he asked incredulously. "No one wants to hear about blood and guts. Who are you, and where have you been all my life?" He grinned at me, and, again, I thought I was going to swoon. "Why on earth would you want to come to some conference, which will likely be a bore to you, when you're on vacation?"

"I'm a primary care doc with Doctors Without Borders. We see weird GI things from time to time, and we aren't always going to meetings and conferences to get the most up to the minute science."

"Doctors Without Borders? Really? I'm finishing an academic post in May-June, and you won't believe this, but I'm actually starting with Doctors Without Borders during the summer." An academic. Ha! I'd nailed it.

"Seriously?" I asked. "Do you know where you're going? My first year, I was in Africa, then this year I'm in Asia, and then next year, I'm headed to South America to open a clinic."

"You aren't Sara James, are you?" his eyes widened.

"Yeah, I am. You aren't Michael Garcia-Obashi, are you?"

"Guilty as charged," he smiled.

We exchanged phone numbers and decided to get dinner and drinks at the next train stop, and we didn't leave each other's side for the rest of the time we were both in Japan. Michael had been divorced for five years. He and his wife had had no children, and she had re-married shortly after the divorce. They had an amicable relationship and had remained friends.

"I know this is a very invasive and personal question, but why no kids?" I asked him when we were sitting in a restaurant bar that first night.

"It was never something I wanted. She really wanted children, and the longer we were married, she realized it was something I was never going to change my mind about. I don't think I have the bandwidth for more than a spouse and my job, and I didn't want to add anything to the mix to take away from either of those things," he said frankly.

"Do you think you might be selling yourself a little short?" I asked.

"I just don't want to find out," he said. "Because the child is the one who ultimately pays the price for any unhappiness I might have a hand in creating."

"I have two kids," I said. "And I have been a terrible mother. I was a happy, productive member of our family unit and then had a miscarriage when my kids were 11 and 12, which messed up everything. I basically deserted my husband and kids and wrecked their lives. We divorced a little over two years ago, but I cut myself out of being a wife and mother around two years before that. My kids are 16 and 17 now."

"Oh, my god, Sara," he said, and he took my hand, and I think that small amount of compassion pushed me over the edge.

The following day, he skipped the conference. We boarded a bullet train and went to Mount Fuji for the day. We took a bus halfway up the mountain. We took photos. One of the people in our tour group said to me, "Would you like me to get a photo of you and your husband with the mountain peak in the background?"

I didn't correct her, and Michael didn't either. I said, "We'd love it. Thank you." He stood behind me, putting his arms around my waist, and resting his head on my shoulder. In one of the photos, I'm looking to the side, right into his eyes, and he's looking into mine. We were smiling at each other. In another photo, we're looking straight into the camera, ebullient, satisfied.

We decided to take a train back to Tokyo the next day and found a small hotel not far from the train station. We stayed in that evening, talking, laughing, and getting to know everything about each other. He had kissed me the night before when he escorted me to my hotel. But we had something. There was something between us, and whatever the something was, it could be cultivated. In the morning, on the train back to Tokyo, we talked about it. Neither of us was new to love, but I hadn't felt this all-consuming feeling since I had met Rob.

"I think we should pursue this, Sara," Michael said. "What do you think?"

"I feel like I would have met you in South America. There's a good possibility we would have gone down this road then. It's got to be a sign that our timetable for meeting bumped us together, randomly, on a train. In Japan. I don't think you ignore that. Do you?" I smiled at him, and I wasn't going to be shy or coquettish. I wanted this thing between us to work...and maybe I was due some good karma.

"Then let's see where this takes us," he said, cupping my chin in his hands and kissing me soundly.

"Promise me something, Michael. Promise me if we don't work out as a couple, promise you'll be my friend, my best friend."

"Same," he said, and we sealed the promise with a kiss.

After his conference and my vacation ended, we spoke on the phone every other night or as best we could manage, and he came to see me four times over my final six months in Asia. I took Michael to meet Claire and her family, and she wholeheartedly approved. She warned him amply of the consequences of breaking my heart. Over the six months of distance dating, though, I knew he wouldn't break my heart. We were very good together and shared the same philosophies on our work and being partners professionally and personally.

When my Asian stint came to an end, I was thrilled to begin my post in South America. Michael and I had decided to share a residence, and I had thought we would stay in South America indefinitely. Of course, my thinking was premature. What if we hated South America? What if we wound up hating each other? So many what-ifs. And the biggest what-ifs were these: What if one or both of us was needed Stateside? What if we had to go back to tend to family matters? We didn't concern ourselves with anything from our former lives, though. I still checked in with Rob but didn't share anything about Michael. I was waiting until I really knew we were solid.

I read the emails from the kids, and sometimes I responded. It was weird for me. I wasn't really much of a mother anymore, and I wasn't their friend. I guess I was this woman who had given birth to them and had been wonderful for many years until I was a ghost of myself. It was embarrassing. If I had been seeing a patient who had all of my symptoms, I know exactly how I would have managed the case. There's a saying that a lawyer who represents himself has a fool for a client. I think for doctors maybe it's the sarcastically rendered, "Physician, heal thyself." But, yeah...I didn't do any of that, and well, we all suffered. I was closing in on my 44th birthday, and therapy was giving me clarity, but I was still a coward and hiding from the mess I'd left behind.

I had a second chance at happiness, though. With Michael. In South America. Helping people who couldn't help themselves. I had to trust Rob and the kids were getting whatever help they needed, and I had to hope they had erased me—at least the last five years of me. At some point, after I felt like I could face them, I thought it would be nice to have a relationship with Jen and Bryan. I didn't know what it would look like, and I didn't know if they would ever be able to love me again or trust me or even want me in their lives. Just like my life was on its own trajectory, all of their lives had moved on without me, and I had to make peace with the fact that I had set them all on a path that didn't include me and might never include me.

***

During one of our video calls after leaving Japan, Michael said, "I know why I'm coming to work for Doctors Without Borders. It's something I always wanted to do. Did you choose it as an escape hatch?"

"I did," I admitted. "It seemed extreme and completely pulled me out of my environment. Africa was so distant that I couldn't just change my mind on a whim. It was deliberate. At the time, I felt like I needed to be away from everything and everyone familiar to me, anything that would ring a bell and remind me of the miscarriage." I moved in a little closer to the screen. I wanted to see every line, every movement of his face.

"Change of scenery, people, circumstance?" he asked, staring right back at me, like we were both trying to memorize every detail of each other and this conversation.

"Yep. Exactly. During that first year, I was surrounded by new sights, sounds, smells, people, and it seemed to revive me. Then I saw my first pregnant patient. She already had four children, and she didn't know how she was going to be able to take care of a fifth child. It was that particular moment when I realized I couldn't escape my triggers, not as long as I worked in medicine in a third world country. Definitely not in primary care." This was the part of the conversation when I had spoken with my therapist where I broke down crying, but now I had reached a point where I could talk about things without feeling like I was the most unfortunate woman in the world.

"What happened?"

"I treated her, took care of her, delivered her baby when it was time, and we found resources for her to take care of the baby or put her up for adoption. After that, I never saw her again. And, I hate to think her pregnancy and baby were the catalyst to my facing my demons, but they were. I started therapy after, granted I didn't actually pull the trigger until I'd reached Asia. Africa was tough for me, but I needed to be there, and I needed to make the decision to leave Africa and work on my own healing. I have come such a long way. Am I 100%? No, but I like to think I'm past the worst of the psychic fallout from my miscarriage."

"I think you've let yourself be incredibly vulnerable with me." He smiled warmly, and I felt something powerful all the way to my core.

"I have. You, my therapist, Asia, and Doctors Without Borders have probably saved my life. Definitely getting therapy was a game changer. And you know, I wasn't in Asia very long before I actually began feeling like my old self. I don't know. This probably sounds weird, but I felt like I started seeing color again, if that makes sense."

"I think I'm happy I met you when I did and not before. You had work to do on yourself. A lot of work. I don't think you would have been open to a relationship before we met in Japan." He ran his fingers through his hair, messing it a little, and I was a sucker for his disheveled look. Beyond the physical, though, he met me where I was, and it meant everything.

"You're probably right. But I feel good about work, about where I am, what I'm doing, and I feel good about us," I said. "Geez. I'll bet you didn't think you were going to be playing psychiatrist tonight, did you?"

The In-Laws

Rob - age 44

Sara's mom, Jo, phoned me at work. It was a Thursday, or as we often called it, Friday's Eve. Ordinarily, Jo texted me or dropped by the house or called when I wasn't at work. Something was wrong. Things had been going smoothly for a while. Erin had gone back to work. The twins were in daycare four days a week, and the grandmas got together at our house once a week and tag-teamed babysitting. Jen and Bryan were doing well, for the most part. When things were going without incident, I always worried the other shoe could drop at any moment.

"Jo, hi. How are you? What's up?"

"Well, I went to the doctor last week for a routine checkup. In the course of my visit, I mentioned I had been bruising a lot. You know how clumsy I am sometimes, but I had been noticing what I like to call 'mystery bruises.'"

"Okay," I said. I didn't like where this was going, and I wanted her to keep talking.

"Well, my doctor also asked how long I'd had shortness of breath," she said.

"You have shortness of breath?" I asked.

"I'm out of shape. I need to start going on walks again. I don't know why I haven't been walking as much. But, yes, it's been gradual, though, this shortness of breath, and I thought it was because I'm out of shape, but I get tired. But the doctor noticed it when he was listening to my lungs. You know the part of the exam when they listen to your lungs and want you to take a deep breath? I took a deep breath and started coughing, and he didn't like the coughing. He says, 'Jo, I don't like that coughing,' and I said, 'Well, I don't like it either,' but what are you going to do about it? You get older and don't necessarily take the best care of yourself, and things start to slip."

"What else did your doctor say?" I asked, not liking where this was going, not one little bit.

"He said he wanted to run some bloodwork, and he thinks he's probably going to send me to a hematologist. He doesn't like the bruising."

Jo had all the bloodwork, and she went to see the hematologist, and it wasn't good. She had a bone marrow biopsy. Howard, Sara's dad, went with her. Bryan took the day off from school, and he went with them, too. Bryan drove them to the appointment and brought them to our house afterward. Tom and Maggie and the kids, my parents, Erin's mom, Tess and Carlotta, and Darcy were all there. We didn't have a theme dinner that night. We took photos, videos, told stories, and Jo kept her composure throughout the evening. We knew she was in discomfort from the biopsy, and we were starting to notice other little things now that we all knew something was going on. She was pale. Was it from the biopsy, or was it part of whatever was wrong with her?

Howard pulled me aside. He was not a tall man. In fact, Howard and Jo were about the same height. The entire time I had known him, his hair had been white, and he was always tan. He smiled a lot, talked little, and when he did have something to say, we all listened. His bright blue eyes were clouded with worry tonight. "We haven't called Sara to let her know something's wrong with Jo. We didn't want to bother her—at least not until we know what's going on. I don't know if we should or not. What would you do if you were in our shoes?"

I pulled Howard in for a hug. He had Jo had been college sweethearts, meeting during the first week of college when they were 18 years old. They had been together ever since, and now, fifty years later, he was terrified of losing his wife and was worried about pussyfooting around his daughter. It made me a little crazy. Sara's parents were guilty of nothing more than lavishing her with love, and she had done to them what she did to the rest of us.

"I think you need to tell her. Come with me. Let's give her a call right now," I said.

"What about the time difference?" Howard asked. I stared at him in stony silence. There would never be a 'perfect' time to have this conversation, and I was angry at the situation that we were all afraid of having an unpopular or less than cheerful conversation with Sara--with it being enough to keep her away even longer. Somehow, we had deified her and made her into an angry goddess who meted out retribution by ignoring all of us who had once worshipped her. I felt the words braced on the tip of my tongue, and it became too much to hold inside.

"I don't give a flying fuck about the time difference. I love Jo like I love my own mother, and I would want to know everything. I hate that you're worried about how to approach Sara, just like Jen and Bryan are. I'm sick of everyone giving her a wide berth. We're calling her, and if we wake her, I don't care."

"Okay," said Howard, his eyes widening at my anger. We called, and we woke her.

"Hello?" Sara asked. "Rob? What's going on? Do you know what time it is?"

"I do know, Sara. I'm calling you right now with your dad. We're calling you because there's a situation. Your mom is sick. We don't know what it is, but she went to see her hematologist today and had a bone marrow biopsy. I think you need to start making plans to come back to see your mom. She's going to need you, and your dad is going to need your support, too."

"Hi, Sara," Howard chimed in. "Your mother would be upset that we're calling you because she doesn't want to be a burden to you."

"Wait, wait, wait," she said. "Can you back up a second and tell me about Mom?"

"She's bruising like a purple people eater," I said. "She's had increasing short-ness of breath and fatigue, and she's been through so many blood tests, like maybe *all* the blood tests, while the doctor is ruling out this or that condition. I think once they get the bone marrow biopsy back, though, they'll know what's happening."

"Okay," she said. "I'll make some calls in the morning and start making arrangements to come back for a while. Dad, is it all right if I stay with you and Mom?"

"Sara," Howard said, running his fingers through his snowy hair then smacking himself on the forehead—like that was the dumbest question of all time, "of course it is."

"Jen will go over to your parents' house and make up the spare room," I said. "I don't want your mom expending any more energy than she absolutely has to. She's lost weight, Sara. She looks good, but pale. It seems like she gets a little paler every time I see her."

Sara gasped. "Got it. I'll figure things out on my end and let you know my travel plans."

Meeting Michael's Mom

Sara - age 43

To say I was nervous about meeting Michael's family, especially his mother, was an understatement. Michael assured me that his family would be very accepting and understanding. They were all healthcare people, too. I didn't know when we would be meeting his family in person, but we both felt like we needed to know each other's families, especially since there was this reality flinging itself in our faces that life is temporary, what with my mom's situation.

Michael's concern, care, and love were everything. I knew he didn't want to have children of his own, and, truthfully, I was in a different place than I had been four years ago. Michael was a quiet strength for me while I tried to find my way back to my kids—whatever that was going to look like. He wanted to meet my parents, my ex-husband, and Jen and Bryan. He wanted to know all the nooks and crannies of my life—my old life and new. I had had video calls with his mom, dad, and his younger brother, who was a general surgeon in San Francisco. They all knew my story. Near panic gripped me when I spoke with his mom the first time. What if she judged me and found me lacking? What if she thought I was a terrible mother? I needn't have worried. Michael's mom was a retired psychologist. At some point, I would want her to meet Jen, since Jen had mentioned wanting to be a sports psychologist.

Before the first video call with his mom, I was freaking out. I hadn't 'met the parents' for over 20 years. "Michael, what do I call your mom? Do I call her Mrs. Garcia-Obashi, or Dr. Garcia-Obashi, or 'hey,' or what?"

"You call her Maria. You're going to be fine. You'll see. She's the best," he said. "Nothing to worry about. She going to love you."

And Michael's mom was wonderful to me. Every time I talk to her, I feel like I'm talking to an old friend. It was clear where Michael had learned his bedside manner. It wasn't until our second video call that I unloaded my backstory on Maria.

"Oh, Sara," she said. "What a terrible thing to experience. I had a miscarriage as well, and it took a little while for me to bounce back from it, but I went for therapy after about a month of feeling terrible, sad, listless, and so emotionally tired every day that I just wanted to lie down and go to sleep as soon as I got home from work."

I nodded. "That's exactly how I felt, but I didn't go see anyone, and feeling all those feelings sort of became my constant companion. If I didn't have the presence of the feelings, then I thought I'd be truly alone."

"You feel what you feel, but if the feeling becomes toxic and separates you from what you love, you need help. You might be able to work it out on your own, but usually not. I'm very happy for you now, though. You've done the work and pursued therapy." I continued nodding in agreement, and I felt the tears stinging the edges of my eyes. I thought about holding them in, but I had also learned about living in the feelings while I experienced them. I wasn't crying about the miscarriage. I was crying about the care and kindness this woman was showing me. All she knew was what Michael had shared with her, and I'm not too proud to admit my failings. Well, now I'm not too proud to admit them.

Michael's mom continued, "Your existence really is a series of journeys, and when you get to the end of this particular journey, there will be another journey, and another, and another; but these journeys aren't all hallmarked by bad times. There are joyful times, too, and you will find the joys far outnumber the sorrows. I understand the sorrows, though. And what you were going through was similar to that saying about not seeing the forest for the trees. But now you see what you didn't see before, and you want to do what you can to make things better. You will have to be patient with your children. You broke their trust, and you will have to earn it back through your actions." She paused, tilting her head a little, like she was trying to see me more closely through the computer screen. "Are you up to the task?" she asked.

"*Now*, I am. I think," I answered. "I'm trying to be real with the kids and let them see me for who I am now."

"Well, Sara, I don't know that you can do much more than that. Don't expect them to rally around you immediately. It will take many, many baby steps to get to a good place with them. Got that?" she asked. "Don't give up if you don't get immediate results."

Michael came up behind me while I was talking with his mom, and he hugged me, and it was exactly what I needed in that moment.

"Ma," he said. "Thank you for the counseling session. Send me the bill." He laughed, and she laughed. I decided I'd laugh, too. We were all laughing, but it wasn't strange or awkward or uncomfortable.

"Oh, you kids. Go on and go save some people's lives or something. I love you, Michael, and take good care of that one," she said pointing at me through the screen.

And here we were. We had managed to find each other, and as much as I had ever loved Rob, I think I loved Michael the nth degree more. Whatever size the nth degree was, it apparently made a difference in the healing process.

After I left Rob and the kids, I found I was grieving everything in my life going to shit, but once I arrived in Africa and my first assignment, I found myself taking care of people who were dealing with death and loss every day, and they weren't setting fire to their lives and running for the hills. I saw the same thing when I moved on to my Asian assignment. That first patient who had me manage her pregnancy in Africa was the catalyst for therapy. I knew it had to happen, but I wasn't ready for therapy until I'd reached Asia. As a primary care physician in a third world country, I couldn't run away from pregnant patients and their babies. It was ironic that I had to run halfway around the world to face my fear and sorrow, even though they'd been right in my face for the two years before I'd started working for Doctors Without Borders. Maybe I needed to be someplace without an audience to my pain.

My goals, written shortly after arriving in Asia were a living thing, and therapy was a must. It wasn't an overnight improvement, but it put me on the road to becoming a fully functioning human being again. It was difficult, rewarding, and the hardest thing I've ever had to do, clawing and climbing my way out of the muck and murk of hurt, loss, sadness, shame, and embarrassment I had allowed to subvert me as a person. Eventually, though, everything became clearer. I had to figure out how I was going to reach out to my children in a sincere way, and I didn't want them to think for a moment the gesture was to assuage my guilt. I wanted us to know each other, and I wanted them to know they were perfect and wonderful, and I didn't know how to do that. Rob was the one who got the ball rolling by giving me writing prompts, and the prompts helped me, too, by reminding me of the best moments of my adult life.

I had experienced journeys of joy, and I had begun experiencing journeys of joy in Asia and South America, and there was no reason I couldn't continue to move forward. It wouldn't be perfect, and I knew parts of my journey were going to be strictly uphill.

Return of the Prodigal

Jen - age 17

Gram is sick. She has aplastic anemia. Her immune system is attacking her bone marrow, which means she isn't making new red blood cells or platelets. I'm not a doctor, nor do I play one on television, but what I understand is that the red blood cells are important for carrying oxygen throughout the body. No wonder Gram has been so light-headed. Then the lack of platelets is responsible for all the bruising she's had, thus the Purple People Eater situation. Usually there are stem cells in the bone marrow, but not Gram's because her immune system is going crazy.

Dad and Grandpa called Mom and told her to get on a plane. I helped Grandpa get their spare room ready for Mom's arrival. She wouldn't be staying with us, which was a good thing because it would just be weird. I placed a sealed envelope on her pillow with a letter I had handwritten. The envelope was decorated with the loops and curves and designs I drew on a lot of the stationery I created.

None of us knew when she would be arriving. Both Bryan and I were driving, but no one gave either of us a second thought by asking us to pick up Mom at the airport. I would've picked her up if anyone had asked, but I would have bitched about it, and I wouldn't have known how to treat her. I pictured the conversation in my head in a hundred different ways, but they all boasted a common thread that boiled down to an imagined exchange of great discomfort and awkwardness.

"Hi, Mom. I'm Jen, your 17-year old daughter. I like running, my boyfriend, my family, my two brothers and sister, my five grandparents, graphic design, nutrition, psychology, and sports psychology. I'm a Capricorn. How have things been for you over the past three years?"

"Did you say your name is Jen? I had a daughter named Jen once. She sort of looked like you. I think I may have seen her when she was 14, but I hadn't really been involved in her life for two years prior. Thank you for picking me up. Do you need the address where we're going?" asked my imaginary mom, bungling through the banter just like I had.

"I'm familiar with where we're going. I'm taking you to my grandparents' house. You might know them. Howard and Jo. When I go over there, I sometimes call their house HoJo's. Get it—like Howard Johnson's? When we arrive, I will show you to the room where you'll be staying. Gram has been too weak to do much housekeeping, and we've all been pitching in to help her and Grandpa."

"Oh? You're with a cleaning crew?" asked my mom, the stranger.

"No. I'm with the family."

"How funny. So am I, I think. I really don't remember all that much about the family, but I've been told I need to be present to provide support."

The stilted conversation would continue on in this vein for the thirty minutes or so it would take to get from the airport to Gram and Grandpa's house. But Uber or Lyft would spare us all from anything similar.

When Bryan showed me the email from Mom inviting him to come to South America to work in her clinic I was equal parts hurt and angry. The hurt and anger were at opposite ends of a seesaw, and depending on my day, the seesaw was balanced between the two, and sometimes one side was heavier than the other.

I couldn't understand why she wouldn't invite both of us. It wasn't like Bryan was going to perform surgery. I could do whatever duties he was going to do. Was she making the offer strictly because she didn't want Bryan to interact with her old partners and office staff? Was it because Bryan wanted to be a doctor? Was it because she wanted to spend time with him? Was it because she might be rewarded by the higher-ups in Doctors Without Borders for getting some free help in the clinic that summer? Whatever the reason, there wasn't a good rationale for her not to invite both of us, and I was leaning more toward being pissed at her. What kind of mother excludes one of her children? But then again, what kind of mother decides to divorce her entire family?

Trent went with me to get the guest room ready and do some light housekeeping. We rooted around in their pantry and refrigerator to make some dinner. Our goal: find the ingredients to make something with a few days' worth of leftovers. I had just put a nice, thick, homemade lasagna in the oven, and Trent was leaning over my shoulder smelling me and smelling the lasagna. He nuzzled my neck when I stood straight again. Spotify played songs from the American Songbook in the background. Trent took my hand and asked, "Would you care for a dance, my love?" He extended his free arm, and I stepped into the frame he created, and we danced in the kitchen. It was slow and sweet. We didn't say anything, and I heard him humming along to the music.

Gram and Grandpa were with Dad, Erin, Bryan, and the twins. We wanted them to come home to a clean house, with the lasagna being an added bonus. The doorbell rang, interrupting Trent and my slow dance, and we broke apart. "I'll get the door," he said. I turned to the kitchen sink and said I would get started cleaning up the kitchen. I sang along to *My Funny Valentine* and then stopped when I heard Trent having a conversation with the person at the front door, and I heard the uncertainty in his voice as well as confusion in the voice of the other person. A woman. I wiped my hands on a blue and white-checked kitchen towel and made my way to the front door to see what was going on. And there she was—my mother.

I felt like I was looking into one of those mirrors that showed what I'd look like 25 or 30 years from now. But, as people, we were nothing alike. My dad didn't let Bryan and me sweep anything under the rug. If there was a problem, we talked about it, and we didn't let things fester. We learned to confront things head-on, and the approach made us better advocates for ourselves.

"Come on in. I'm Trent, Jen's boyfriend," he said, holding his hand out to my mother. She shook his hand. "Sara, right?"

"Yes," she responded, and then her gaze caught me.

"Jen," she said. Trent turned to me, offering an uneasy smile.

"Sara. Mom," I sputtered, then tried again. "Mom. I don't know if anyone knew you were arriving today. Dad didn't say anything, and neither did Gram and Grandpa."

"When I made my flight reservations, everything happened so quickly, I didn't have time to sit down and send an email or make a call. I had to find fast transportation to the airport, and I barely made my flight. Then my connection was very short, and the first flight was delayed, so there wasn't any time to call, text, or email. And voila. Here I am," she said and offered a tired smile.

"Trent and I made up the guest room for you, and there are clean towels in the guest bath. I imagine you'll want to get settled, maybe relax, shower or something?" Oh, my god. I was up-talking. I cleared my throat. "We just put a lasagna in the oven for dinner tonight, and it should be finished in about an hour if you're hungry."

"That sounds fantastic. You're fantastic," she said. "Wow. Lasagna. I can't remember the last time I had lasagna." She shook her head, marveling, then turned behind her to get her luggage and start the trek to the guest room.

When she was out of earshot I said, "I am a fantastic girl, aren't I?"

Trent answered, "Such a fantastic girl." He pulled me against him, and we watched my mother's vacated path, almost expecting her to have left something behind like planes leaving contrails in the sky. After a bit, he said in a low voice, "That was so weird. She didn't approach you to hug you or anything."

"To be fair," I said, "I didn't offer her any contact either. I kept my distance, and I called her Sara before I called her Mom. Probably not the best move. I didn't gush or fawn over her." I paused. "I don't know. I probably could've done more." Could I, though? Besides sending her occasional emails and receiving short, stilted replies, she was a stranger who looked a lot like me, but she didn't think like me. She didn't, at least anymore, actually know me. I was the fucking valet. It was a lot like the conjured conversation. So weird. I felt weird, and I hoped she felt weird. Even if I had been a distant relative, wouldn't she have hugged me? It was her move to make—not mine.

"She's your mother and a grown-ass adult," he whispered. "She could've done more, too. You're not responsible for everyone's feelings, emotions, and reactions. You're allowed to be a kid." Trent stopped himself for a moment, looking up at the ceiling like it had the answers, then continued. "I think she's probably gun-shy and may try to earn your regard. Just a guess, though."

"Boyfriend, you're being mighty charitable," I said.

Mom 1 and Mom 2 Have Coffee

Sara - age 44

I talked to Rob after my run-in with Jen. I did not handle it well. He suggested I speak with Erin because his emotions were all over the place. Erin took the receiver from Rob.

"Sara, hi," she said. "It's going to be strange meeting you under these circumstances. Everything has got to be strange and foreign to you right now with your mom being sick, then being back in the US after almost three years. There's bound to be some culture shock."

And I think I might have loved her for not jumping in and telling me what a shit mother I had been for the last five years. She could have led off with a zinger, and she chose compassion. "I saw my daughter for the first time in five years, and I just froze," I said a propos of nothing.

"Sara, none of us is perfect. You had no idea anyone was going to be at your parents' house when you arrived. It's okay that you were shocked. You both were," she said, and this woman was doling out grace like she had a truckload of it.

"I should have been prepared that I could have run into anyone at any time, and I should have..." I trailed off. I did not know what I should have done, but I was pretty sure what I had done was the wrong thing.

"You know what? Spend some time with your parents tonight. Let them fawn all over you. Get a good night's sleep. Why don't we get together tomorrow? I'll pick you up. Does that sound all right?" She was so nice, even knowing what a pit of despair I had left for her to clean up.

"That sounds really nice," I said.

My parents came home a little later, and the smell of the lasagna Jen had made perfumed the house. "I smell something tasty," my dad said. "Smells like our Jen has been here."

And then he and my mom looked over to the couch where I had been napping, and they both jumped a little. They didn't expect me today. I hadn't had a chance to communicate my travel arrangements with anyone.

"Surprise," I said, throwing up jazz hands.

They rushed to me, pulling me close into their collective embrace. My mom covered my face with her kisses, and my dad may have tried to squeeze the air out of my lungs.

"Sara!" Mom exclaimed.

"Baby!" Dad boomed.

"Mom. Dad," I said, and I cried because I hadn't had any clue how much I needed their touch, their warmth, and their love—that certain something that just about every parent has for an offspring.

We had dinner together. I showed them photos on my phone. Africa. My clinic there. Asia. My hospital. Claire. Claire's family. Japan. Mount Fuji. Michael. South America. Our clinic. Our small house. They smiled and made all the right comments, but there was more than one elephant in the room, and the easiest elephant to tackle was, sadly, Mom's aplastic anemia. After she updated me on the schedule of events and what the doctors had said, we lapsed into a lull, leaving the other elephant.

"When are you going to see Rob, Erin, and the kids?" Dad asked.

"Funny thing," I said, after swallowing a bite of Jen's divine lasagna. "Jen and her boyfriend were here when I arrived. I botched it big time. Erin is picking me up tomorrow to talk."

Mom patted my hand. "I promise you're going to hit it off with Erin."

I showered after we ate, and then lay down in my childhood bed, sleeping nearly twelve hours straight. When I awoke, I thought, 'Brand new day, Sara. Choose wisely.'

My parents had placed Mom's medical records on the kitchen table, and I gathered them up, sorting them in chronological order, looking at her labwork, then looking at the physician notes from her visits. I pulled up some articles on my computer, and I called a friend from med school who had become a hem/onc specialist with the Mayo Clinic. My mom's best chance at a cure would be a donor match, and sibling matches were typically best, but my mom and her siblings had all been adopted, leaving me as her next best chance.

Mid-afternoon arrived, and there was a knock at the door. I looked at the time on my phone. It had to be Erin. I had seen her photos, and she had popped on to a couple of the video calls I'd had with Rob, but nothing prepared me for what I would encounter in person. She was tall, about as tall as I was, and she wore her hair in a braided bun, shot through with golden highlights. Her skin was smooth, youthful, and to look at her, I couldn't imagine twins living inside her slender frame. "Erin. Oh, my god. You're gorgeous. Come on in. Let me grab my purse."

I fled the room, gathering my wits. I was no slouch in the looks department, but Rob had upgraded with Erin. No question. I grabbed my bag, and we went to a coffee shop called The Magical Fruit. "Okay, that's hilarious," I said. "How long has this place been here?"

"Maybe three years or so? I'm not 100%. It's been here a minute." Erin paused and leaned in toward me, "They really have great coffee. Their beans are magical." She laughed, and it was a sweet tinkling sort of laugh. When she said 'magical,' she wiggled her fingers like she was casting a spell, and spoke the word in an exaggerated sing-songy way. She was simply fantastic.

When we sat down with our drinks and homemade scones with clotted cream, Erin said, "You're new to me. Talk to me. Tell me about you. Clean slate. I know stuff, but ignore it. Set the record straight for me." She paused, forcing me to look her in the eye. "Please."

Erin made me feel safe, much like Claire did when I met her. I told her about meeting Rob. She smiled, her eyes taking on a faraway look, like she was imagining him 20 years ago. I told her about when I was growing up, going to college, med school. We discussed the good parts of being mothers. And I finally told her about the miscarriage, my eyes misting over. When I talked about it, I consciously tried to dissociate, knowing if I didn't, I would fall apart in a horrible way in a public place.

Erin responded by taking my hand. She used her other hand to dab at her eyes with her napkin.

"You're going to have some hurdles, Sara. They aren't going to warm up to you or trust you—at least not right away. You're going to have to deal with some anger and hostility. I want you to close your eyes and visualize something. Imagine being in the hospital with your mom. What would happen, how would you feel if she didn't make it through any of her treatment? What if you lost her?"

I gasped, shaking my head back and forth. I pictured my mom, so much thinner than she'd been nearly five years ago, her eyes looking huge and sunken in her gaunt face. She was so pale, fragile looking, like a China doll. One of those dolls I looked at but couldn't play with. She'd have to be put on a shelf, and if she fell, she broke apart.

"Open your eyes," Erin instructed. "You got to see what it would look like with your mom leaving you involuntarily. Knowing how that felt, think about Jen losing her mom, but she lost hers voluntarily and didn't get an explanation. Think about your own mom, leaving without telling you why. Think about your own mom ignoring you during a time when you really needed her to help you grow up."

I nodded. I needed to talk to my therapist. Erin got to the heart of putting things into perspective for me.

"Do you want to come to our house, spend some time with your kids?" Erin asked.

"I'm not prepared to meet them, but if you think I should…"

"I'll call Rob. He'll be able to get a good read on the situation," she replied.

She made the call, and I was a little disappointed not to see the kids today. "They need a little time today to get used to the idea of seeing you. They want to know if you could come for dinner tomorrow." Erin's head tilted when she asked me about the next day.

"Yes," I said. "Yes. I want to see them tomorrow. I have everything I've documented based on Rob's prompts. Tomorrow would be great." Erin firmed things up with Rob. She showed me photos of the kids, both hers and mine, the house, Rob, Rosemary and Sage, the family gatherings. They were happy, and I needed to be happy for them. I had no right to expect their happiness to revolve around me. And the truth of it is: No one's happiness should be lit by a single source. We have to find happiness, recognize it, and celebrate it wherever we find it.

Game Plan
Bryan - Age 16

I came home from school knowing something was up. Dad was already home. He had Bryn on one hip, and Jen had Walker strapped to her in the Baby Bjorn. "Uh, hey, guys," I said. "Dad, you're home early. What's up? And, Jen? You know that kid is way too big for the Baby Bjorn. You're going to hurt your back."

"Well," Dad said, "Erin is having coffee with your mother." Dad glanced at Jen pointedly, then looked back at me. "Your sister was ambushed at your grandparents' house the other day, and it wasn't fair to either your mom or your sister because neither was prepared to see the other like that since her one visit back at our old place."

"Seeing Mom was good and bad and weird and uncomfortable, " Jen said." I don't know if I need to close myself off to her or what. I don't know what she wants, and I don't know what I want. And it's so stupid that she's here and she hasn't even reached out to either of us. If Trent and I hadn't been at Gram and Grandpa's, would we even know she'd gotten back into town?" She covered Walker's ears gently, and whispered, "It's so fucked up."

"I'm ambivalent," I said. "I could take her or leave her. If she hurts you, game over. We have a mom, and she is Erin. She has loved us and mothered us. She could have kept us at arm's length, but she pulled us to her like we were her own. As far as I'm concerned, we had one mom who was great, and then she died. Then we got another mom, and she has been more than I could have ever asked for."

Dad said, "Do me a favor. Let's hear what Erin has to say when she gets back from meeting with Sara. Okay? I will back you up 100% in whatever you decide." Dad's cell phone was ringing. His ring tone for Erin was *The 1812 Overture.* He loved it because it reminded him of some movie about baseball from when he was a kid. Every time he heard the music, he smiled.

"Hi, hon," he said. "The bigs and the littles are fine. How did your coffee date go?" While Erin was talking, Dad was looking around the room at Jen and me. He motioned for me to take Bryn from him. He started making his way around the family room, picking up dog and baby toys, and throw pillows. He was straightening up. Jen looked at me for help.

"I think Erin is bringing Sara, Mom, whatever, here with her," I said.

"No," Jen said with finality. "I am not prepared for that. Two ambushes in as many days is not fair."

"Erin, honey, Jen and Bryan aren't ready to see Sara on short notice. Could you explain that to her? Can we shoot for tomorrow? Let's at least debrief when you get home, then go from there. Okay?" Dad said.

Dinner was quiet. Normally, there was chatter, laughing, conversation, but no silence. There was the gentle clinking of silverware tapping on dishes. I could hear Dad's jaws clicking when he chewed. He was a tooth grinder, and I figured the jaw was eventually going to give him problems if his molars didn't give up first.

Erin cleared her throat. "Okay, family. It looks like I'm going to go first. Sara is here to support Jo, first and foremost. She knows she wrecked your lives at a particularly terrible time in your development, and she has received the help she needs. She started therapy while she was in Asia, and she's still having sessions now that she's in South America."

Jen grunted something that sounded like, "Ha. Are we a stop on her apology tour? Is she going to throw herself on her sword, do a bunch of chest beating, gnashing of teeth, beg for our forgiveness?"

And holy shit. I don't think I'd ever heard that much acid in my sister's voice before. I don't think Dad had either. We were all kind of stunned into silence.

"What?" Jen asked. "It's what we're all thinking, isn't it?" Jen put her fork and knife down. "I am so sick of putting myself out there for her with my emails and hoping for scraps of validation. She sucks."

Jen continued, "I've been in therapy for almost, what four years, five? Does she think that going through therapy will make us roll out the red carpet for her and offer her congratulations? I think not."

We were all silent, staring at Jen, who never blew up like she had blown up over the past days since Sara had come back to town. "Good for her. She's been in therapy, but she didn't do a damned thing about us. She hasn't made any effort to clean up her mess. I have gone round and round on this, and I don't need her anymore. I don't want her anymore," Jen's voice softened, and she was crying. Erin got up from her seat, pulled Jen out of hers and just held her.

Erin's face was buried in Jen's hair, but we heard her loud and clear, "Forgiveness doesn't mean you become best friends. It doesn't mean Sara is going to waltz in here and put you to bed at night and listen to your hopes, dreams, and prayers. What it does mean is this: She is sorry. She understands now that things turned sideways for her, and she didn't get the help she needed. Her being sorry doesn't undo anything that was done to any of you, but forgiveness means you can let go of the hurt if you want. You can let go of her, too, if you want. It means that you can shake off some of the negative feelings and mental energy going into hating someone or even yourselves. You can let go of the guilty or conflicted feelings you've been harboring toward her all this time. Forgiving her isn't the same as giving her a free pass. Forgiving her allows you to continue to move on with your lives with or without her being a participant."

Jen asked in a very small voice, "What would you do if you were in our shoes?"

"I can't tell you, honey, because it didn't happen to me. My cogs and springs up here," she pointed to her head, "are set up very differently than yours. What's right or wrong for me may be the opposite for you. And, I want to state this very plainly. I love both of you, just like I love those two babies that are sleeping right now. I did not give birth to you, and I know Sara's your mother, and I cannot take her place, and I'm not trying to take her place. If you choose to include her in your lives, then I am not going to be offended at all. Do you each understand me?" Erin looked over Jen's head, giving me a pointed gaze, "Bryan, do you understand?" I nodded. "Jen, do you understand?" Jen nodded, wiping her eyes. "It's up to you to determine what, if any, role Sara has in your lives."

"What does she want from us?" I asked.

"Besides your forgiveness, I think she wants to be like a weird aunt or family friend or something. I honestly think she doesn't know. She'd like to know about your lives, but I think she's so committed to her work with Doctors Without Borders that I don't know that she has room for much else. I think it would be good for you to let her tell her story, and only after you've heard what she has to say, when you have the other pieces of the puzzle...well, make your decisions then. Okay?"

We both nodded. Dad was completely star-struck by Erin. She was a force, and I couldn't have asked for a better mom than she was. Bryn and Walker were two lucky little kids.

Jen said, "I will listen to her with prejudice. That's the best I can do for now."

Two Roads Diverged

Rob - age 44

Erin and I were lying in bed. She wedged her cold feet in between my warm feet. She rested her head between my shoulder and chest. I stroked her hair. She'd been wearing it in braids and hadn't tied it up for the night yet. Erin broke the quiet by saying, "Sara has a boyfriend. He's still in South America. They've been together for a while, maybe 6-9 months or so. Sounds serious. She didn't want to say anything to you in case it didn't work out. He's a doctor, too. They're thinking of getting married. They want to make sure their future assignments are together."

"Really. Well, good. I hope she finds happiness," I said. It felt so incredibly strange to think of someone who was supposed to have been my life partner moving on with someone else. But isn't that exactly what I had done?

"I'm a little surprised she didn't find someone sooner," I said. "I don't know. Maybe she couldn't start a new relationship until she addressed her problems. What else did she say about the new guy?"

"His name is Michael. Her face lit up when she talked about him. They're living together, work in the same clinic, and are both very committed to two things: their jobs and each other. I think they connect on physical and intellectual levels that are completely in sync. I know you two had a special relationship—otherwise you wouldn't have married her. We have a special relationship, and I love our relationship. I love you, and I love our family and all the extra people we've built into our family unit along the way. I think my life is so much richer than it ever was before. I think Sara has something sort of like that with Michael."

"I think of Sara and me as two roads that intersected for a while. Eventually, our roads branched off. My road was the main road, and it was paved and maintained and got wider. Sara's road stayed small and meandered off onto a gravel road, then a dirt road in a completely different direction. Eventually, though, a town sprang up around her road, and then it was paved and maintained, and it became something new, and it didn't even run parallel to the old road. It became something that serviced a different town or city with different cars," I said.

"I like your main road, Rob, and I like the cars that kept driving down your road." She kissed my jaw, and I turned toward her kissing her deeply.

"Did Sara have the blood draw today to see if she's a match for Jo?" I asked. Erin fluffed her pillow and positioned it on my shoulder.

"Early this morning," Erin said. "They're putting a rush on everything and should have results back in 3-5 days. As soon as Jo's doctors know if Sara can be a donor, Jo would have to get a central line put in so that the doctors can start the conditioning process for preventing Graft-Versus-Host-Disease." Erin shuddered. "Jo is going to be going through a lot very, very soon if Sara is a match. Sara will make her donation under general anesthesia, and she'll be sent home afterward. I think Michael will probably come up here to be with Sara right after her bone marrow is harvested—that is if she's a donor match for Jo. I don't know what Sara's plans are if she isn't a match. I don't know if she'll stay for a while to support Jo through the transplant. Apparently, all the fun and games really begin for Jo *after* the transplant. If Jo has the patient education packet handy, we should offer to make copies for everyone. Jo and Howard will probably need meals, and we'll need to get a box of N95 masks and hand sanitizer to keep viruses and bacteria away. Even if Sara isn't a match, it would be nice for Michael to come up to meet her parents, and I suppose the kids, if they decide it's what they want to do."

We were quiet for a while. I thought Erin had drifted off, but she said quietly, "I don't know why you wouldn't want to link up all the pieces of your life. Do you think Sara will stay around for a while to help after the transplant?"

"I don't know. I really don't," I said quietly. "What's the plan for tomorrow? Is she going to come here to spend some time with the kids?"

"Yeah, I think that is the plan. She's kind of in a holding pattern while the bloodwork is being processed. Do you want all of the grandparents here when she's here, or do you want to keep things small and have it be just the kids and her, and then we can be available if anyone needs an assist?" Erin asked.

"I think the less is more approach is probably best," I said softly. Getting to this point had been something akin to a miracle. I had kept hoping over the years for some kind of rendezvous between Sara and our children, and I think I had finally accepted it might be a Sisyphean task and wishing or hoping for more was in vain. Now, Sara was on the same continent as her parents and children, and the success or failure of the relationships was definitely going to rely on her.

We turned out the lights, and it was a long while before I fell asleep. When Sara and I were first dating, we went to some of the local bars with college friends of mine who were visiting. One of my buddies said to me, "I know you really like that girl, but I can't put my finger on it. She's going to break your heart. And I sincerely hope I'm wrong." We didn't invite that guy to our wedding. Now, though, I'd love to call him up and tell him he was right. But the thing is this: Without Sara, I wouldn't have Jen and Bryan. Without going through the heartbreak, I wouldn't have found Erin, and we wouldn't have Bryn and Walker, and, yeah, it's like Erin said, my life is so much richer.

Special Session
Jen - Age 17

"Jen, I'm so glad you wanted to schedule an extra session" Dr. Bennett said. He was a short, stocky man. He wore glasses with thick lenses, and his eyes were magnified to the extent that it often looked like he could see into my soul. I knew he couldn't, but, man, it was something that made him a really good therapist.

"I'm grateful you were able to fit me in on such short notice, and my brother wants to get worked into your schedule soon, too," I said to my psychologist.

"Well, let's start with you. Okay? Tell me what's going on," he said.

I explained the whole situation about Gram's aplastic anemia, the transplant, and Sara showing back up and wanting to pry her way into our lives.

"I want you to think about something, okay. I want you to visualize your feelings. Imagine they are living, breathing beings, and you are the zookeeper for them. You decide who gets fed and watered and who gets skipped. If you skip some of the animals too often, they're going to die, right?"

"Sure," I answered.

"Let's talk about hate, hurt, and negativity," he said. "Do you want to continue to feed those animals? Before you answer, let me throw out one more thing to consider. You have a limited supply of food. If you choose to feed hate, hurt, and negativity, you don't have enough to feed hope, love, and happiness. Who do you want to feed?"

"When you put it that way, I know who I need and want to feed. It's just so hard when feeding the others has been part of my life for so long. How do I skip the bad animals?" I asked.

"First of all, hurt isn't a bad animal. You have a right to feel hurt, and you have a right to feed it, but at some point it becomes bloated and obese, and it breeds other feelings that demand feeding. It's tough to know when to cut off feeding hurt, but I think you know the answer to that as it applies to your situation."

"I would rather feed the others, Dr. Bennett. But how am I supposed to act toward Sara?" I asked.

"Great question. How would you like to treat her?" he asked.

I was quiet while I thought over my options. "Well, I could act like she's someone I've just met. She can become a friend, an acquaintance, or remain like a stranger or distant relative. She doesn't have to be anyone of significance, or she can be whatever I want her to be, but only if it's something she's willing to be. Right?"

Dr. Bennett nodded. "What else are you thinking? I can see there's more you want to say."

"I guess she'd be like any new person I might meet. We'll uncover what kind of role she's capable of playing. I can't ask her to be a duck if she's chicken, and I can't ask her to be a chicken if she's a duck."

Dr. Bennet gave a small laugh.

"What if she rejects us or me again?" I asked softly, holding tightly to the tissue I had grabbed when I entered Dr. Bennett's office.

"What animals do you want to feed? Which animals raise you up? Are you willing to accept what she can give or not? The choice is entirely up to you. You have the power to choose which animals to feed or skip them altogether."

We looked at each other. I nodded in understanding.

"I'm not here to give you the answers, Jen. My job is to help you uncover the answers on your own. I think the more you think about what we've discussed, whatever decision you make will be the right one for you."

And the more I thought about it, the more I didn't want to short-change feeling hope, happiness, and love from all the other people in your life because of her.

"So, it would be okay if I decided she's just this strange woman I see once in a blue moon, and it's okay because it's my decision what kind of space she occupies in my life. I don't give her any more power or sway than I permit her to have."

"I think you're on the right track, Jen. I really do. I want an update at our next session, and if you need to schedule something sooner than next week, I will work you in. Got that?" He patted my back as I walked out of his office.

When got home, I went directly to my bedroom. I grabbed my journal and began to draw the animals in the zoo. I drew myself in, too, and I drew in a small bowl of rice or oats or whatever. I sat there for a while. There were definitely times when I fed the good animals, and there were times when I fed the bad ones, and there were times I had let the hurt become large and dangerous. These were no one's choices but my own. It was up to me to figure out how to deal with Sara and feed the animals who really needed to be fed. Since the run-in at Gram's, I knew who'd been fed, and it made me feel terrible. I didn't need to feel terrible. If Sara wanted to feel terrible, then she could feed her own animals.

Video Visit

Bryan - age 16

"**D**r. Bennett, hi," I said, once the computer connection was established for the video visit I had with the psychologist. He pushed his glasses along the bridge of his nose to be able to see me better on his monitor.

"Bryan. Tell me what's going on, and how you're doing," he said, smiling broadly.

"Sara's back. She's coming over for dinner tonight. I'm worried about Jen. I'm worried about me," I said.

"Understandable," he said. "Here's the thing, Bryan. You can worry about Jen, but you can't control her feelings or reactions or how she handles things. You can control your own feelings and reactions, though." He steepled his fingers and rocked them back and forth slowly.

"I got that. I think I'm worried that if I don't mirror Jen's feelings exactly, she may feel betrayed, and I don't want to do that do her. You know?"

"Give your sister and your relationship some credit. You're different people. When Sara left, yes, you were both abandoned, but your sister feels it in *her* way, and you feel it in *your* way. Think about it like this. Let's say you go to a department store and try on a jacket. It fits you really well through the shoulders, but the sleeves are too short. Your buddy tries on the same jacket. The shoulders and sleeves fit great, but he can't get the zipper to go up because he's got the wrong size. Same jacket, different people, different fits."

"Okay," I said drawing out the second syllable.

"The two of you are very open with one another. You two don't keep secrets from each other. Why don't you try trusting her and talking to her about what you're talking about with me? Tell her exactly that your feelings toward Sara may be very different than Jen's. It's okay. Trust her and talk it out, hmm? Do you want to talk about it with her? If you don't, then don't. It's up to you what you want to share." Dr. Bennett's eyes looked enormous through his thick lenses, which was spellbinding. I couldn't look away.

"You concentrate on you and allow yourself to experience seeing Sara. Allow yourself to form your own opinion, and you make your own decision. Maybe the two of you will come to the same conclusion, and maybe not. However it turns out, you're both right, and you're both entitled to feel whatever it is you feel. Then we reconnect and talk about processing your feelings in a productive way."

"I mean, I guess that makes sense. So, I'll just have the experience and see what comes of it. No worrying about Jen's reaction." I had no idea if I was capable of not trying to get inside Jen's head, but we were both older now, and I think it was time for me to let go.

"Bryan, you must remember something. You are Jen's brother, not her therapist. You don't need to take on her feelings and feel responsible for providing her with coping mechanisms. Give yourself a break. Is that something you feel comfortable with doing?"

I had no idea. I'd been getting inside my sister's head for so long. I would worry about myself first. Shit. What was that all about? I'd do it, though.

We spoke for a while longer, focusing on only me, which felt very invasive, but Dr. Bennett had been right. I'm a teenager, not a therapist, and I needed to quit hiding behind trying to fix everyone else. I couldn't live with these people and constantly be in a state of trying to fix them, especially since I needed to work on being a kid.

"Can you do me a big favor, Bryan?" Dr. Bennett asked before we signed off.

"Sure," I answered.

"I'd like to have you come in for a session after you see your mother. Actually, I'd like each of you to come in separately after you see her."

"Okay. I'll pass the message on to Jen."

I walked into Jen's room, and I said, "Listen. I just had a session with Dr. Bennett. Let's hear what Sara says and form our own opinions."

I was doing what Dr. Bennett said and remaining open-minded enough to have feelings independent of others. "No strategy session?" she asked, frowning but then brightened. "Hey, do you want to play Battleship?" We had the set from when our dad was a kid, and we spent the time calling out coordinates and sinking each other's boats.

Erin and Dad were cool about giving us a free pass not to help with the kids or getting dinner ready. The doorbell rang, and Jen and I stopped the game and looked at each other. We were each other's mirrors in that moment, and I saw angst, trepidation, hurt, confusion, anger, and wariness written all over her face. Then I started laughing.

"Why are you laughing? Are you finally cracking up?" Jen asked.

"No," I said, then told her about everything I saw written on her face. "Then I started thinking, 'what if all of that were actually written on our faces?' We would be like Post Malone or Jelly Roll or whatever, only we'd just be covered in feelings." Jen smiled, then she laughed, too. Not the belly busting guffaws I was issuing, but enough to get us moving out of her room and down the stairs.

First Date with the Kids

Sara - age 44

I think I understood what it would have felt like when Anne Boleyn went to the guillotine. She probably felt very shaky on the inside, her blood warming or icing over (one or the other) in her veins, and yet, she had to hold her head up, not betraying any of the fear she felt. Walking into Rob's house, arriving at 6:30 pm on the nose, I felt all those feelings and also like I'd drunk a full pot of coffee. My nerves jangled, and I was a nanosecond from running out the door I had just entered.

Erin answered the door, and Rob hovered behind her. Their little ones were on the floor simultaneously trying to eat and play with some plastic blocks. And, again, she stunned me. Erin was beautiful, ethereal, really. She wore her hair in braids, had clear caramel skin, and light brown, almost golden eyes. Her smile was genuine and warm, and I could see how she would be easy to love. I had once been easy to love, and I hoped Erin never changed. I hoped she continued to be the soul-soothing balm to these people I had left behind. "Sara," she said and hugged me. "You found us all right, I trust?"

"Waze brought me right to your door," I said sheepishly. "You have a lovely home," I continued.

"Oh, I can't take credit. When Rob bought the house, he hired our friend Maggie to decorate. Her instructions were to make the place feel like home." She smiled and pinkened a bit as she shared. "But, thank you. We do like what Maggie pulled together, and over time, we've all added our own little bits of flair here and there."

Rob said, "Welcome, Sara. We're keeping dinner pretty informal, and Erin and I will get out of your hair and leave you to it with Jen and Bryan. If you need us for any reason at all, though, we're just in the next room." Rob was still built like a swimmer, and he still looked like the guy I fell in love with when I was 22. He had smile lines bracketing his mouth, and there were some crow's feet beginning to appear along his eyelids, but they made him look mature in a good way, like he'd been living a good, happy, and fulfilling life. In a way, I wished I had been part of his life, but I knew I couldn't go back and undo everything that had happened, everything I had done—or not done.

And then there were Rosemary and Sage. They bounded into the room, circled around me without jumping up on me. They were noticeably older and slower. Time was a robber of vigor and speed, among other things. I thought briefly about making a list of stolen items at the hands of time's thievery.

"Can I take your jacket or bag or anything?" Erin asked.

"No. I have some things in here for Jen and Bryan. I can hang onto everything," I said. "Are they here?"

"They are," Rob said. "I peeked in on them a few minutes ago, and they were playing Battleship." No sooner had Rob finished his sentence than Bryan and Jen made their way down the stairs. They didn't hurry, but they didn't drag either. They were casual and at ease with each other, and as they approached the bottom of the stairs, they made eye contact with me. I gasped. I had seen Jen the other day, but I hadn't seen Bryan for years. He had grown, filled out, and he was a blend of Rob and me. My beautiful boy. And my beautiful girl. I didn't know how I could have left them. I realized I was staring.

"Is it okay if I hug you both?" I asked.

They looked at each other and at Erin and Rob, and I saw Rob nodding his head. "Sure," Bryan said, and his voice was deep. He had gone through puberty, and I had completely missed it. I hugged each of them. Jen didn't pull me to her with enthusiasm, and I didn't expect she would. Maybe after we all talked, we could get to a point where we could try to move forward in some way. This felt like a first date or a blind date, and I had no idea how the evening would end. I was determined to get to a second date with my kids if they were open to the idea of seeing me again.

Jen broke the silence following the awkward hugging by saying, "Why don't you follow us? We'll have some dinner and talk. Bryan and I decided you could ask us anything. Is it okay if we ask you anything, too? If you have boundaries, we want to respect them."

"Sounds fair," I said. "You can ask me anything."

Once we were seated around the table, the three of us looked at each other, and I decided I would break the ice. "I've been preparing for this for close to two years with therapy, and it took me a long time to get to where I am today. I still have work to do, but I am leaps and bounds from where I was before. I've learned a lot about grief and post-partum depression. It's still a tough thing for me to talk about, but I want to answer or discuss whatever you want."

Everything was on the table and set up for us to make some sandwiches. There were chips and sides and drinks. The kids made their sandwiches. I noticed Jen cutting her sandwich into the little triangular quarters and trimming the crusts off. She was a perfectionist. Everything about her screamed meticulousness and planning and a personal quest for perfection. I would not say that my teenage daughter was someone who was carefree, and I was pretty sure I had a hand in causing her to be this person who thought through everything all the time, and I wanted to cry when I thought of what I may have robbed from her.

Bryan sat next to Jen, and he took in the room, Jen, me, the food--everything—like he was putting a puzzle together and he needed to get all the like pieces grouped. He was a hawk, and he was deliberate and mindful. He rose from the table, taking his glass, and said, "I'm going to get some water. Would anyone like water?"

I held up my glass, "That would be great. Thank you."

"I'll take some, too," Jen said.

Bryan delivered our drinks, and we began eating. It was silent but for the sound of our chewing. "All right. I guess I'll get things started," I said. My messenger bag lay on the chair next to me, and I reached inside it, producing two bound stacks of paper. "I've been working on this for a while. These are stories and essays and memories I've captured, for you to get to know me. I know you have memories from before the miscarriage, when we were a functioning family unit. We had animals, a big yard, and a big life together. And then I turned into someone you didn't know, and I think that may be the version of me that occupies the biggest part of your perspective of me. And I'm more than that person. I would like you to read these when you have time, but between now and then, I want to answer questions, and I want to tell you some things." I laid the packets on the table gently, then I shook out my hands. "Whew. Okay," I said.

Jen asked, "Do you regret marrying Dad and having us?"

"Oh, gosh, no," I said. "You two are the two greatest things I've ever done in my life. I did a terrible job being a mother and I've done things I regret, but being with your dad and having you two will never be a regret."

"Why didn't you get help, you know, after the miscarriage?" Bryan asked. He looked at me directly and would not lower his gaze.

"I thought I could fix myself. I thought eventually I would be all right and things would go back to normal, and then I got stuck in the bad feelings and it became a new normal for me. And I was so wrapped up in feeling alone and terrible, I didn't pay attention to anyone else's needs. I was in a dark place and didn't want to drag anyone else into with me, but, as it turns out, I dragged you all to some other dark place, and you will never know how sorry I am to have put you through it." I noticed Jen and Bryan looking at each other, and maybe my eyes were playing tricks on me, but I may have seen an eye roll from Jen. That was fair. They weren't buying what I was selling, at least, not yet.

"Why don't you call, visit, write, email us? I started sending you emails as a kind of online diary, thinking you probably didn't read anything I sent, and then sometimes you would respond. Until you sent us the message saying you were reading our messages, I had no idea anyone was at the end of anything I sent. You don't initiate any communication with us. When you sent us the message that you were reading what we were sending, I thought, 'Why even bother to answer at all?'" Jen asked.

"I didn't know you wanted an answer," I said, and even to my own ears, it sounded like the lamest excuse in the world.

Jen said, "Well, here's a solution. You could have called to ask about the email messages."

"You're right," I conceded. "I have been a selfish, cowardly asshole, and I didn't know what to do. I probably should have asked. As for the calls and communication with you two...I can only say I'm ashamed of and embarrassed at being a terrible mother. I have never failed at anything, until I had the miscarriage, and then I felt like I was failing at everything. I think having this sit down with you two is up there in the top ten hardest things I've ever had to do." When I said 'asshole' they looked at each other, and I think they wanted to laugh, but I hadn't earned anything but scrutiny from them.

"Sara. Mom. God. I don't even know what to call you," Bryan said. "I'm sitting here, and I'm looking at you, and Jen looks just like you, and I see parts of me that I've inherited from you, but it's like you're a stranger. I can't figure out what box to put you in. You look familiar, but you aren't familiar. What I can't figure out, hell, what none of us could figure out, is why you would invite me and not Jen, too, to work in your clinic. Do you have any inkling of how shitty it made my sister feel? In case you didn't know, it was a total dick move." I was still a shitty mother. I should have included them both, but in my heart of hearts, I knew Jen would decline, and I didn't want to be rejected by her. After the thought dawned on me, I felt like an even worse person and human because wasn't that exactly what I kept doing to her? I kept an unfulfilled hope spiral in operation, continually directed toward Jen.

"I am so sorry. It was never my intent to make anyone feel bad, and when you're saying everything now, I know I should have invited you both, and I...I really was a dick, wasn't I?"

They both nodded.

"I was only responding to you with the idea after your message about working in my former practice. If Jen had said something like that, too, I would, of course, have extended the invitation." I knew this was a lie, and both of the kids knew this was a lie, but I couldn't come up with a reason for not inviting Jen to South America. The more I thought about it, though, the more I think Jen was like a mirror of me—the biggest difference being she hadn't screwed a bunch of people up. She was a reminder of everything I had done wrong because she had the misfortune of looking just like me.

I laughed a little, "You guys know what? I have so much more work to do in therapy. And this is probably the worst possible time for me to have a breakthrough. You can be sure I'm scheduling a session with my psychologist right after I leave here."

They looked at each other. "Sara," Jen said, "Bryan and I have been through so much therapy we could probably counsel you ourselves." And then she did something unexpected. She laughed, and then Bryan laughed, and I sat there with my jaw hanging open. Literally.

"Well, for what it's worth," I hollowly offered, "if either of you would like to work in the clinic, I would love to have you."

"Thanks, but I'm speaking for the both of us," Bryan said evenly. "We are staying here. Jen's applying to colleges in the summer. Her boyfriend is leaving for college in the fall. My girlfriend is applying to colleges this summer, too. I'll be making college visits in the summer and fall, and I would like to work here in the US. No visas to mess with. It's just simpler all the way around. I am grateful for the offer, though, but you can see how the optics of the situation were a little stressful to me and distressing to Jen."

"Point taken," I responded. I tried to look Jen in the eye, but she wasn't looking at me. She was looking everywhere but at me. "I am really failing here, and I have learned to deal with failure. I want to stop failing the two of you. I'm not perfect, and I'm not going to be perfect. I have to know when I'm missing the mark, but you have to give me the grace to course correct. Please tell me when, you know?"

"As a mother, you were a good mother," Jen said. "Then this stupid ball of cells upended our entire family, and you became a really shitty mother. It was a fucking ball of cells, Sara!"

My feisty girl. She didn't hold back. Bryan stared at her. She took a drink of her water, and her face returned to its natural color, not the flame-infused look she had brandished a moment before. I didn't want to say anything, and I thought I heard footsteps in the other room. Would Rob or Erin poke a head in to calm the situation? I hoped not because I felt like I deserved every single thing my kids were throwing at me. I owed them answers, and I also needed to be a landing place for all the feelings I had left for them to deal with on their own.

"Okay," said Jen, looking me in the eye. "Here's what I want to know. What do you want from us? Do you envision having a relationship with us? One of us, both of us, neither of us? What do you hope to achieve? Why are you sitting here talking to us tonight? Do you want our forgiveness? Are you looking for a fresh start or a clean slate or what?"

"I wanted to explain myself. I know I don't deserve it, but I wanted to ask for your forgiveness. I would like to have some kind of relationship with you, and I'll be frank. I don't know what I can give. I don't know what's too much or too difficult, and it's a moving target. If you want to keep me at arm's length, I can respect that. If you're open to an evolving relationship, I can probably accommodate that, too, because I'm going to keep up with therapy, and I'm assuming I'll continue to get better," I answered. I could feel sweat on the back of my neck and on my scalp. My hands were getting sweaty, and I worried I was going to mess everything up. My stomach was churning, and I worried my sandwich was going to make a reappearance. "My questions for you two are whether or not you would like to have a relationship with me, and, if you do, what does the relationship look like?"

It was very quiet, and I could feel my pulse in my neck, and I wondered if they could see that I was entering into panic mode. Bryan spoke first. "I would like to have a relationship with you. I think maybe if you could begin with me by serving as an advisor or mentor that might be good. If the relationship evolves, then we'll cross that bridge when we come to it."

Jen spoke almost as soon as Bryan had finished speaking. "I kind of think of you as a distant relative right now. It was very difficult early on when I thought of you as my mom who didn't give two shits to send an email, call, or send a birthday card or anything. I did finally reconcile things in my mind, though, and once I did, as long as you were on another continent, you were an emotionally and geographically distant relative. Now you're here. I wanted to see how this dinner went, and I wanted to hear what you had to say before I made up my mind on what I wanted."

"Okay. That makes sense," I acknowledged.

"I will never trust you," Jen said, and it felt like she had punched me in the stomach. "I will listen to everything you say, but I don't think I will ever trust you. I have forgiven you. Hating you took too much mental energy out of me. I'm angry, and that's what you've been seeing mostly since you've been here, but I don't hate you. Not anymore. Anger fades, but right now? Hearing all this 'relationship stuff' from you? I don't believe you. I don't think you believe yourself either. I think you're trying to tell us what we want to hear. All we want is honesty."

We all sat there quietly. I couldn't meet their gazes. Of course they were completely within their rights to call me out, and Jen had my number. She had been on the receiving end of my shortcomings for over four years.

Jen cleared her throat, and placed her napkin on the table, then she picked it up again and began twisting it in front of her before she continued speaking. "With therapy, I learned to forgive you. It made me feel better because I was conserving energy I could direct toward other things. Maybe someday we'll be friends or something, but in my mind you're like Lucy, and I'm Charlie Brown, and I keep wanting to kick the football. I should know better than to trust you aren't going to pull the football away from me. I'm tired of trying to kick the football. I'm tired of landing on my ass and being surprised. I'm tired of not learning my lesson. You hurt me in a way no one else in my life has ever hurt me, but I have forgiven you. I just can't put myself out there for you again. Maybe someday." She paused. "I do want you to know I don't hate you. I learned to forgive, and I learned how to be a healthier person because things were very dark for a very long time for me."

"Do you not want to see me while I'm here for Gram's transplant?" I asked.

"I'm all right with seeing you. We can work toward having a relationship. I will be cordial, and I will be honest with you. I won't hide my feelings from you, and if you or I have expectations of one another, then we need to articulate them. I think that's fair," Jen said evenly. "Do you feel like you can share your expectations with me?"

"I think I can," I answered. "What you've said seems fair, and I will honor and respect any boundaries you establish, and I am optimistic."

I took both of them in. Bryan continued looking directly at me. Jen looked between Bryan and me, assessing where everyone seemed to be landing, emotionally, in the room.

"I am optimistic that we can grow something between the three of us. I don't know what it will look like, but I didn't have much in the way of optimism for several years, until I'd started therapy myself. I want you both to know that whatever it is you need or want from me, I will do my damnedest for you." I paused for effect then looked down at my plate while I spoke the next bit. "One of Jen's emails said she hoped I was sheltering in my shell and would come back out again, and it resonated profoundly. I was sheltering, and it took me a long time to figure out how to get back out to the rest of the turtles."

When I looked back up at the two of them, Bryan looked confused, but Jen nodded her head. "I'll tell you later," she whispered.

"Do you think you'd like to get together again this week? Would you like it to be just the three of us? I would like to see you both again, but I don't want to come on too strong," I admitted to them.

"I think," Bryan said, "it would be good for you to give me your cell phone number. Let the two of us process everything from tonight, and we will figure out what our next meeting will look like. We *will* want to get together, though. We just need to take a beat to get ourselves aligned with what would be best for us. I will, with 100% certainty, call you tomorrow, though." It looked like I had made the cut—there would be a second date.

"Sara," Jen said, and hearing her call me by my first name stung a little every time I heard it from my kids' mouths. "I'm not trying to be a ball buster here, but I don't believe you, and I can't imagine you believe what you're saying. We all have limits. You need to figure out what your limits are with the two of us. Don't over-promise and under-deliver. Rethink what you've just said, then come back to us with what you truly think you can offer for the future."

Bryan, who had been quietly watching the exchange finally said, "You can't change the past. You can't undo what you've done, and even a heartfelt apology over four years later doesn't suddenly make things better. You do realize the relationships are irreparable, don't you? Whatever closeness you thought could be restored isn't going to be restored by your apology. The relationships we had with you are dead. We are all starting over, and your actions or non-actions are what will define how we all operate with one another." He paused for emphasis. "We don't know you."

And those four words felt like a sucker punch to the gut.

Vasectomy

Rob - age 44

Sara finished dinner with Jen and Bryan. I didn't hear any screaming or crying. When she said goodnight to Erin and me, I didn't notice any distress on Sara's face, and it was possible I saw a glimmer of, not hope, but thoughtfulness and determination in her eyes. Jen and Bryan called Erin and me to join them in the family room. The two of them looked very sober, and they were incredibly matter-of-fact in their retelling of their dinner with their mother.

"Well," I said. "Is it too soon to ask how you want to proceed?"

"I think so," Jen said. "I need to mull things over. She's like some long-lost relative to me. I don't know how much I want to let her in the door. By the same token, she could be like a pen pal or something like that. She's my mother, but I don't know if she's ever going to be my mom again. Erin has been my mom." Erin moved to the couch, sat next to Jen, and took her hand, giving it a light squeeze. Jen continued, "I know there are plenty of kids whose parents are divorced, and they have great relationships with both their mothers and stepmothers. But my mother chose not to be a mom, and one part of me would like to give her the opportunity to be a mom again, but how can I trust she won't freak out again and disappear?"

"I understand, and I'm not going to try to persuade you or lead you to possible solutions. Only you can know what's right for you. But if I can offer one thing: Think into the future. Think one year, five years, ten years, and twenty years ahead. What do you envision your family relationships will look like? What do you want them to look like? Maybe that can help you decide how you move forward," I said.

Bryan, said, "I need to sleep on everything. Mom-Sara gave us each a packet of documents to read. I think I'm going to turn in and read a little bit before I go to sleep."

"Same," said Jen. She hugged Erin, then crossed the room to give me a kiss on the cheek. "Goodnight, Dad."

After the kids had left the room, Erin said, "My dad died when I was pretty little, and I don't have a lot of memories of him, but the memories I do have were good ones. It's too bad Jen and Bryan's good memories are hidden in the shadows of a whole bunch of bad memories and feelings for Sara, but I understand, and I count myself very fortunate not to have to be in their shoes." Erin shook her head back and forth, and it was obvious she had more to say, and I would wait until she was ready to say it. Erin was honest, frank, and transparent, and she didn't let things fester, either.

Eventually, Erin and I made our way to bed. We hadn't even been in the room for the dinner with Sara, Jen, and Bryan, and we were both emotionally exhausted. While we lay in the dark, Erin said, "I think you should get a vasectomy. Our family is complete, and we don't need any surprises."

"Boom," I said. "That's a bomb. Why are you thinking about this right now?"

"I'm thinking of you and Sara and the surprise pregnancy. I cannot even fathom why a doctor couldn't figure out birth control. She has to understand biology," Erin's voice faded in the darkness.

"You get that we let alcohol stamp out all rational thought after that wedding reception, right?" I quipped.

"Yes, of course I do," she paused, laughing and continued, "I know how alcohol works."

We were quiet again, and in the dark, I could almost hear the gears turning inside her skull. "I don't want to stay on the pill," Erin said. "The hormones aren't good for me, and I think a vasectomy is a good option. Plus," and now I could hear the smile in her voice. "After you have the vasectomy, you have to ejaculate like 100 times before you go for the confirmatory test that says you're not sending out any more swimmers."

"A hundred times, eh?" I asked.

"Yep," she said. "It might be fun." She poked my side, and I grabbed her hand before she could start tickling me in earnest.

I pinned her underneath me and whispered into her neck, "We'd use condoms until I'm in the clear, then?"

"Mm-hmm. Would you be all right with condoms?" she answered, her free hand finding its way into my pajama pants.

"Sure," I said, adjusting my position to give her better access to where I hoped this quiet, night-time discussion was leading. "For the record, I agree. Our family is complete. I'm happy. Are you happy?"

"I'm deliriously happy," Erin said. "I have two babies and two bonus kids, and I have you. My cup is full, and after I get these pants off of you, maybe you can top off my cup...if you know what I mean..."

"Darling, I always know what you mean."

Over coffee in the morning, I thought about Erin's fear of miscarrying a surprise pregnancy. I also thought of the four mouths we were currently feeding. I think this thing with Sara was like an after school special for birth control, or maybe a public service announcement to say alcohol impairs judgment. I also thought Erin had a feeling that a pregnancy loss might break me, her, the kids, and/or our whole family because of the precedent set by Sara. Erin had to know she was stronger than giving up and running away. But I agreed with her. Our family was complete.

Everyone is Okay

Sara - Age 44

"I'm a match. I'm so relieved. The advances in the treatment of aplastic anemia make Mom's prognosis pretty good." I beamed as I looked at Michael's face on the computer screen.

"When do you want me there? I've been pricing flights, and I can get on a plane in the morning. I have to finagle transportation to get to the airport, but there is a flight." Michael looked tired, excited, and incredibly handsome while he tried unsuccessfully to pull up something on his cell phone.

"I have an idea," I said. "Why don't you arrange transportation to the airport first, then see what kind of flights are available. It doesn't make sense to book something you may or may not be able to make."

"Right. I'm just so excited for your mom, and I miss you like crazy. I realized I can't be in this remote place without you." He ran his fingers through his hair, and when his hands came away, he looked even more handsome than he did before, the tufts of his silky black hair shooting in different, nearly artistic, peaks on his head.

"Tell me how dinner went with your kids," he said.

"Hmm. It was good, and it was a disaster, and I have to have hope," I answered.

"Oh, yeah?" he asked.

"Well, they don't trust me, and they don't believe me, and I think I don't even believe some of the stuff I told them. As it was coming out of my mouth, I thought, 'Is this realistic?' and I knew it probably wasn't. They agreed to get together with me again, though, which is promising. I need to be honest with them and with myself. I don't want to spend a lifetime apologizing. Jen said she forgave me because it was easier to forgive and quit hating me. She was very direct, and it was like being stabbed in the stomach."

Michael said, "Oh, honey. I'm so sorry, but you wanted to know, right?"

"Yeah, and I realized I have a bunch more work to do in getting myself sorted out," I admitted. I looked into his eyes, thousands of miles away. He looked at me, and the corners of his eyes turned up. I didn't even need to see the rest of his face to see his warm smile.

"I miss you, too, and I love you," I said. "We're going to see the hematologist today to get all the details and the schedule for Mom's conditioning and then we'll also get my procedure scheduled. We'll round out the day with Mom's central line being put in. Depending on how that goes, she may get to come home, or they may keep her overnight if there are any complications."

"Oh, my god," Michael said slowly, shaking his head back and forth. "How long is she going to be NPO?" He knew I got hangry if I went too long without food, and he assumed my mom was the same way if she had to go the entire day with nothing by mouth prior to her procedure.

"Relax," I said. "Everything should be done by noon. We have the first appointment of the day with the hematologist." I smiled.

By the time I met Michael, I was, mostly, a functioning adult human being, capable of giving and receiving love. Michael. There was a rush of warmth through my body every time I thought of him, pictured him, his smile, his essence. I didn't know it was possible to have such a visceral response to another person. Jen and Bryan knew about Michael, and they knew they would be meeting him. My mom and dad knew about him and would be meeting him, too. When people talked about things' coming full circle, well, I guess this is what it felt like—not like George Costanza from Seinfeld and the episode where 'worlds collide.' I was ready for everything. Everyone meeting each other, the bone marrow transplant. Everything. And it would be okay. I would be okay.

The Bike Ride and Information Dump

Jen - Age 17

Bryan and I rode our bikes around the neighborhood, and we talked about the packets our mother had given us. I stayed true to what I had initially said. I forgave her, but I didn't know how to trust her. She seemed sincere, and she had made herself vulnerable by giving us all of her writing prompt responses. She had so many beautiful memories. She reminded me of Gram's sterling silver flatware. One day, Gram took all of the utensils out of a little wooden chest, and the inside of the chest was lined with shiny red satin. Lying inside the chest were dull, black and gray, mottled forks, knives, spoons, and serving utensils.

"Yuck," I said. "What happened to all this stuff?"

"You want to see something amazing?" she asked.

"Of course," I answered.

Gram picked up one of the teaspoons and a soft cloth, and she poured a little bit of cleaner on the cloth. She began to rub the spoon, and eventually, all the gritty and grimy-looking stuff disappeared, and the spoon shone bright and silvery.

"Silver oxidizes and turns dark. You have to polish it to restore it. It will eventually tarnish again, but if you give it a little love every now and then, you can keep your silver looking shiny all the time." She placed the polished spoon next to the chest and reached in for a couple more utensils. She handed me a knife. "Here, sweetie. Why don't you start with a knife. They're easy to polish." We continued polishing the silver, and what originally looked like something I would have thrown in the trash ended up looking the complete opposite. We had a pile of dazzling precious metal.

My mother's written memories were a benefit to all of us. We got to know her through her writing, but she had a chance to polish the silver of her life, too. Eventually, she would shine, and I could appreciate her taking the initiative to recognize what she needed to do, but I didn't know if she could ever fully restore everything that had been tarnished.

Bryan broke my reverie, "Are you going to cut your hair to support Gram?"

"Hmm," I answered. "We haven't received anything from the doctors that her conditioning drugs will cause her hair to fall out. I will take her to the salon, though, and if she's getting a pixie cut, then I will, too. What about you?"

"Well, I don't think the pixie cut will look great on me. I was thinking I would get a high and tight cut or a burr or something," Bryan quipped and flashed me a winning smile. "So, uh, what's going on with you and Trent these days?"

"Holy subject change, Batman!" I exclaimed, and volleyed with, "So, uh, what's going on with you and Darcy these days?"

Bryan rolled his eyes. "You promise you won't freak if I tell you this?"

"No freaking," I said.

"Well, we were thinking about getting married after I graduate. She'd be finishing her freshman year in college. We'd go to the same place, either live in married student housing or get an apartment. We want to be together, and we don't want anyone else," Bryan said.

"But you're going to miss out on stuff. Both of you. What about fraternities or sororities or just being young and dumb?" I asked. "Are you ready to be that poor?" Bryan laughed out loud. I must have had the craziest look on my face. I wasn't too proud to want to stay on the family payroll as long as possible, and marriage sounded like a sure way to getting kicked off the payroll and wandering into the territory of being self-sufficient. Yuck. Adulthood could wait. "Bry, are you *that* desperate to be an adult? From my vantage point, I think it seems like it sucks."

"We both have our college funds, and we'll both qualify for financial aid and scholarships. Honestly, depending on where we go, with our grades, we could get full rides. We've talked about what we'd be missing out on, and 'young and dumb' is our biggest obstacle. We aren't sure if we feel the need to be young and dumb. We're both very driven, you know? I would marry Darcy today if I could. We don't want to be apart at the end of the day. We want to come home to each other and be together, eat, laugh, study, watch TV, love and sleep in the same bed. We're both going into science fields. Darcy has decided on dentistry, and I'm doing medicine, and we will be able to support each other. We'll be able to have a baby when she finishes dental school. We sort of have things planned out."

"Well," I said, "I want to support you, but you know what Mom's favorite proverb is: Man plans. God laughs." I thought about my relationship with Trent and what it would look like if we married after I graduated from high school. We were definitely together, but I also wanted to have some flexibility to be young and dumb. I think I wanted to join a sorority. I wanted to explore business and psychology and do some internships, and I knew Trent was of a similar mind. I wanted to run track and cross country. There were things I wanted to do, and getting married was a big deal. It would force us to grow up before we might be ready to be in that headspace.

This next school year would be very telling. Trent was going away to college. We would see each other, but it might not be the same, and we were prepared for it, and we were going to do our best to make it all right for each other. I wasn't planning to date around, and I didn't want him to date around either. I wanted us to work out in the end. In my mind's eye, I still saw us running together every day, and it would be heartbreaking to lose my running partner and the man who helped me put myself back together. I knew I loved Trent with every fiber of my being, and I knew it meant only wanting the very best for him—whatever it might be, and if it didn't include me, I had to learn to be all right with it. But I hoped it did include me.

"Don't get her pregnant until you can afford to pay for a baby," I said. "Condoms are your friend. I'm going to buy you a giant box at Costco."

We pedaled along in silence for a few minutes. Bryan wouldn't graduate for two more years. A lot could happen in two years. Anything could happen. My mind was blown, though. What if they grew apart during Darcy and my freshman years in college? What if they were just too young, too idealistic? They'd hypothetically be married before they could drink alcohol legally. What if they began to resent each other when they saw all the fun their friends were having? I looked forward to college because it was going to be the next chapter, a chance to try out my independence, and then there was the option of being young and dumb.

"I can hear your gears grinding, Jen. Relax," Bryan said. "We still have to get through your guys' senior year. As much as we love each other, we're two years away from getting married. If we're going to do this, we have to lay the groundwork with all of the parents, and you know Darcy's parents are a shit show."

"Yep. That's going to take some work. What do you think Dad, Erin, and Sara will say? I mean, how do you think they'll react?" I asked.

"I have an idea, but really, I don't know. I could see them going either way, and to be frank, I don't care what Sara thinks. She hasn't even met Darcy."

"Sure, sure. What if you guys turn into Darcy's parents? Oh, my god. That would be a nightmare," I said. I did wonder what everyone would say about the two of them getting married as teenagers, though. "Hey, stop! Look! It's a tulip tree and it has flowers on it!" Bryan circled back around, and we dug in our pockets for our cell phones and took photos. "Have you ever seen a tulip tree with actual flowers on it?" I asked.

"Nope. Never have. I didn't know there were male and female tulip trees. This is pretty wild." We showed each other our photos. If the homeowners had been looking out their windows, they might have thought we were casing their house and not fawning over their tulip tree. All the grandparents would be impressed with our photos. And then I thought of Gram, having to avoid people for a while during her conditioning chemo for her transplant. I would send her a text.

"Hey. We need to make sure we have plenty of masks. I don't want Gram to get depressed about being left out of things," I said.

"Right. Good thinking. I think we have some left from the pandemic, but they may have been the cheapies and not the most effective," Bryan said.

"Oh, my god, Bryan. We sound like we're 80 years old. Let's go home and have some Ovaltine or Grape Nuts."

After we'd put our bikes away, we entered the house and found Dad, Erin, Sara, and a very good-looking man with jet black hair and deep dark eyes sitting at our dining room table. When he smiled at Bryan and me, I think I felt like I was looking directly into the sun. Shit. Was I dazzled? Is that what it felt like to be dazzled? Like, there was this insanely attractive guy, and I hadn't even given a thought to Sara. She was just background noise in the face of this TV-star-looking man. Where in the hell had she found him?

Sara and the man both rose. The man was swoon-worthy. Wow. He was tall, but not as tall as our dad, and he was built more like a runner. Dad still had the broad shoulders of a swimmer. But this guy Sara had brought with her, wow. I knew I was staring, and my jaw may have dropped. When Sara began moving her arms as if to present us all to one another, I collected myself. I glanced at Bryan, and he was staring, too.

"Jen, Bryan, I would like you to meet Michael. He's my partner. We work together, and we *are* together. I feel silly being over 40 and calling him my boyfriend, but he is my boyfriend and partner. This feels so awkward. He's mine. That's how I think of him, and I haven't put a label on him beyond the fact that he's mine." She turned red. It was funny seeing our mother on the hot seat. It was funny when Erin and Dad were discovering each other and professing their love for one another in front of all of us.

We all exchanged handshakes and awkward hugs. Michael broke the weirdness, though, by saying, "I have been so looking forward to meeting the two of you. Your mother has talked about you and shown me photos from social media, and it's just so nice to meet you both in person." Bryan may have responded in kind. I don't know. I was a little spellbound. Holy cow. I think I was supposed to respond, too, because I felt Bryan nudging me with his elbow.

"Thank you," I said trying to perform a smooth recovery and decided to throw a little dig Sara's way. "We don't know much about you, I'm afraid, because we have really only had one conversation with Sara since she's been back, but it would be nice to get to know you while you're here."

Bryan threw in some more niceties. He was good that way. "We are looking forward to spending some time with you and hope you won't be a stranger while you're here. This isn't insanely new to the two of us. We got to know Erin when Dad was getting to know her, and she's become part of our family. And then we have a little brother and sister, too."

"Yes," Michael said. "I got to meet them when we arrived. They were just going down for their afternoon naps. They are beautiful."

"We think so," Dad said, overly bright. "But we're a little biased." He clasped Erin's hand and gave her a squeeze. She gave him a reassuring smile that said he didn't need to try so hard.

"I wanted to give you an update on Gram's bone marrow transplant. I'm a match, which means I'll have surgery, and bone marrow will be harvested from my hips. My recovery will take a week or two, and there will be some hip and maybe some leg pain. Not a big deal. Gram is going to have nine days of conditioning chemotherapy and radiation prior to receiving the bone marrow transplant. There have been some changes to the treatment recently that have had much better outcomes. Gram's recovery will take a while." She took a deep breath, took a sip from the water glass in front of her, and I saw her hand shaking, "My bone marrow will be processed by a lab, and then Gram will have an infusion through the central line that was placed. Then we wait a few weeks to see if the graft takes. With the changes to the treatment protocol, there's less of a chance of Graft-Versus-Host-Disease—which is good. Gram will get more drugs to prevent rejection, and she will have to be somewhere germ-free, like the hospital, for around a month. We can visit, but we're all going to have to wear masks, and Gram will need filtered air. After she leaves the hospital, she'll continue with the hematologist for frequent, regular visits to monitor for complications. I'm planning to be here for around six weeks, and Michael's planning to be here for something less than that, but we haven't made any travel arrangements yet for his return to our clinic."

"Shit," Bryan said. "That's a lot."

"It is," Michael said. "Your grandmother is going to be going through some stuff, and she's going to be pretty sick for a while. Your grandpa is going to need support, too, because it's terrible to see someone you love going through something that makes them so incredibly sick and fragile." Sara took Michael's hand, just like Erin and Dad had taken each other's hands earlier.

"Tell us what you need and when you need it," I said. "We are here to help out, and we're pretty industrious. We have people who will jump in and lend a hand at a moment's notice, too."

"May I hug you both?" Sara asked, and she seemed sincere. Bryan and I looked at each other and nodded. She approached us tentatively and wrapped us in a tight hug. This was causing a tight feeling in my chest as I realized it was the only the second time I had been held by my mother in over five years and both hugs had occurred within a week of each other—after nothing for a very long time. And I hugged her back.

Michael broke the weird tension of the hug, saying, "I'm here for moral support and to help anyone and everyone in any way that I can. Just to forewarn everyone, I don't do well with downtime and will find things to do. Please don't be shy about telling me to butt out if I get in anyone's business or crowd you or anything." He seemed a little nervous, too. "But, what I'm trying to say is that I'm here. Whatever anyone needs."

THE QUANDARY

BRYAN - AGE 16

The world kept turning. Gram had chemo and radiation, and Sara had the bone marrow harvest. Michael hung around a lot and cooked meals for everyone. He had a lot of energy, and it was obvious the guy wasn't used to having downtime. When everyone was at the hospital, he cleaned Gram and Grandpa's house, cut the grass, found things to fix. He came to our house and mowed our grass. Sometimes when he ran out of things to do, he would get the shopping list from Erin and go to the grocery for us, and then he'd cook something. I couldn't even begin to imagine what Michael would be like when he retired.

When Grandpa was home from the hospital, visiting Gram, he tried to keep his distance to minimize any exposure to anything weird or tropical he may have brought back with him. He and Dad seemed to get along great. When Dad was home from work, the two of them would sit on the back porch and have a beer. Dad even introduced Michael to Tom, and the three of them picked up tickets for a basketball game and made a night of it.

Bryn and Walker were walking and running around like little terrors. We had to keep a close eye on them because they would get into everything. Michael said, "They're like Thing 1 and Thing 2 from The Cat in the Hat!" When Michael really started laughing, it was contagious. He cackled. There wasn't any other way to describe it. The first time the twins heard him, they cocked their heads and stared. It was a priceless moment watching them as they tried to puzzle out what this grownup was doing and why he was making crazy noises.

While Sara and Michael were in town, the third quarter at school ended, and Jen and I brought our grades home. We also had worksheets for planning our schedules for the following year. I had left everything on the kitchen table to go over with Erin, Dad, and Jen after finishing my homework. Hello, calculus, my friend. When I came back downstairs, Michael was looking over my transcript and had the school's course listing up on his laptop.

"Find anything interesting there, Michael?" I asked. I didn't have any secrets or anything, and strangely, it didn't bother me that he had helped himself to my stuff.

"First, sorry if I have overstepped. I saw everything on the table and was getting ready to set the table for dinner, and then I couldn't resist. Again, I am sorry about that. But—" and here he drew 'but' into three syllables. "Did you know right now, you have enough credits and AP classes and that you could graduate with Jen next year? I was looking at the State Board of Education, and at the end of next year, depending on your course load, you would be able to meet all the requirements to graduate. You and Darcy could start college together."

"Really..." I said and let the thought sort of take on a life of its own. "By chance, did you look at the classes I'd need to take to graduate early?"

"I did," he said, and the guy looked so proud. "I figured out first and second semester, and kept you filled up with AP classes. You'll meet all the requirements and have enough credits to start college as a sophomore. My guess is that Darcy and Jen will also be able to start with sophomore standing, too." He paused. "Man, I wish they had all this stuff when I was in high school. That was kind of a dark time for me. I couldn't wait to start college."

"Nuh-uh," I said, disbelief lacing my response. "Look at you. You're like a model and a brainiac doctor."

"Ah, my friend, I was a very late bloomer, and kids weren't kind. I'm half-Asian and half-Latino. I didn't really fit in with any group, and I was alone a lot, until my younger brother started high school. He was actually cool, and I sort of became less of a dork by association."

"I never would have guessed it," I said. "So, what if I *did* graduate early? My birthday is after the cutoff, which makes me one of the older kids in my grade. I'd turn 18 toward the end of first semester of my freshman year. Not the worst thing. Hmm. I need to think about this. Could you do me a favor and not say anything to my dad or anyone? I want to process this before I breathe life into it."

Michael smiled, "You got it. It's sort of exciting, though, isn't it?"

I went back to my room and texted Trent.

Bryan: You up for some ice cream after dinner?

Trent: Sure. What's going on?

Bryan: Want to run something by you.

Trent: Gimme a clue.

Bryan: Nothing bad. Just need your opinion and want to bounce some ideas around.

Trent: Does Jen know, or do I need to keep it quiet?

Bryan: Quiet for now.

I would need to start doing college visits now and take the SAT or ACT. I hadn't done a prep class or even taken a mock or practice test. It was time to make a list and then go over it with Trent. He would ask good questions and play devil's advocate. He would be objective and candid and keep emotion out of the discussion, punching holes into the suggestion or telling me the whole thing was do-able. After Trent, then I'd talk to Jen and Darcy to get their take, and then Dad and Erin. It was a huge change to the plan that had been set in motion when I was in kindergarten. I would go from being one of the older kids in my class to being one of the younger kids. The age thing didn't bother me, though. It was mainly the suddenness of a change in possible circumstance.

There was a knock at my bedroom door. It had to be Jen.

"Bry?" she called.

"Yeah. What's up? Time for dinner yet?" I answered and volleyed a question back to her.

"Uh, yes. Five minutes. Trent was going to come over to do some studying, but he said the two of you were going out. Everything all right?"

"Oh," I said. Jesus, Joseph, Mary, and all the saints. Word traveled fast around here. "I wanted to get his opinion on some stuff, you know, guy stuff."

"But you're okay?" she prodded.

"Yep. Nothing to worry about. I'll hit you up soon enough. Don't you worry," I said injecting a smile into the last bit.

Over the past five years, when something bothered one or the other of us, Jen would come into my room, or I'd go into hers, and we would sometimes talk, sometimes remain silent, and we'd press our foreheads to one another. We'd sit on the floor or on one of our beds with our heads pressed together for anywhere from a full minute to three, four, or five minutes. We hadn't done the forehead thing for around a year, and now when I really needed her to hear me and I needed the sibling closeness, I'd go to her and hold her hand and give it a good squeeze. Jen was a little different. She would summon me, and then she would have flip charts. Once she had graphs. Another time, she had prepared a PowerPoint presentation. She wanted to keep her emotions at bay as much as she could while she presented her case, and then afterward, I'd see everything—all the feelings, conflicting emotions, worry, care, and concern.

I opened my door, and there she was. "Jen, have I told you how fortunate I am to have you as my sister?" I slung an arm around her neck and pulled her in for a hug. "Do you know how much I love you?"

"As big as the universe?" she always asked.

And I always affirmed, "As big as the universe."

THE IMPROMPTU SESSION
SARA - AGE 44

My kids are good people. I can see they rely on each other, but they have a healthy respect for Rob, Erin, all of the grandparents, their romantic partners, and the parents of their partners. I know I had a small part in it before I fell apart, but I don't credit myself with the poise and maturity they both display. I haven't been here for any of that development. I wonder how much of it came from modeling their behaviors after people they admired or if it was the result of adaptation for gaining a grasp on what was deemed an acceptable response to the cards they had been dealt. But, I look at them, and I'm proud.

My hip doesn't hurt anymore. The bone marrow harvest was two weeks ago, and Mom's transplant went without issue five days ago. I am so proud of how she has faced this and how well she's done with everything that's been thrown at her. Look at me with all this pride in my kids and my mom. Michael decided he wanted to stick around for the first week after Mom's transplant, even though I told him it would be fine to head back to our clinic. He'll be here for a few more days, I think. He hasn't booked his return plane ticket yet. I'm completely heartsick about his leaving, but we did long distance before, and we can do it again for a relatively short time.

Mom's in the hospital for at least another two to three weeks, and Dad's been going back and forth between home and the hospital. He's tired, so tired and so worried. Michael has been doing a lot of dropping off and picking up. My leg hurts just a little bit, and I don't feel up to driving yet. I think Michael is waiting until I'm at least 90% and able to drive without having the pain in my leg before he feels comfortable leaving. I'm staying until Mom is out of the hospital and I feel that she and Dad have things under control a little bit, which is maybe another three or four weeks. It depends on what Mom's hematologist says and how my dad feels about his ability to take care of Mom when she comes home.

We have a conference with the hospital's social worker coming up where we (the family, and 'the family' is a small village) and the social worker talk about coordination of care when Mom is released and what services we may need to use to support Mom's recovery. It's a lot. I'm a doctor, and I'm realizing this is a lot. Michael is a specialist, and he said, "Wow. This is a lot. Are you sure you don't want me to stay longer? I might be able to come back and relieve you for a few weeks after she comes home." We'll have a better handle on everything after our conference, though.

The dogs warmed up to me much faster than my children. Jen and Bryan are coming around very slowly, and I overheard them talking and saying I wasn't like a mom but more like a weird aunt who popped in every once in a great while. Being transparent here, I was eavesdropping. When I heard their voices, I just sort of hid behind the door frame and listened to their conversation like some kind of creeper.

When I got back to Mom and Dad's I looked at the time and sent an email to my psychologist to see if she could provide some ad hoc counseling in the next twelve to twenty-four hours. I sent an email, and she quickly responded she could fit me in early in the morning.

I awoke in plenty of time for the session, didn't even need to set an alarm. I logged on to the patient portal, and there she was, Dr. Mary Burgess, the woman who probably saved my life.

"Good morning, Sara," she said. "Talk to me about everything. I'm surprised you didn't reach out sooner. You've got to be facing a lot of stressors."

"I would say, 'you have no idea,' but you really do have an idea," I answered. I filled her in on the transplant, and she was pleased it was going well.

"How are Jen and Bryan? How are you doing with the two of them, and how are they acclimating to Michael?" Mary asked.

"You know what's funny? I think they're all much more open and accepting of him than they are me," I answered.

"Well, to be fair, he didn't abandon them. They get to know him as an entirely new person without a broken track record. He doesn't have ground he needs to make up—like you do," she said.

"Ouch," I said.

"Well, we can't brush the past off the table because it figures in so prominently with the kids, right? And if you choose to ignore the past, you're insulting the two of them." She paused. "Tell me, what have you done with Jen and Bryan while you've been back?"

"I had dinner with them. We talked. I introduced them to Michael. I've seen them twice," I answered.

"Only twice? In all the time you've been there?" Mary countered. "Are they or are they not a priority for you?"

"I'm gun-shy," I said. "I was listening to them talking to each other. They didn't know I was within earshot. They said they sort of liked me but didn't know me and after I go back to work, after my mom is faring better, they have no idea when or if they're ever going to see me again. I did tell Rob what I had overheard, and he said, 'What did you expect, Sara?'"

Mary replied, "Rob is right. You have to give them some time, and you have to give them actions to show your commitment. What does that look like to you? Are you going to continue to be gun-shy? If you are, then why did you even get together with them in the first place?" She paused and drummed her fingers on the table in front of her. "I know and you know we've talked about this before, but you are going to have to make some tough decisions for yourself that will affect Jen and Bryan. We're kind of at the moment of truth now. Do you even know what kind of relationship you want to have with them? Do you know what you want it to look like? Have you thought about the effort required to create the relationship, and do you have the wherewithal and personal fortitude to forge that relationship? If what you're able to do falls far short of what you envision, it's better off for everyone if you're the weird aunt. Who are you going to be, Sara?"

"I've been thinking about this a lot. Following through on what I want to promise. Here's the thing. Now that I'm here and I'm in the moment, I want to promise the kids the universe. But here's the other thing. I love my job, and I am 100% committed to serving my patients. When Michael and I met, he said his two priorities were his wife and his job." I stopped talking. I needed to hear myself. "While I've been gone, and even before that if I'm being candid, my priorities shifted to my job and only my job.

"I have become very comfortable with just the one priority, and it took work to make space for Michael. I don't know that I have room for more while I'm in South America, and I don't know if I want to come back to the States when I'm ready to be finished with Doctors Without Borders. I can visit. I should visit. But if I'm looking at the structure of my life as it is now, I don't think I can promise my kids much at all. I can be a distant relative or friend they hardly see. I can be someone who doesn't promise much and doesn't deliver much either." I gave a weary sigh, shrugged, and leaned my head onto my hand.

Mary looked at me, scrutinizing me through the monitor. "Are you sure? Do you think you can stretch just a little? You made room for Michael, and I'd say that was a much bigger stretch than what you'd be doing for your kids."

"Yeah, but there's the proximity factor. He's right there with me, all the time," I said, and it sounded like an excuse even to me.

"Sara, I can't make you be a mother to your kids. Whatever relationship you have with them is going to have to be something you want and a commitment. You cannot drop the ball. I will tell you this, though, as a caution. If you don't want to function as a mother, then don't make it an option. You may *want* it, but don't offer yourself if you *can't* do it."

"That's a lot to think about," I said. "I'm going to journal what we've been talking about. Maybe I'll get some clarity by writing about everything.

"I think that's a good idea, Sara. Will you set up another visit when you've come to some conclusions? I'd like to talk again in two days if that suits".

I had a lot to think about. I still knew I had limitations, and I needed to stop being all pie in the sky and hoping the kids would magically welcome me back into their lives. Because the truth was: I would be leaving again, and I would be leaving them behind...again.

And the Hits Keep Coming

Rob - age 44

On a sunny, Sunday afternoon Tom, Michael, and I were sitting in the generic sports bar about a mile from our house. Literally—not the mile distance but the bar's being generic. The name of the bar was Generic Sports Bar. The menus looked like the labels on the generic products in the grocery store. The sign outside the bar had large lit up black letters spelling out GENERIC, and underneath in smaller letters (same font) were the words Sports Bar. Inside, though, the ambiance was anything but generic. There was a lot of polished wood, comfortable pleather booths, and televisions everywhere. On the tables in the booths, there were small monitors where we could choose whatever game or match we could possibly want to view. This place was Mecca for people who loved sports and had ADD. At any given time, there were people playing trivia, watching college or pro rugby, soccer, baseball, basketball, football, hockey, curling...you name it. All the sports, all the time because there was always some streaming service playing back games or matches from 20 to 40 years ago in addition to anything that might be happening today.

"So, I think the cat's out of the bag, isn't it?" Tom asked. "Is Bryan going to graduate with Jen and Darcy?"

This had been the shock of shocks when Bryan came to talk to me about graduating early. He had made a list of pros and cons, had talked to Trent, then Jen and Darcy, and then he came to Erin and me. "Michael, man, you could have given me a heads up you had done the analysis of Bryan's transcript before you pitched the idea to him. I'm not mad or anything, and I feel kind of stupid that I hadn't picked up on the possibility before, but when Bryan came to us to discuss the situation, I think I could have been knocked over with a feather," I said.

Michael looked sheepish. "I'm so sorry. I got caught up in everything, and then Bryan walked into the room, and I couldn't contain myself. I have to tell you, though, it was the best puzzle going through his transcripts and the course catalog. What did he decide to do?"

"He's going to take the SAT and ACT. He'd be doing both tests without the benefit of a prep class, though. If he does well, then he's going to apply to schools in the summer when Jen and Darcy are making their applications. I think he's going to apply regardless, and then re-take whichever test seems like a better fit for him and get in a prep class. He's been doing some mock tests with Jen and Darcy." I sipped my beer. "I don't know that I'm emotionally prepared for both of them to leave home at the same time," I said, shaking my head.

Tom nodded knowingly, "I hear you. Maggie and I both get weepy when we think about Trent leaving us in August. Bridgette will miss him, too. She's been pretty clingy, and she insists that Trent take her to her piano lessons, dance class...whatever she can think of...just to get that extra bit of time with her big brother. How's Jen been?"

Michael chimed in, "Can you hold that thought for a second? Do you guys want to watch the Michigan -North Carolina NCAA final game from 1993...Chris Webber's timeout?" Tom and I both nodded. The Timeout. I remembered that with crystal clarity. Probably one of the most memorable moments in college basketball I would ever remember.

"Jen has been all right. She knows Trent is going to go somewhere and run. She's been getting scouted by Division 1 schools since her sophomore year. She totally downplays her talent. Her grades are great, and I think she's going to be able to go wherever she wants. She'd like to go somewhere warm, though. Has Trent decided where he's going? Jen would like to go wherever Trent goes. She knows it might not work out that way, but they think they can keep their relationship intact regardless of where they go." I knew I was raising my brow when I said the last bit. The two of them loved each other, but they were 17 and 18 years old, and once they were apart from each other, who knew how things would work out for them? Do you think he'll run for a D-1 school?"

Tom swirled the beer around in his pint glass. "I don't know. In case you didn't know it, Rob, Jen is—in my humble opinion—an elite runner. Trent is a strong runner, but I wouldn't say he's an elite runner. He might get to run for a D-1 school, but it would have to be for a smaller school. I don't think he's going to run for the Penn States of the world."

I coughed a bit, "Whoa, whoa, whoa. You think Jen's an elite runner? I know she's really great, but I'm her dad. She's been scouted ever since we moved here, but aren't there always scouts at track meets?"

Tom coughed into his beer mug, "Uh, no, Rob there aren't. You've just become accustomed to seeing them at all of Jen's meets. They're coming to see her run. Have you talked to any of them yourself?"

"Well, some of them come ask me if she has committed to anywhere, and I tell them she hasn't even begun applying to colleges." I stopped talking. "I'm an idiot, aren't I? Like, I'm an hour behind everyone else in the room." Michael and Tom just stared at me and then began nodding slowly. "I wonder if Jen has been talking to them. I should probably talk to her, shouldn't I?" They continued nodding. We drank our beers in companionable silence. When we had emptied our mugs, Tom hopped up to order another round.

Michael said, "I'm adding in my two cents here because I have so much downtime and I love puzzles. Rob, have you looked at Jen's stats beyond her school and the state records for her events? She's way the hell up there. She's been performing above a lot of the Division 1 women for the last year. These are women who are anywhere from two to four years older than she is."

Tom returned to the table with a pitcher of beer. While Tom poured, Michael continued, "When I come over tomorrow, I'm mowing your lawn. No, that's not a euphemism," Michael said, smirking at Tom and me. "But I'll bring my laptop. I created a spreadsheet with all the top female runners for the last five years, and then all the current US records and all the world records for Jen's events. I even made some scatter diagrams to visualize where she's performing. It's fascinating." His eyes began to glaze over as he talked about the data. Tom and I stared at

Michael. "What? I told everyone up front that I don't do well with downtime. I look for things to do, and this was one of the things I stumbled upon."

"I have to tell you guys that we've always wanted to be supportive of her running and encouraging, too, but I've always tempered it with her only sticking with the competitive side of it as long as it's fun. When it stops being fun, when the training is a drag and something she dreads, then she should just run when she wants and for enjoyment or fitness or whatever she wants to get out of it," I said. "You know, I'm not sure if Jen is even tracking her stats."

Tom said, "She and Trent keep spreadsheets with their personal times and are basically competing against themselves. Their goals are to improve their personal bests. They don't track records of other people or anything."

"Jen's running has always been *her* thing. I've stayed out of her way because early on, her running wasn't healthy, and it was a bone of contention. She's had coaches, nutritionists, sports psychologists, and we did all that to get her healthy—physically and mentally. Again, I know she's a fantastic runner, and I know her running is therapeutic, but I didn't know she would be considered elite." I rubbed the stubble on my jaw and chin. I looked at Tom and Michael, shaking my head in wonder. "You should come over tomorrow, too," I said to Tom. "Bring the whole family. Michael, do you want me to call Sara to extend the invitation, or do you think she'd be all right coming with you?"

"This is so weird. She's your ex-wife, but you're my friend, and she's my girl-friend-partner, probable future wife, and I think you and I have the relationship. I'll ask her to come. If she seems iffy, then you invite her."

We watched the rest of the 1993 Michigan-North Carolina game with the timeout and technical foul that sealed their fate. The look on Chris Webber's face was heartbreaking because he knew instantly they were out of timeouts.

When I got home, Bryan and Erin were going through toy catalogs. My cell phone started buzzing, and I looked to see who was calling. Jo.

"Jo, hi. How are you?" I asked. Unprompted calls worried me.

"I think I'm doing very well, in fact, better than expected," she said. "They aren't seeing any signs of Graft-Versus-Host-Disease yet, which I think is wonderful. I may be getting my hopes up prematurely, though. But the doctors are talking about letting me go home a little bit sooner because I'm doing so well."

"That's great news," I said, and relief washed over me. Jo had been like a second mother to me over the years, and even when Sara left us all, Jo and Howard remained fixtures in our lives. And even now that our lives had changed and included Erin, Rose, and two rapidly growing toddlers, she and Howard had never shied away from the expansion and had embraced everything about it.

"I was wondering. I know you and Michael have become close. Do you think he and Sara might be interested in getting married before they go back to South America? Sara said they've talked about it from the standpoint of continuing to be assigned together as a unit in their work, which makes sense. I would so love to see her settled, you know? I'm not sure how Jen and Bryan would handle it, though. This is one of the most unorthodox conversations I've ever had with anyone, but you would probably be the most logical person to deal with any fallout with Jen and Bryan, and I wanted your thoughts."

I clicked my tongue against the roof of my mouth a few times. "Let me run some hypotheticals by the kids later. Jen's out with Trent, I think, and it looks like Erin and Bryan might be starting to plan Bryn and Walker's birthday party. Geesh. Time. It's a beast, you know?"

"Thank you, Rob. You are a wonderful son-in-law and father, and at some point, I'll get to add another son-in-law to the mix."

The day was getting stranger and stranger. In the other room, Bryn was walking around, and Walker was chasing her, reaching out for her hair. Bryn looked up at me, made eye contact, and said, "Not nice!"

"My little sister does not put up with anyone's shi—stuff," Bryan said proudly.

"That counts as a swear, Bryan," Erin said. "You owe me $5, please. I'm delighted to put it in the swear jar for you," she added sweetly and put her hand out, palm up.

"Fine.'" Bryan pulled his wallet out of his back pocket, and when he haphazardly popped a $5 bill out, a condom came with it. Erin, Bryan, and I all stared at the packet on the floor like it might sprout wings and fly out of the room.

"Yeah, uh, so...funny thing," Bryan said.

"No. Not now, and not here." I held up a hand to stop any further talking. "Let's go to your room, okay?" And if the moment couldn't be more awkward, Darcy came through the front door, loaded down with a tote bag and her backpack.

"Hi, everyone." She made a bee-line for Walker who lit up every time he saw her. "This little guy is going to be riding a skateboard before we know it." Darcy looked at each of us in turn, reading the room. "I'm interrupting something, aren't I?"

"Nah," Erin said. "We're looking at toys, and batting around ideas for the kids' birthday party. Bryan and Rob were going to look into some SAT or ACT prep classes. You want to throw in your two cents on party themes?"

"Love to," Darcy said, smiling.

Bryan and I exited the room. "When is your sister getting home? Might as well do all the talking all at once."

Bryan tugged his phone out of his front pants pocket and texted Jen.

"They're on their way back right now," he said.

"Good."

The Thrill and Agony

Sara - age 44

"Michael, honey, can you please help me with something?" I stood on a ladder trying to balance a heavy box between my head, shoulder, and sternum, while holding on to the ladder with my free hand. I started laughing a little because if falling from a ladder in my childhood home was the cause of my demise, in spite of the crazy situations and pathogens that had crossed my path over the past couple years...well, then, wouldn't that be rich?

Michael arrived, held the ladder steady for me, and eased the box out of my hands. "Hey, whoa. You do realize this is a two person job, don't you?"

"I didn't realize it at first. Then I started picturing my death, and I realized I had bitten off more than I could chew. It's still hard for me to ask for help when I face a problem. My first urge is to be The Little Red Hen and do everything myself. Not the wisest option when I'm half in and half out of the attic," I said, a bit discomfited.

"Did you find what you were looking for?" Michael asked.

I nodded. The box was full of my old yearbooks from high school and college, along with some of the journals I had kept back then, too. There wasn't going to be enough time for Jen and Bryan to get to know me as much as I wanted, and I had hoped to give them a glimpse of who I was when I was their age. Maybe they would see bits of themselves in some of the pieces of my past. It was a heavy box, though; but when wasn't the past a heavy thing?

Michael held onto my hips longer than necessary before easing the box away from me. "I've been thinking," he said. "If you're on board with your mom's request for us to get married before we go back to South America, then I think we should do it."

"All right. Let's do it."

Michael set the box on the floor a few feet away from the ladder and backed up enough to give me room to descend the ladder without incident. When I reached the bottom and turned around, he was down on one knee and held a small jewelry box out to me."

"Marry me, Sara," he said earnestly. "Be my wife. Make me the happiest man in the world and agree to spend the rest of our lives together. I love you on a nearly elemental level, hell, maybe even a sub-atomic particle level. Every part of me has been calling out to you across this globe we inhabit. There wasn't going to be a circumstance where we wouldn't cross paths, but the timing had to be just right, and we had to move onto the right squares on the game board. Please say you'll be mine and want me to be yours officially, because we do belong to each other even without all the paperwork."

I was crying. I leaned down and took his precious face in my hands and kissed him for everything I was worth. "Yes, yes, yes. Let's get married."

He sighed, standing, and sliding the ring onto my finger. It wasn't a diamond, and I knew it wouldn't be a diamond. We wouldn't be adding valuable gemstones to anything until we were back in the States on a more permanent basis. The white gold band had beautiful mill grain and scroll work all along the outside. "Look on the inside of the ring," he said.

It was inscribed with our initials and the date we met in Japan. "It's perfect. I love it, and I love you." We called my mom and dad to let them know, and then we called Michael's parents and brother. With Mom's immunity compromised, we decided we'd go to the courthouse and tie the knot there. We'd figure out getting a video of the ceremony and then we would share it with our parents. Eventually, we'd make our way to California and spend time with Michael's family, but it wasn't going to be on this trip.

I think what I realized was that my parents were getting older, and I wasn't going to have them for another forty or fifty years, and with Mom's situation, I wasn't sure I would have her five years from now or even a year from now. If it made her happy for us to put our plan in motion sooner than later, we would do it.

Michael and I called Rob, and we put him on speaker. We told him our news, and he asked if I'd like to share with Jen and Bryan. I could hear him calling the kids' names while he held his hand over the microphone on his phone.

"Guys," he yelled. "Can you come here for a minute?" I didn't want to remind him the mute button existed for a reason, but it would have been splitting hairs.

A few seconds later he said, "OK. They're both here. Go ahead."

I told them the news, and silence followed. I didn't know how I would have reacted had I been in their shoes, but this complete non-reaction floored me. My guess was that Rob was telling them to say something.

Jen was first. "That's great. Congratulations to Michael, and best wishes to you."

Then it was Bryan's turn. "Yeah, um, congratulations. When is the big day?"

Michael jumped in to answer because I wasn't hiding my distress due to the kids' apparent apathy. "We were thinking of going to the courthouse tomorrow."

"We wish you both every happiness," Jen said somewhat robotically. "Why right now? Dad told us you two would probably get married, and it makes sense. I was just curious about the timing."

"Ah, sure," I responded. "You two know we wanted to get married to ensure we'd be sent to the same places in the future. Gram has a lot of time on her hands while she's in the hospital, and she wants to see everyone's plans are set in motion in case..." My voice broke here, and I had to stop talking because the reality of losing my mom was hitting me. She didn't want any loose ends in case she didn't make it. "Sorry. You know, though, right?"

I heard a hitching sound and realized one of them was also facing the reality that Mom might not do too well in the long run. In a low, quiet voice Bryan said, "We know. I think we didn't realize you were going to move so quickly. But we do understand the reasoning—and now—the timing."

After the call, which went stranger than I expected, Michael and I, who had been on Cloud 9 before, looked each other in the eye and realized we were on

Cloud 8.9. But, dammit, we were going to get married. We were going to help the people who needed us most; and now I realized there were people here who needed us, and before we got in too deep with the dynamics of being part of a larger family unit—outside of what I could manage with just Michael and me—I knew without sitting down and doing any formal problem solving that I didn't have the wherewithal to maintain the relationships and the level of intensity the relationships would require.

Rob called a few days ago about a condom that Bryan's wallet had produced, and I basically told Rob that he needed to handle it. Bryan and Jen likely did not put an ounce of credence into anything I would have to say to them. They didn't trust me and had told me as much. I could not and would not be a disciplinarian or authority figure to the two of them. I don't think I could even mentor them in any meaningful way. Michael and Bryan had managed to form an interesting bond, and Rob and Michael had become friends. In talking with Michael, he planned to maintain the relationships. It was sobering and humbling to realize I had limits and couldn't stretch beyond them. I loved Jen and Bryan enough to know I wasn't a role model for them and that we could love one another from arm's length. I was going to be the weird aunt, but being or doing more was beyond my limits.

Michael was surprised by my revelation. "I see you every day in clinic, and you put yourself out there for our patients all the time."

"I know, but family and patients are different. I can advise patients on certain things but not others. My kids need to be advised on all manner of things, and I've been checked out long enough that I'm not qualified to offer an opinion. I don't want to take the intensive course on parenting teenagers. We're leaving here, and I know I'll be back again, but I won't be back for long stints like this one unless something goes terribly wrong."

Michael pulled me into him and breathed into my hair before saying, "Did Rob say anything to you about Jen's running and her stats or about Bryan graduating from high school a year early?"

"He did. You've been very bored and busy and looking for things to do, haven't you?" I asked with a little sass in my tone.

"I have a lot of free time. There are only so many meals to cook, houses to clean, lawns to mow, clothes to launder. I would probably offer to watch Bryn and Walker, too, but I think I'm way out of my comfort zone with toddlers," he said sheepishly.

"I'm sorry I haven't been around more. I want to see my parents as much as I can because we can't see the future, and..." I didn't want to add anything to my thoughts that could point to this visit possibly being the last time I would see one or both of them ever again. There are 'last times' that sneak up on us, and Time is a beast, stealing away this and that and leaving us with less of some things and more of others, like aches and pains, uncertainty and confusion, birthdays, hearty laughs with the people we love. Did I know the last time I read bedtime stories to Jen and Bryan would be the last time? Did I know the last time Rob and I had sex would be the last time we had sex? When I was child on the cusp of becoming an adolescent, did I know the last time my mom tucked me into bed would be the last time? No, no, and no.

Michael drew his head away from me, far enough that he was looking me in the eye, and his gaze held love, concern, and truth. "Stop. No apologies. I knew you were going to be very busy when I decided to join you here. I have actually enjoyed the time. I think I forgot what it felt like *not* to be steamrolling through the day. This has been a nice break for me, and I've been able to do some self-discovery and rediscovery, and I've made some friends, one of whom is your ex-husband. And, yes, I have a lot of energy and an almost pathological urge to fill all my waking time with activity."

I remained quiet. There was the sting of oncoming tears, and I could feel my eyes getting glassy. Michael saw me getting ready to break down. "Hey, hey, hey," he said. "No crying. Your mom is doing great, better than even her doctor expected. Your dad is doing great. He's going to need a little help getting into a groove when your mom comes home, but you'll be here to get things onto an even keel. Jen and Bryan are going to graduate in a little over a year, and before you get any weird ideas in your head, I'm telling you this: We are going to make the trip for their graduation. Your daughter is probably going to make a Division 1 track and field team at some point, and I'm going to keep adding her data into my spreadsheet. Your kids are going to be successes in whatever they decide to do because they have an incredibly supportive group of people in their lives." Michael paused, a small smile on his lips. "When we get back to work, things are going to be much the same, but we will be married, and I love the feeling I get when I think about your being my wife. Not only that, I get to be the luckiest guy and be your husband." I smiled back, a small smile, but he saw it, acknowledging how I felt. "I guess I get to be the weird uncle, then, don't I?"

"Rob probably already knows how everything is likely to play out, don't you think?" I asked quietly, and Michael nodded. "He's always been very perceptive, and I think he was doing the right thing to let me be with the kids and figure myself out. But I know he wouldn't have allowed anything to mess up the kids, which is a testament to who Jen and Bryan are. I think they're stronger than anyone I've ever known, and they're intelligent, perceptive, and very open in their communication."

"You know how they got that way?" Michael asked. "They have spent a lot of time in therapy and learned coping tools and acquired coping skills. If you hadn't left, who's to say what would have happened? This life we lead is an adventure, full of twists and turns, obstacles, easy stretches, and roads pock-marked with potholes. But you know what? We persevere. Jen and Bryan and Rob have persevered, and they are adept at recognizing the potholes and getting around most of them." His smile became a little bit sad.

"I do need one thing from you, though. When those kids send you an email, you need to respond. I don't know if they're going to continue to send you emails or not, but if they do, you're going to send a reply. Even the weird aunt answers email. Okay?" I nodded. I could answer emails. I could even call now and then. And, maybe, in the future, I would be able to be more and do more. Promise less, deliver more.

The next morning was a blur. Michael and I went to the courthouse, the same one where Rob and Erin were married, and we put my cell phone on a little stand and took a video of our wedding. We didn't know the witnesses. They were getting married right after we were, and we offered to be their witnesses, but they had already supplied their own. We uploaded the video for both sets of parents and Jen, Bryan, Rob, and Erin to view. We were official. Man and wife. We had a signed piece of paper that said so. While Dad was at the hospital with Mom, Michael and I high tailed it home to consummate our marriage. His flight back to South America was booked for the next afternoon. Mom was scheduled to come home from the hospital the following week, and then I would return in a week or two after that.

Mom was doing so well, and there were no signs of Graft-Versus-Host-Disease so far, and it looked like the transplant had grafted as planned. We were all praying every day, sending good thoughts and wishes into the universe, doing whatever we could to pay it forward in the hopes of returning good karma. I could see the spring in my dad's step returning. He had been cautiously optimistic about everything and had turned a corner to being openly optimistic. Mom's color was improving all the time, and she seemed to be gaining a bit more energy every day. We couldn't have asked for more, except for her not developing aplastic anemia in the first place. I felt very positive about how everything was going, and I kept my fingers crossed that the rug wouldn't be pulled out from under all of us.

Dress Shopping

Jen - age 17

Bryan made the decision to graduate early from high school. We took the SATs at the same time, and he scored 25 points higher than I did, and I had even taken a prep course. Not to take anything away from him, but he's a very good test taker. We drove to school on a crisp morning in the Spring. Bryan was well-prepared for the test. He had pencils, erasers, and a protein bar. When we parked, he left his phone in the glove box. I, on the other hand, scurried around the house looking for pencils and erasers, my ID, tissues, and a bottle of water. Normally, I am so perfectly prepared. I'm a 'never let them see you sweat' kind of girl, but on SAT Saturday, I was not my usual self.

Bryan and Darcy were aiming for Northwestern, and with their grades, activities, and test scores, I didn't think they'd have any problems being accepted. My top two were going to be Stanford and University of Florida. UCLA was the runner-up pick. I wanted decent weather and a top notch running program. Trent and I wanted to attend the same school, but we weren't sure he'd be picked up by a Division 1 school. He's a strong distance runner, and there had been some interest in him from University of Florida. We decided, though, it would be important for us to make the best choices for ourselves individually, not as a couple. If we were at the same school, fantastic; if not, we'd try to make our relationship work long distance. And, honestly, the biggest test would be Trent's freshman year in college and my senior year in high school. I didn't want him to miss out on anything because he was shackled to me. He was kind of offended that I referred to myself as shackles. We would play it by ear.

Darcy and I shopped for prom dresses together. We went to the mall, hit the food court, ending up with sticky fingers from the Orange Julius. Darcy commented, "My mom said when she was a kid, they used to put an egg in the Orange Julius drinks to get it to froth up in the blender. Can you imagine raw eggs being served in the mall nowadays? It's a recipe for a lawsuit."

We wandered into the bathrooms to wash our hands before trying on dresses. "How do you think you'll wear your hair for prom?" I asked.

"What you see is what you get," Darcy deadpanned. "My hair does one thing, and this is it." She pointed to her head. "How about you?"

"Mmmm. Maybe part up and part down? I still want to look like myself," I said. "And you do know you're the prettiest girl in school, right?"

"Oh, pe-shaw," she said, the prettiest blush coloring her cheeks and neck.

We knew we would be looking at dresses in the junior department, but I also wanted to hit the ladies' special occasion dresses. They seemed to be better made and more sophisticated. Of course, we would steer clear of anything looking like a mother of the bride or groom dress. Erin and I had looked for dresses one time for an event she and Dad attended, and she was concerned about looking matronly. "Dear god, I don't want to look old before my time," she had said, laughing.

Darcy found an ice blue strapless sheath that hit her mid-thigh. The fabric was silk charmeuse and felt incredibly luxurious. She found a wrap to go with the dress in a midnight blue accented with the same blue in the dress. "I'm going to wear my mom's silver Jimmy Choo's." She made a 360 degree turn in the three-way mirror.

"Wow," I said. "You look beautiful. Bryan's not going to know what to do with himself." And she did look beautiful. The blue of the dress set off the blue in her eyes and highlighted the perfect blonde in her hair. If my hair only did one thing and always looked as good as hers, I would be thrilled with that one thing.

I envisioned a ballgown for myself. The ballgowns were big and bulky and took up a lot of room on the dress racks. Teenage girls attacked prom dress shopping like big game hunters, and the store was already fairly picked over in late-March. Proms in the area weren't scheduled until May. Advanced planning was a requirement if you were even thinking of going. All this to say, the search for the perfect ballgown was a bit more onerous. Eventually, we found *the* dress.

It was dark green, strapless, had a belt, and pockets. Pockets! If I were going to design my own dress, this would have been exactly what I would have designed. The green was so dark, it was almost black, and the way the skirt swished when I walked and when I did the 360 turn...gosh...I felt like a princess. I looked at Darcy, and she stared at me, mouth agape. I gently pushed her lower jaw up to close her mouth.

"Oh," she paused. "Jen. Oh. Please tell me you're going to get this dress. You are perfection."

I smiled a little bashfully. "Yeah, I think this is the one."

We took pictures of each other and sent them to our families and grandparents.

"Are you buying an outfit for the After-Prom?" I asked after we had paid for our dresses. My dress bag was enormous.

"Not sure Bryan and I are going to the After-Prom," Darcy said. "We were thinking about staying somewhere after the dance."

"Oh?" I asked. I knew they had already had sex. The Great Condom Incident had answered all speculation.

"Yeah," she said. "We're going to look so nice, and it's a special night and all, and we just want to be together."

"What are you going to tell your parents?"

"I think I'm going to tell them I'll be with you. I mean, I will be with you for at least part of the night," she said. "Is that all right?"

"Sure. I'm just wondering what Bryan will tell Dad and Erin."

"I think he's going to be pretty upfront about it, especially with the Great Condom Incident in the rearview now."

I thought a beat, "I'm not sure about that. He won't want to wave his sexual activity in their faces. He's probably going to say he's staying with Trent, or that he's going to the After-Prom and then breakfast right after sunrise."

"Ah. We're going to need to get all of our stories straight for the parents, I suppose," Darcy said. "What about you and Trent? Any big plans? Are you guys going to...you know?" Darcy raised a brow with the inquiry.

"We're going to go to the After-Prom, but we decided we would wait on the 'you-know.' We love each other and all, but I think I want to wait. It's been drilled into my head that I need to wait until I can afford to pay for a baby, and number one: I can't afford to pay for a baby; and number two: I don't want to take a chance and wind up pregnant and messing up my chances for a running scholarship. There have been so many times where, in the moment, it would be so easy to get it over with and just do it, but then I keep thinking, 'Do I really want my first time to be in the spirit of getting it over with?'"

"I get it," she said. "I know Bryan talked to you about marriage while we're in college, but we're not doing that. If he wants to join a fraternity, or if I want to join a sorority, or if there are things we want to do that really only lend themselves well to our being students, being married would be an obstacle, and neither of us wants to have any regrets. We're planning to get married while I'm in dental school and Bryan's in med school—and that's if everything goes to plan."

"I don't know if I'm doing the right thing putting my running before Trent, but he and I have the rest of our lives to be together if we're meant to be together. I may only have a few years left of competitive running. I love to watch my times improve. If I didn't commit to seeing how far I could go with my running, barring any injuries, I would have the biggest regrets. I'm committing to myself first because this is probably the only time in my life I'm going to be able to do what I need to do to be the best runner I can be." I stopped myself. "Does that sound selfish?"

"No. It sounds like you're putting things into perspective, and you've really thought things through," Darcy replied. "Not to switch gears, but I'm switching gears here. What's happening with your, um, Sara, and how's Gram?"

"Gram is doing great. She's home. Michael flew back to South America. Sara comes around a couple times a week. She tries to relate to us, but she's also keeping her distance, because I think she's afraid of over-promising. She'll be around for another week or so, and then she's going back to Michael. He's good for her. Dad, I swear, misses Michael, and so does Tom. I don't think Dad expected to spark this weird friendship with Michael, but they got to be pretty tight while he was here, and Sara is just sort of on the sidelines, you know? Dad won't miss Sara when she leaves, at least, not like he misses Michael. It's weird, but I don't try to understand."

"How do you feel toward Sara? Bryan just sort of acknowledges that she was someone who was the focal point of his life, and that person is gone, like dead. Sara is like this relative you guys don't know very well who exists on the outer edges of your lives," Darcy stated, and I knew she was exactly right. We reached her car, carefully placing our dresses in the backseat.

"I told her I had forgiven her. I think the forgiveness was more for me and my peace of mind than anything. But we're never going to have the mother-daughter relationship we could have once had. Maybe someday we'll be friends or something. Who knows? My mind is clearer now, though. I don't really think about her. I don't worry about not being enough anymore. Getting to that point was a major breakthrough for me," I gave a small smile. "Ick. I'm getting maudlin. Put on some music."

"You got it," Darcy said, and queued up a playlist while we navigated away from the mall.

"I can't believe we knocked out prom dress shopping in one trip!" I said.

A Little Consulting

Sara - age 44

"Michael, did you know Jen did some kind of process improvement certificate? She wound up having time in her schedule where she only actually has to go to school four days a week, and on her fifth day, she spent the time doing this certificate," I said. We were sitting in our very small house, fanning ourselves with medical journals, and enjoying what little cool there was in the early morning.

"That's great," Michael said. "What are you thinking? I can see the wheels turning in your head."

"Well, I think we could use some process improvement in the clinic, and maybe Jen would want to help us remotely or something. What do you think?"

"It's definitely worth a conversation," he said and reached across the table to squeeze the hand that wasn't waving a medical journal in the air.

It was a Saturday when I called Jen, and she picked up on the first ring. "Sara, hi. How are you? How's Michael? Gram is doing great!"

"I'm so glad to hear that," I said. I knew Mom was doing all right because I had checked up on her the night before, but it was a relief to know everyone else was checking up on her, too. "So your dad said you had completed a certificate for process improvement or transformation."

"I did. It was pretty cool. Great applications, and it speaks to my need for organization," she said.

"I was wondering if you'd like to put your certification to the test and help me with something. You don't need to come here or anything. I think we can accomplish what we need to accomplish in a web meeting or something."

"Probably, sure," she said. Her voice sounded happy, hopeful, unguarded. "Before we get to brass tacks on this, I need you to do a little homework to help me prepare. Okay?"

"What do you need?" I asked. I couldn't believe how well this call was going, and I prayed I didn't screw it up.

"There are two things you need to think about. 1. The problem. Summarize it in one concise statement; and 2. An opportunity statement. When we're trying to solve a problem, we want to turn it into an opportunity to improve something."

I started thinking about problems in our clinic and in our community. I practice medicine in a third world country. I can't get through a single day without something going at least a little bit off kilter. And I decided the problem was the problem. This whole exercise would be so exciting. Everything about tonight would be a 'win' for me.

"Where do we start?"

"We start with your opportunity statement. I don't need to know the problem. I need to know where you see an opportunity for improvement. We are always looking for positives and opportunities—that's why I call it an opportunity statement."

"Okay," I said slowly. "My clinic has an opportunity to be more organized when we are required to be flexible."

Jen was silent on the other end of the call for a moment. She was thinking. "Can you give me an example?"

"Sure. We run our clinic with a schedule of appointments, but if there's a heavy rain with flooding, it brings out the snakes, and we get an influx of people who've been bitten by the snakes. They take priority over our regular schedule of patients. Or sometimes, a woman from another village will travel up to a couple hours to get to our clinic to give birth because we're closer than her nearest hospital. She won't have had any pre-natal care, and we have to deliver her baby not knowing what we may be getting into. Or sometimes, we'll see someone with appendicitis. Basically, anything that isn't on the schedule throws the entire office into a tizzy. The staff aren't equipped to change gears, and the patients don't understand why they were next in line to see the doctor, but now they have to wait an additional hour or two or three..." I was getting a little stressed just thinking about it.

"I see. You have an opportunity to create a new routine for schedule disruptions. Let me think about this a little bit. Do you have index cards or Post-its? I don't think this is going to be crazy to work through, but it'll help if you have some tools."

She gave me the list of what I would need, and we made plans to speak the following weekend. After I hung up, I turned to Michael, "I can't believe how well that went. She's going to be able to help us." Michael smiled widely.

The following weekend, Michael and I got on a web call, and we had all the supplies Jen had told us were the bare minimum for developing an action plan.

"Once we get through this process, we'll be able to write a plan. You'll be able to measure the results of success or failure quantitatively, too. I think you'll be happy with the solution or range of solutions to try. But buyer, beware: It's an iterative process. You may need to make small adjustments. I'll go over all of that, though, and you'll know how to document and measure. You'll be fine."

Eventually, we had the workings of a solution mapped out, and it was good. I shouldn't have been surprised Jen gave more than 100% in everything she did. When we wrapped up, I thanked Jen profusely. "Jen, this has been more than I ever dreamed of when I called you the other night. I thought we would brainstorm, and that would be it. But this was so much more, and it makes so much sense. You are incredible."

"Don't get too excited. I'm using the tools and methods I learned through my certification programs. When I tell you there's nothing new under the sun, I'm telling you, 'There's nothing new under the sun.'" She laughed. I laughed. Michael cackled, but we were all laughing. Together. And it felt great.

Later that night, lying in bed and holding tight to Michael like a baby opossum hanging onto its mother, we talked about our time with Jen, focusing on what it had meant to me. "I don't know if working with Jen today has done anything for our relationship in the long run, but it felt special to me. What about you? What do you think it meant to Jen? I'm proud of myself for initiating contact. I need to do that more, I think. Do you think I have it in me to do that?"

Michael rolled onto his back, and I perched my head on his chest. "I think only you have the answers. What I can tell you, though, is that you're stronger than you think you are, and you have more capacity than you think you have, and you have so much more love to give than you think you do, and you're no longer as broken as you once were. Would it be so bad to put yourself out there for Jen and Bryan?" I could hear Michael's heartbeat beginning to speed up. "Sara, I've only known the two of them for a couple weeks, and even I love them. And you know I have very little room in my heart for loving new people," he answered, ending with clear mirth in his voice.

"I love you, you know," I said.

"I know," he said.

"You want to get it on?" I asked.

"You don't have to ask twice," he said. "And for the record, I love you, too."

Ah. The magic words. And I climbed on top of him and rode him like we were in the Kentucky Derby.

Epilogue: Six Years Later

Erin

Rob and I stood side by side on the walk in front of our house, arms wrapped around one another. It was a bright, clear morning in late August, that special time of year when the days are warm, sunny, sometimes hot, but the mornings' fleetingly gripping onto a chill and the faintest whiff of decaying leaves. My babies, my youngest babies, Bryn and Walker, were weighed down with their backpacks and talking back and forth with one another about where they would sit on the bus this year or if they would have assigned seats. They would turn seven just after Labor Day, and today was the very first day of first grade.

The bus came to a gentle stop, and I don't know why it always shocked me that the tires screeched when the brakes were applied, but it was a thing. The kids looked so tiny as they made their way to the bus, its doors opening like jaws. Oh, my gosh--what am I saying? The bus is a wonderful, wonderful vehicle that transports children to school, and the wheels go round and round all through the town. There.

We watched them climb the steps, greet the bus driver, and make their way to their seats. They both looked out the windows and waved to us. I rubbed at my eyes, which seemed to be a little leaky this morning.

"You okay?" Rob asked. We turned our heads, watching the stop sign arm of the bus fold back to the bus's side, and the bus proceeded on to its next stop to gather more children for school.

I turned toward him when the bus had turned the corner and was out of sight. He leaned down, placing a kiss on my forehead. "I am," I managed to croak.

We went back to the house to call Darcy and Bryan. They decided to get married right out of college and were getting ready to start their second years of dental school (Darcy) and medical school (Bryan). They opted to stay in Chicago, and their apartment was taking shabby chic to a whole new level. We offered to buy them furniture, and Darcy's parents offered, too. But they wanted to do as much as they could on their own. Of course, they did get a lot of good stuff on their wedding registry. Their one year anniversary passed two months ago, and we all made the trip to Chicago to celebrate with them and have a piece of one-year-old wedding cake. The icing was definitely a little stale, and maybe more than a touch freezer burned, but the cake was still as good as I remembered it from the wedding reception.

It was a fantastic weekend to be in Chicago. We purchased tickets for a Cubs game from some scalpers and overpaid, but it was so worth it. Bryn and Walker loved Wrigley Field. We made a pit stop at the Billy Goat Tavern, and the kids weren't impressed. Bryn's question after we ordered our food was, "Why don't they have Coke?"

And her brother acknowledged, "Maybe it's the Billy Goat Gruff Tavern."

When we took them to Navy Pier, they wanted to ride the ferris wheel non-stop. We had no idea when we arrived at Navy Pier that our children would be so enamored and want to stay there as long possible. I thought all the little shops would bore Walker to death, but I was completely surprised. There were enough stores with extremely diverse merchandise that he viewed the whole experience with complete wonder. I was terrified I would lose track of my children in the mad crush of people in such a confined space.

We visited as many of the big tourist places as possible during the weekend (hello, Museum of Science and Industry—my wallet is much lighter after spending time in your gift shop), and I would hazard a guess that we succeeded. We saw fish, cavemen, planets, rocks; ate popcorn, pizza, hotdogs; and took a very nauseating (for me) elevator ride to the top of the Willis Tower.

I have a very good strategy when visiting museums, especially with children. We each chose one must-see exhibit, went to the exhibits, then moved on to the next museum. Everyone wins, and no one winds up over-tired and there's still the excitement of going back again in the future.

We were stopped several times during the weekend by people who wanted to tell Rob or me how beautiful our children were and what a handsome family we made. There were also the people who I could tell were trying to put the pieces together of who belonged to whom, 'Are those people a family? I shouldn't stare. I should look at my shoes, or over their heads, or well, anywhere but directly at them.' Rob and I always had a laugh because we knew we looked different, and we knew our children were beautiful, and we knew we were anything but invisible. Michael once told us about growing up and not fitting in with the Asian kids or the Latino kids. Right now, Bryn and Walker were just children, and they hadn't experienced having to find 'their people.' Right now, everyone was 'their people,' and I hoped it never changed, but in my heart, I knew how people were, and I knew things would change. Rob and I talked to other interracial couples to see how they handled the situation, and I didn't think we'd ever be perfectly prepared, but we sure were trying to get to the point where we could answer questions and potentially soothe hurt feelings and hearts. We knew in our bones what was coming, and it turned out, Michael's mom was a fantastic support to us.

Sara and Michael decided to remain in South America instead of taking on other assignments after their first year opening their clinic. They made the trip for Darcy and Bryan's college graduations and stuck around for their wedding. Bryan insisted on seating me (as the mother of the groom) in the front row with Rob, and I insisted that he would also escort Sara. He did as asked, and I think Sara was touched, and I know it was the right thing to do. She and Michael sat a bit farther down the pew, and Rob and I were right on the aisle. We had the primo seats. We put all the grandparents in the second pew to make sure they had aisle access, too. There were so many of them just on our side of the church because we had grown a family, a rather large family.

The maid of honor was Jen. She took a year off from school to focus on training when she received an invitation to try out for the Olympic track and field team. She took a bronze medal in one of her events. And to think that girl didn't know she was an elite athlete. Our family made a fairly formidable entourage, and Jen was able to finagle a dozen seats for us for the opening ceremonies. She beamed as she walked with the rest of Team USA, and I don't know that I've ever seen her look more 'herself' than she did during her events. All of her work, drive, and focus were channeled into a compressed moment on a world stage.

Jen decided to go to University of Florida. She couldn't say no to the weather. Trent spent his freshman year at UCLA, and the distance was tougher on him than he thought it would be. He missed Jen, and he missed his family. He knew if he transferred to be with Jen, he wouldn't be running competitively. Knowing the trade-off, he transferred. He's in the last year of his MBA. Jen should be graduating at the end of first semester this year. Her plan is still sports psychology, but she's been talking about an MBA, too. Graduate school is definitely in her future, but none of us knows what shape her future is going to take. It will include Trent, though.

He and Jen had come home for the fourth of July. Jen was in the backyard with Bryn and Walker, playing Simon Says. Trent looked out the kitchen window to keep an eye on things. If we didn't know better, it might have seemed like he was getting ready to rob a bank. He was so shifty-eyed at that moment, trying to keep tabs on everyone and everything.

Rob said overly loudly to Trent, "Erin can be the lookout, and I can drive the getaway car."

Trent visibly relaxed. "Erin, Rob, I want to ask you both for your blessing and allow me to ask Jen for her hand in marriage."

Rob looked at me, and I nodded in silent agreement. Rob said, "Son, nothing would make us happier than to see you two married. Yes, you have our blessing and permission."

Trent looked relieved, and then he seemed to ignite. He went out the back door. "Hey, Bryn, Walker. Your mom and dad need you to help set the table for dinner."

Trent walked over to Jen, and they made their way to the swing set on the edge of our property. She sat on one of the swings, and she looked worried. I could only imagine Trent saying something like they needed to talk--words no one wants to hear. But then he got down on one knee, producing a jewelry box from his back pocket. Jen started swaying, and Trent quickly got to his feet, catching her before she hit the ground. While he supported her in one of his arms, he clumsily maneuvered the ring out of the box and slid it onto her ring finger. It looked like he was blowing on her face. Rob and I were laughing so hard. He was snorting, and tears were running down my face, and I couldn't catch my breath. We stopped each other, though, to see what would happen next. Jen's eyes fluttered open, and she smiled up at Trent. We saw her nodding in the affirmative before gazing at the ring on her finger. He gently lowered her to a seated position on the ground and joined her there, then pulled her to him. The next bit was a lot of kissing. We stopped looking out the window.

Around five minutes after the proposal, they came into the house. "Guess what?" Jen said. We all looked to her and Trent, and they said, "We're getting married!" She held her hand out to show us the ring, and the two of them were bursting with joy.

Bryn ran to Jen, hugging her tightly. "Am I going to be the maid of honor?"

"Of course you are," Jen answered. "What color do you want to wear?"

"Orange!" Bryn said.

Jen looked to Trent, shaking her head back and forth, with a happy, relaxed smile. "I guess we're having an orange wedding." We all laughed.

Rob and I covertly called Tom and Maggie while Jen was passed out to let them know what was happening. They had been planning to grill out with us for the fourth anyway, but with the proposal, we wanted them to arrive earlier. We would all want to see them sooner rather than later to celebrate the engagement and the holiday. Bryn adored Bridgette, and Walker had a tiny crush on her. In his eyes, she was like a movie star, and with her being eleven years older than our seven-year olds (thank the lord), she was unattainable.

Six years had passed since Jo's bone marrow transplant. She was doing very well. No evidence of recurrent disease or any new disease. Sara's visit to make the donation helped repair some of the damage done to her relationship with her parents, but Jen and Bryan regarded her more as a distant relative. They communicated periodically and had an amicable relationship, but she was still

'Sara' to the two of them, and when they introduced me to their friends, they introduced me as their mother.

My mom, Eva, and Jo had started going on girls' trips every year, and they had been talking about asking one or both of Trent's grandmothers if they'd like to join, 'but only if they can promise not to be a drip.' I look at my wonderful boys and men, and my amazing, magical girls and women, and I look at myself, and well, I think I am living such a fantastic life.